D0948747

KILLING CYNTHIA ANN

Other fiction by Charles Brashear:

*A Snug Little Purchase, How Richard Henderson Bought
Kaintuckee from the Cherokees in 1775*
(La Mesa, California: Associated Creative Writers, 1979).

Contemporary Insanities, Short Fictions
(Arroyo Grande, California: The Press of MacDonald &
Reinecke, 1990).

The Other Side of Love, Two Novellas
(Denver: Alan Swallow, 1963).

KILLING
CYNTHIA
ANN

a novel by

Charles Brashear

Texas Christian University Press
Fort Worth

Library of Congress Cataloging-in-Publication Data

Brashear, Charles.
Killing Cynthia Ann : a novel / by Charles Brashear.
p. cm.
"Historical notes and bibliographic essay on Cynthia Ann and
Quanah Parker": p.   .
ISBN 0-87565-209-3 (alk. paper)
1. Parker, Cynthia Ann, 1827?-1870 Fiction. 2.
Texas—History—Civil War, 1861-1865 Fiction. 3. Indian
captivities—Texas Fiction. 4. Comanche Indians Fiction. I. Title.
PS3552.R3276 K5 1999
813'.54—dc21
99-27674
CIP

Contents

On The Pease River,
8 Dec. 1860

Náudah paused and looked up from stripping the flesh and striffen from a fresh buffalo hide. A few steps to the east, several women—friends and relatives—bent over buffalo hides pegged out among the tipis in various stages of curing and tanning. The sliced meat hung on drying racks. Nearby, Nobah Joe, subchief in charge of the camp, bent his gray head forward, absorbed in attaching a flint arrowhead to a shaft with a fresh, elastic piece of buffalo sinew that would shrink tight when it dried. His braids, wrapped in ochre and russet ribbons, kept falling forward, obstructing his view of his work.

"Aren't you worried, Nobah?" Náudah called, sitting back on her heels and scanning the flat horizon to the south.

Nobah grunted. A woman's idle chatter was hardly worth an answer, even if she was the favorite wife of Peta Nocona. He glanced around. The sun shone warmly on the camp of some twenty Comanches on the banks of Mule Creek, a tributary to the Pease River. He muttered a little prayer of thanks to the sun; they had already endured two snowstorms this season. It looked like a bad winter approaching. He sniffed the air: a bit too much moisture. A chill that defied the sunshine told him another blizzard was coming.

On all sides, a small grassy rise one could hardly call a hill hid the Comanches from view, but also prevented them from seeing out. A buffalo trail led south up to a low, flat ridge and disappeared.

"Shouldn't we post lookouts?" Náudah continued.

"Thank Gekovak for the warmth," Nobah said aloud and held up his wrinkled arms, as if to embrace the sun. "Snow and ice will hug us too soon." He looked off to the north. He could see a little blue line down close to the horizon.

"You know what I mean, old *esa-kwita*,"[1] she said, letting out a short breath in exasperation. "The Tejanos. The bluecoats. We never know where they are." Her daughter, Toh-Tsee-Ah, carried a flint scraper and toddled around, mimicking her mother's work on the buffalo hide. On the other side of the skin, her adoptive sister, Trades-It, her hand and arm permanently disfigured from a childhood fall from a horse, scraped striffen with a steel trade knife. She smiled in sympathy at Náudah, then went on with her work.

"*Tahuh nurhmurh-ne*,[2] 'Our People,' is the strongest tribe on the prairies. You know that," said Nobah Joe. "What tribe would dare attack us?"

"The Tonkawa, the Pawnee, our traditional enemies. The Tejanos. The bluecoats," Náudah said, ticking them off on her fingers. "Only the Mexicans at Santa Fe are peaceful, but they have been known to attack others."

"Ha!" Nobah scoffed, not looking away from his work. "Not even the Tonkawa would attack a camp of women. What tribe would have the courage to attack a camp of women?"

"I don't know why I even talk to you," said Náudah, standing up and adjusting her medicine bag so that it hung at her side inside her dress. Her hands trembling, she walked over to the horses, thinking she had better make sure that everything was ready for the unforeseen. She wore a loose velvety deerskin garment tied with soft straps across her shoulders. A ring of pearly cowrie shells sewn to the leather formed a low yoke on her breast and identified her as the wife of an important leader, and a hem of leather fringes swished below the knees of her leggings.

She ran her hand over the muscled rump of her dappled gray mare, which Peta Nocona had named Wind because she was so

1. Esa-kwita, literally, "Wolf turd," an ambiguous term. Excrement and references to excrement were generally negative, but the wolf's medicine was among the most powerful, so anything coming from a wolf denoted power. One of the most successful and respected Comanche chiefs was named Esa-kwita.

2. "Nurhmurh" is the Comanche word used to refer to all members of all clans collectively, the broadest possible translation of "all my relations." It is pronounced with very weak "r's," almost as weak as the British retroflex 'r;' "-ne" is a suffix that denotes "person of-" or "people of-." Thus "Nuhrmuhr-ne"—"people of our extended clans"—should be translated

fast. The surcingle was a bit loose, but she didn't tighten it—the poor animal needed some respite from a constant girdle. The bridle thong was a different matter; that had to be ready to ride at a moment's notice. A rabbit-skin bag tied to the surcingle contained enough pemmican for one day, a small amount of fire starter, a few Mexican matches and a small flint knife. She touched it to assure herself that all was ready. Then she walked back to her buffalo hide. To steady her breathing, she tried humming a little Comanche song about prairie flowers to her daughter.

Nobah finished his arrow and started another, considering the possibility that she was right. Maybe Náudah was just too anxious. She had spent her whole time with Our People hiding from the white men, the *tosi-taivo*. She had been taught to seclude herself when any of them came around, to run into the bushes if they spoke to her, to make invisibility her best defense. That had made her edgy and suspicious. She saw danger when there was none. Like a rabbit, she dodged the shadows of limbs when there were no Eagles in the sky.

"Nobah, have you seen Quanah and Pecos?" Náudah asked.

"Your sons are out fighting the rabbit wars. They can take care of themselves." Nobah inspected the bindings on the arrowhead; it would make a fine weapon for his sister's grandson who was just approaching warrior age. A little pine pitch from the mountains near Santa Fe, a week's journey to the west, would help—if he only had some. He would ask Peta Nocona to trade for some of the glue next time he went west to a Comanchero gathering.

"I've heard that bears curl up in safe, warm holes in the western mountains and sleep as long as the ice and snow lasts," Náudah went on, wiping her cheek with a forearm covered with dried buffalo blood. She tried to wrap her arms around Toh-Tsee-Ah to imitate a bear robe, but the baby squirmed out of her grasp and dropped the flint scraper on the buffalo hide.

"I've heard that," said Nobah, glancing at her.

Strange, he thought, that she should almost read his mind. Many people said she had special powers—*puha*, strong medicine. Maybe those blue eyes saw into other people's heads. Maybe that's why Peta Nocona was so devoted to her, though everyone knew she

"Our People," rather than "The People," according to Thomas W. Kavanagh, "Political Power and Political Organization: Comanche Politics, 1786-1875." (Ann Arbor: University Microfilms, 1989).

was one of the best workers in the camp, one of the best at curing buffalo robes.

"I'd like to live a while that way," Náudah went on. "Curled up in a bearskin, warm and well-fed. And not wake up till the prairie is in bloom."

"That's for bears," Nobah answered.

"I know," she sighed. "Still, I'll be happy to get to winter camp and set up my tipi."

"Three days more and we can pack the meat and skins," Nobah countered. "Then we can move." He glanced at the northern horizon; the little blue line, a coming blizzard, was getting bigger slowly.

"Ha!" scoffed Náudah. "The hunters will bring more fresh meat and hides to cure. They always do."

"Be glad that we have food to eat. With the Tejanos and bluecoats killing so many of Our People. . . ."

"Oh, I am. I am glad." She wiped sweat from her upper lip. "I just wish we were safe on the Washita with a hill to stop some of the wind. Or I wish we were all bears in some safe cave in Palo Duro Canyon. I wish we were home."

As a Texas Ranger patrol came upon a buffalo trail that led to a slight rise overlooking the Pease River and the surrounding plain, Captain Lawrence "Sul" Ross spotted an Indian encampment clustered tightly on the flat right in front of a stream flowing in from the southwest to the Pease. He motioned his troop to take cover behind the flat ridge, then called his orderly: "Ride back and tell Cureton where we are and that he should come on up." He waited until the messenger was out of ear-shot, then turned to his men: "Get ready for a fight, boys. You twelve over here, go east a little ways. Get around behind 'em downstream and cut 'em off. The rest of you, let's charge right through 'em. Shoot everythang that moves. I got a nice Colt six-shooter for the first man that kills and scalps a Indan."[3] He held it up at arm's length, turning it right and left, so all could see.

Ross really wanted to find some Comanches to kill. He had been out to the Llano Estacado and the canyons along its eastern escarp-

3. The cap-and-ball six-shooter that Lawrence Sullivan Ross carried in the Pease River Massacre survives. It is in the Texas Ranger Museum in Waco, Texas, engraved: "To C.R. Gray on occasion of your first scalp—L.S. Ross."

4. Ross (1838-1898) was wounded in 1858 just before he had to go back to Alabama to finish his studies in Military Science at Florence Wesleyan College. For more on Ross, see *The New Handbook of Texas*, Ron Tyler, et. al. eds. (Austin: Texas State Historical Association, 1996), vol. 5, pp. 688-689.

5. Sam Houston, first president of the Texas Republic, had long been sympathetic to the Indians: he had lived among the Cherokees for a time in Tenn-

ment in the summer of 1859 and got in a couple of Indian fights, but they weren't very satisfying. Not only were the wily redskins hard to catch, but he'd taken a bullet in the fleshy part of his left leg.[4] He really wanted revenge for that wound. He especially wanted to catch that damned Peta Nocona; that'd make his reputation.

Of course, it was not just for his reputation. The land had to be made safe for women and children. The abominable Indians weren't using the land anyway. Why didn't they just move on and leave it to someone who would, someone who would create a peaceful and prosperous community?

In 1860, Ross had persuaded Texas Governor Sam Houston that another troop of Texas Rangers was needed to protect the settlers in Parker, Palo Pinto, and Jack Counties, as well as the sparsely populated regions along the upper Brazos River. Peta Nocona and his warriors had killed 168 people on the Texas frontier in the last year alone. Reluctantly, Houston gave Ross a commission as captain of Rangers and the charge to raise a volunteer regiment to punish Peta Nocona.[5]

Sul hardly had a regiment. He had convinced forty volunteers to follow him, and he had twenty regulars on loan from Captain Nathan Evans of the 2nd U.S. Cavalry at Camp Cooper on the Clear Fork of the Brazos. Many of his men had been meat hunters in Kentucky before the game was thinned out. They'd shoot at anything wild, just because it was wild and just because they could shoot. Vaguely, Sul knew they hunted and killed Indians in the same spirit—for the sheer fun of it. As much as he might disapprove of their motives, the results were right: the savages had to be cleared out.

And then there was that snotty-nosed upstart, Captain Jack Cureton, with his ninety volunteers from Bosque County. Who needed him? You practically had to tell him where the ground was before he could hit it apissing. Like now, they were stringing along two miles behind. How could they get in a fight by hanging back?

Sul felt confident at the head of a twenty-five-man advance scouting party. He had an excellent lieutenant in Tom Kelliher and the best guide that Texas had to offer in Charles Goodnight, who had been on the frontier since the age of nine. And his men were willing to ride hard, even when their horses were almost worn out, like now.

essee; he once had a Cherokee wife and Cherokee children; and he had been a strong advocate for the property rights of the Texas Cherokees and all Indians. Mirabeau Lamar, second president of Texas, announced he would rid Texas of all Indians and sent his troops riding through the Cherokee settlement, killing everyone in sight.

But times were changing; Houston had come to believe that the continued attacks by the Comanches along the Texas frontier could no longer be tolerated. So he had agreed that the Comanches on reservations along the Brazos River in Texas should be removed to Indian Territory and that more force should be used to catch Peta Nocona, war leader of the Noconi Band of Quahada Comanche.

6   The last thing he needed was some pussy-foot to take care of.

He judged the other twelve were in position by now, then glanced around to see that everyone was ready. He raised his six-gun like a sword and gave the signal to charge.

With a lurch in her heart, Náudah saw the Ranger skirmish line before she heard the first shot. "Enemies! Tejanos!" she screamed, sweeping Toh-Tsee-Ah into her arms and running for cover behind one of the tipis. She saw her sister, Loves-Horses, look up in surprise at the sound of charging horses and gunshots, drop the meat she was carrying and run for her horse. Trades-It stumbled on a pegged-out buffalo hide, caught herself with her crippled hand, then scrambled to her feet.

Two war women owned trade guns. With two warriors, they came out of the remuda, using their horses as shields, and quickly formed a half-ring around a group of women and young girls in the middle of the camp. They fired impulsively, then didn't have time to reload. Their bows and arrows, or even war axes, would not be of much use against the Rangers' six-shooters.

Nobah had mounted his bay horse and was riding along the defense line. Somehow, he had found his lance, which had a blade made from a Mexican bayonet. He lifted it like a scepter, screaming at the warriors, "Don't shoot too soon!" He was too late.

In panic, Náudah pulled Toh-Tsee-Ah against her body and raced for Wind. No time to tighten the surcingle. She leaped on the dappled gray mare and reined Wind downstream. In front of her, frightened horses kicked up dust that mixed with the smoke and stench of the gunpowder. She heard screams. Her way was blocked forty steps away by women and teen-agers in the open, jerking when bullets hit them, little fountains of their blood spurting toward the river. She saw another group of Rangers in a little clump galloping behind the Comanches, getting ready to race around and around them, as if they had caught a herd of buffalo in a surround and could take their time in killing every last one.

One of the war women screamed in Comanche, "Prisa. *Run!*"

Women dashed toward the river, not knowing in the dust and smoke that they were running right into the second body of Rangers. They fell in a volley of bullets. People near horses grabbed hold of a mane and swung up, then tore off.

Náudah saw Nobah racing toward his teenaged granddaughter, Tena. He grabbed Tena's arm at the same time as she seized his, and he swung her up behind him at full gallop. They sprinted upstream to the west, while most of the other horsemen were galloping downstream. Náudah kicked her dappled gray and headed upstream.

She and Wind quickly caught up with Nobah and Tena on the big bay horse. They crossed the little stream, and, as soon as they were in the open, Náudah turned her pony slightly to the right, thinking it was best to scatter. There was no time to wave goodbye.

As Captain Ross rode through the Comanche camp at full speed, he noticed buffalo hides pegged out for drying, meat hanging on racks, women lying dead with their scrapers still in hand; but no bucks. Hell, it was a damned squaw camp, not a war party at all.

Still, he could hardly contain his excitement—nothing like a charge to get a man's heart pumping.

Ross already knew what he would report to General Houston: "The Indians, unconscious of our presence, had gotten out on a level plane and were never apprised of our approach until we were within 200 yards of them, in full charge; consequently many of them were killed before they could make any preparations for defense."[6]

Sul and Tom Kelliher saw the two riders cross the creek to the west and spurred their horses in pursuit. "I wanta get one by hand," yelled Kelliher. Sul smiled to himself. He had complete confidence in Tom Kelliher in hand-to-hand combat. When the rider on the dappled gray veered off to the right, Kelliher followed.

Sul followed the bay. When he was close enough, he fired. The Comanche at the back jerked with the hit, then fell, dragging the

6. As quoted in *The Galveston Civilian*, 15 Jan. 1861; see Margaret Schmidt Hacker, *Cynthia Ann Parker: The Life and the Legend* (Texas Western Press, 1990). "Plane" is Sul Ross' spelling of plain.

8   lead rider off. Sul saw at once that the dead one was a teenaged girl. Damn! he didn't like killing squaws, even if they were Comanches. You couldn't hardly tell the men from the women in their winter hunting shirts and leggings.

The lead rider was an elderly man. He was shaken up by the fall, but quickly got to his feet and lifted his lance to fight. Ross shot him in the right arm, breaking the bone. The man fell over, then got up, his useless arm dangling.

"Quien esta?" asked Sul when the dust had settled. He'd like to know who it was he was about to kill.

But the man did not seem to understand Sul's Spanish. He just glared at the Ranger in defiance. He held his lance in his left hand, feinted threateningly toward Sul, and howled challenges.

Sul stood up in his stirrups and looked around, spotted Antonio Martinez, his Mexican servant who spoke Comanche, and yelled, "Tonio! Over here!"

As Martinez rode up, Sul swung around. "See if you can tell who this feller is."

Antonio asked the man in halting Comanche, then in Spanish, what his name was: "¿Cómo se llama?"

The man fired back a rapid string of Comanche, his throat growling with the hatred.

"What's he say?" asked Sul. He rested his hands casually on the wide saddle horn.

Antonio was having trouble getting his horse to stand quietly after so much excitement. "He say something Nocona, I think."

"Nocona? Peta Nocona?" cried Ross, swinging down to confront his foe directly. "Have we caught Peta Nocona?"

Again Martinez spoke to the man. Again, the man answered rapidly.

"What's he say now?" Sul did not take his eyes off the Comanche.

"Gekovak. His word for the God. He say the God give the sign if he no do his job as jefe, I think."

"Chief?" asked Sul, astonished. "You mean, we've caught Chief Nocona?"

Antonio just shrugged. "I dunno. He say Nocona."

"Well, I'll be damned! Ask him to surrender, Antonio."

Martinez again spoke.

The man responded by screaming a war whoop, rushing forward, and thrusting his lance at Sul.

Sul jumped back, but did not parry. Damn! the man had spunk. To be as gray and withered as he was, to have a broken arm, and still be willing to fight. You really ought to respect a man like that.

Sul looked around, trying to figure out what to do next.

"Capitán," said Antonio. "The Noconis, they kill my family long time 'go. They keep me the slave. That is how I learn el lingo Comanchero. My familia no get the revenge. Quiero la venganza now."

Sul studied Antonio for a moment. He could see and understand the hatred in the man's face. He understood a man's need to retaliate. He glanced at the Comanche; there was no surrender in his eyes, nothing but defiance. "All right, Antonio," said Ross. "You can take your revenge."

Antonio pulled out his pistol and, without hesitation, shot the old man in the head. One of his braids and part of his skull flew two yards away. Nobah was dead before he hit the ground.

Sul took the warrior's lance, his belt knife, his medicine bag, the leather hunting shirt, the drilled-stone necklace. He'd send them to General Houston with the greetings that Sul Ross had killed the owner.[7] He hacked off the other braid, threw it aside, and took the man's scalp as a personal souvenir.

Tom Kelliher pursued his warrior without firing. He wanted to catch him by hand. The Comanche was a good rider; several times, Tom had almost gotten in a position to stop him, when the rider got away. But that couldn't go on forever. The Comanche's pony was no match for Tom's superior gelding.

As Tom closed in for the grab, the Comanche suddenly reined in and turned to face Tom. Shit, it wasn't a warrior at all; it was a

7. On 2 Jan. 1861, a report in the *Dallas Weekly Herald*, told how Ross and his Rangers had caught and killed the notorious Peta Nocona, leader of the marauding Quahada Band of Comanches. The news fit the Texas mentality perfectly; Ross was an instant hero and was later elected Governor of Texas. It would be many years before the error was corrected. Antonio had killed Nobah Joe Nocona, Peta's servant.

damned woman. And on top of it, she carried a child. She raised the baby up so Tom could see her and cried, "Americano! Americano!"

Kelliher barely managed to rein his horse aside to keep him from colliding with the Comanche pony. Then he rode quick circles around the woman. His heart was beating fast and his breath coming in short, exaggerated gasps.

The woman held the baby in one hand and held the other in the air to show that she didn't have any weapons. Her teeth chattering with fear, she cried out repeatedly, "Por fávor, no me mate. Por fávor, no me mate." *Please, don't kill me; please, don't kill me.*[8]

Tom saw a substantial woman, leather-skinned and muscular, with a large bosom, though her leather dress fit her like a sack. Her hair was greasy and matted.

Kelliher let his gelding slow to a walk. He stroked the animal's neck to calm him and sized up the situation. There was nothing to do but take her back into the camp, a prisoner. To think, he'd run his prize horse more than three miles, just to catch an old squaw. Crap! He motioned for her to ride back to camp, then he fell in behind and drove her pony. The horses' breath streamed white in the chill December air.

As they rode, the woman began to weep and moan in a combination of Comanche and Spanish. Tom only caught that she was worried about what her sons would do without their mother, or if they were dead.

"Mis hijos," she cried. "Mis hijos. ¿Están mis hijos muertos?"

When they reached Nobah's naked and scalped body, Náudah screamed, "Nobah! Nobah!" as if she could wake him up. Her heart skipped and her breath caught when she saw that the bullet had taken away a large part of his skull, making his scalp hardly worth the taking, but that hadn't stopped the Ranger. The ochre and russet ribbons were unraveling from the loose braid.

Her captor was right behind her. She heard the man cock his six-shooter, and he rammed his horse into hers. She whirled to face

8. Spanish—the language of trade with the Spaniards and Mexicans—was a second tongue among most southwest Indian tribes. Many Indians had been taught Spanish by missionaries and learned their catechism in Spanish.

him, screaming, "No me mate! No me mate." She shielded Toh-
Tsee-Ah in tight against her body.

Kelliher motioned her to continue toward the camp.

They passed Tena's body, too. She had been stripped and scalped. The blood across her face made her hardly recognizable. "Tena, Tena," she wailed, getting ready to dismount and see if she could do anything. Again, she heard the pistol of her captor cocking.

She couldn't race away; he'd be able to shoot her and Toh-Tsee-Ah. She felt like racing Wind right into the chest of his horse; maybe she could upset his mount, throw the rider to the ground, and get away. But she saw that the Tejano was too good a rider for that to happen. There was nothing she could do but scream in fury and frustration. Oh, if she only had a weapon! She thought of the small, flint knife in her medicine bag, but it was too little to kill a man.

Back at the camp, she saw several bodies of her friends and relatives. Her captor let her race ahead to them, because there were so many Tejanos around. Most of the Rangers had dismounted and were walking around among the dead, taking scalps, collecting the Comanche's garments, and any necklaces, knives, or bows and arrows they could grab.

Náudah set Toh-Tsee-Ah down to toddle and found the body of Trades-It, which almost made her vomit. Trades-It was naked. Her bent arm had been broken again and she had been scalped. Náudah lunged at the nearest Tejano, beating at his face and neck with her fists. The Tejano slapped her with the back of his hand, sending her sprawling among the dead. He pulled out his pistol, ready to shoot her, then hesitated; he couldn't just kill her in cold blood. He wanted her to be running. "Git up!" he commanded.

Náudah squirmed back and reached again for Toh-Tsee-Ah. Bumping against Trades-It's body, she saw that Trades-It's vagina had been cut out. Some Tejano was wearing the bloody little pelt as a hatband. Ughhh! 'Our People' had been right. The despised Texans were worse than Tonkawa. The Tonkawa only cut strips of flesh from their captives, roasted them, and ate them in front of the captive's eyes. But these Tejanos were savages.

The Tejano with the pistol had gone back to collecting loot.

Náudah searched through the dead, looking for her sons,

Quanah and Pecos. She found Loves-Horses, She-Smiles, Wind-in-the-Oaks, Yellow-Legs, Gripping-Stone—they had all been shot several times, stripped, scalped, and their vaginas cut out—but she did not find her sons. She felt torn between rejoicing that her sons may have gotten away and screaming out in fury and protest at all the killing of her relatives.

A Ranger with a full mustache came in from downstream, leading a Comanche pony that had a body draped across it. "It's jist a goddamn squaw," yelled the Ranger when he got within earshot of the others. "Had to chase her more 'n a mile, 'fore I could hit her. Bill's is the same thing."

Náudah could see that the body was a grown woman, not her sons. "Mis hijos!" she cried, grasping the arm of one hairy Texan after another. "¿Dónde esconden Ustedes mis hijos?" *Where are you hiding my sons?* She began screaming and wailing the funeral chant.

Kelliher was back; he dragged her roughly to a little clump of men. She thrashed against his grip, trying to hold her baby and at the same time beat at him with her free fist, screaming "No me mate! No mi hija mate!"

Antonio questioned Náudah in Comanche and Spanish. It was hard to progress—the woman was wailing and weeping hysterically the whole time, "No me mate, por favór. No mi hija mate. ¿Dónde están mis hijos?" She refused to meet her captors' gaze, but always kept her eyes averted.

Other Rangers straggled into camp with dead Comanches draped across the captured ponies. Each new body brought a wail from the woman.

"Well?" asked Ross, after Antonio had talked with the woman a few moments.

"She is wife of Peta Nocona," said Antonio. "She weep for her esposo y dos hijos."

Seems natural to weep for a husband and sons, thought Sul. Like any woman. "Ah, Antonio, don't tell her just yet that Peta Nocona is dead."

When she heard her husband's name, the woman stopped her
wailing and turned to Ross, appealing in a string of Comanche and
Spanish. He could see her hands trembling, as she reached out
toward him. All Sul understood were the words, "Peta Nocona."
But he was suddenly stopped by her appeal. Beneath the grime and
blood, there was something different about this woman.

Then, through her weeping and thrashing, he saw what it was:
she had blue eyes. Every Comanche he'd ever seen had brown eyes.
He examined her closer. Her skin was dirty, tanned, and looked
thick; she'd been up to her elbows in meat and blood, the filth all
over her face, plus the grime she'd gotten by handling the dead
Comanches. He studied her face closely. She didn't have those
high cheek bones.

"Are you a white woman?" he asked.

The woman didn't understand. She spurted out another string
of breathless words that contained "Peta Nocona."

"Antonio, ask her if she's a white woman."

Antonio spoke, then translated her reply. "She Comanche. Wife
of Peta Nocona. She demand where are her boys. She crying por
sus hijos. She ask, 'you kill her sons?'"

"Damn me, boys, if we ain't got a white woman here," said Sul.
"Been held captive so long she can't speak English any more. Ask
her if she's a captive, Antonio."

Again, Antonio translated her reply. "She no captive; she
Comanche. She want to know what to happen with her boys."

Sul looked around the plain. Everywhere, his men were taking
scalps or picking up weapons and personal articles that had
belonged to the Indians. They were stacking the stripped bodies in
neat, straight rows. "Sergeant," called Sul. "Do you have a report
on the battle yet?"

"Yessir," said the sergeant, his left arm embracing a bundle of
booty. "We captured about forty mules and horses, some of them
with brands. Probably some they stole. Charlie Goodnight and one
other are tracking a couple of bucks that got away. There are sixteen Comanches dead, all but two of them women, and a few
young girls. No wounded."

"Any young boys among the dead?" asked Sul.

"No, sir," said the Sergeant. "No young boys. And no prisoners but this woman and her little girl. No loss of personnel or equipment on our part."

"Antonio," said Sul Ross, "tell this woman—and be nice about it; we got a white woman here—tell her that her boys must be okay, 'cause there ain't any young boys among the killed or wounded."

After Antonio translated, the woman gasped and wept anew, but with a difference. She looked at Ross thankfully, choking through her tears, and said, "Oh, grácias, capitán; grácias."

Sul looked at the flat rim of the northern sky. Some nasty weather was brewing; they'd need to find some shelter soon. "And ask her, Antonio, if she'd mind coming along with us back to Camp Cooper."

"She come," said Antonio. "She no got the choice."

Náudah glanced at the ring of Texans around her. Practically all of them had thick, bushy mustaches and wore floppy felt hats. She searched frantically for a way to get away. Even if she and Toh-Tsee-Ah could leap on Wind, the Rangers would hem her in instantly. Oh, if she only had a decent weapon: at least, she could kill a couple.

Beyond the Rangers, she could see the row of bloody and naked bodies of her friends and relatives. The sight made her stomach jump and her throat tighten. The Rangers had stacked some on top of the others, like logs for the fire. She retched, but did not vomit. Trembling, Náudah hugged Toh-Tsee-Ah close against her doeskin dress and waited for them to kill her.

Then with a jolt, she realized that they weren't going to kill her. Worse, they were taking her prisoner for later tortures.

The baby, sensing her mother's worry, began crying, and Náudah, unable to reassure her that everything would be okay, began crying with her.

"This way, ma'am, if you don't mind," said Ross, as he touched the brim of his hat.

Camp Cooper

"I'll bet she's Cynthia Ann Parker," said Captain Nathan Evans, commanding at Camp Cooper on the Clear Fork of the Brazos River. "It all fits when you get down to it. She's about the right age. Quahada band. And last time we heard anything, they said she was married to a chief. It fits. I'll bet she's our long-lost captive."

"She's our captive, that's for sure," said his interpreter, Horace Jones, in his patient drawl. "You have to watch her ever single instant, or she'll try to get away."

Evans looked out the window of his headquarters building. The rest of the camp, except for the two-story mess hall and supply room, consisted of two short rows of wood and canvas barracks. The wooden floors and partial walls of other rows had been abandoned and the canvas roofs removed a year ago after Robert Neighbors, the Indian agent, escorted the Comanches to a reservation at Cache Creek Valley in Indian Territory.

"Where's she now?" Evans asked, turning back to Horace.

"Over by the corral," Jones replied, gesturing with a gloved hand. A two-inch leather fringe dangled from the gauntlet of his glove and along the yoke and sleeves of his buckskin hunting shirt.

"Mr. Ross and Captain Palmer are trying to get her to talk to Ben Kiggins."

"Does Kiggins know enough Comanche to make anything of it?"

"Well, he was a captive as a kid. He has a kid's understanding of the lingo. And Martinez knows enough Comanche to understand, but he don't know enough English to tell us what he knows."

Captain Evans took his seat at his desk, his blue uniform slightly rumpled from an early morning patrol. "Well, take the woman over to our quarters and tell my wife to give her a bath. And see if she can't find some decent clothes. We'll try to talk to her later." His tone of voice said make haste.

Horace Jones turned to go out.

"Oh. Horace, have you tried to talk with the woman yet?"

"Not yet," admitted Jones. "I was out on patrol and just heard about her when we got back."

When Captain Innis Palmer returned to headquarters, he reported to Evans, "She's awful emotional. We can't hardly get her to quit shaking and blubbering. And all she can do is cry about her boys." Like many men of his time, he wore bushy side-whiskers but kept his chin and neck clean-shaven.

"Any luck?" asked Evans.

"Not much more than we already knew. She still says she's the wife of Peta Nocona. She keeps asking about her two boys. We told her again and again there weren't any boys among the killed, so they must have been out somewhere else. That calmed her down a little. Mrs. Evans has her now."

"Well, I guess we'll see soon enough," said Evans. "Take her to the mess hall when she's ready."

When Mrs. Evans brought the woman and her child to the mess hall, the captive was quiet and subdued. Captain Evans sat at a table, twirling a pencil. His company clerk took notes. Captain Innis and the other officers stood impatiently around the tables. Sergeants and other non-commissioned officers had crowded into the area not reserved for officers.

Toh-Tsee-Ah wore a Little Bo Peep cotton print dress with puffy sleeves and a billowy skirt. Náudah wore one of Mrs. Evans' cotton print shirtwaists but was barefooted.

"I swan, I thought we was never goin' to get all the grime off of her," said Mrs. Evans. "But we finally did a pretty good job, don't you think? She insisted on cutting her own hair. I have to say I was pretty glad. I didn't cotton to the idea of washing all that greasy mess."

"Cutting the hair is a Comanche sign of mourning," said Horace Jones. He felt a deep sympathy for the woman, an understanding of the pain behind the gesture.

"And she won't let go of that grimy little purse she wears on a thong under her dress. Nastiest thing I ever saw."

"That's probably her medicine bag," said Horace. "Where she keeps little tokens of her most sacred experiences."

The woman was of medium height, blue-eyed and brown-haired, in her mid-thirties. Her little girl was about two years old, though not yet weaned. A pretty child with an upturned baby nose and dark eyes and hair, she could toddle and talk quite well. The woman's body was thick without being fat, which only showed that she had worked a lot and would be capable of enduring more. Her skin was sun-darkened and leathery, but now they could tell, even more than before, that she was a white woman. She kept her face down, refusing to make eye contact with any of the whites.

"Well, Mr. Jones," said Captain Evans. "Let's try your tongue at talking with her."

Jones offered a greeting in Comanche: "Meeku takwuh Ta-ahpuh makaaruhu." *Let us together nourish the Great Spirit.*

The woman looked at him, surprised, making eye contact briefly. She seemed to notice his buckskin hunting shirt for the first time. Jones smiled at her, but she remained impassive.

"You got any little bit of food I can give her?" asked Jones, looking across to Evans. "A Comanche never pow-wows until you've exchanged some rituals." Captain Evans nodded to his orderly, who went out to the kitchen for food.

Horace Jones tried to get the woman to sit at the officers' dining table, but she refused. She shook her head, glancing furtively at the shoes and legs of the men in blue uniforms who had moved closer. She retreated toward Mrs. Evans. Jones could see her touching her medicine bag through the cotton dress. She was probably repeating some silent charm for protection. Finally, Jones pushed aside the table and sat on the floor, inviting the woman to sit also.

Slowly, cautiously, the woman began to sit cross-legged on the floor. Mrs. Evans reached for the baby, saying, "Here, dear, let me hold the child while you're a-talking." The woman jumped up and back, glared at her, shook her head violently, and pulled the child closer. "Es mi hija," said the woman, "no se mate." Wild-eyed, she looked around at the circle of men surrounding her and began to cry. "No me mate, por favór, no me mate."

And she continued with a breathless rush of Comanche. *"Are these Texans? Please don't let them kill me, don't kill my baby. They are Texans, aren't they? They've killed my relatives, and I don't know what has happened to my sons. They are Texans, aren't they? I won't tell them anything. Maybe they won't kill me. Please don't let them kill me."*

"What's she saying?" asked Captain Evans, gesturing with his pencil.

"She thinks we're going to kill her and the baby," said Jones, flatly and matter-of-factly, his head down so that he would not have to look at any of them. "She thinks we're going to get all the information out of her that we can, then kill her. She's heard that's the way Texans do things."

"Well, tell her we aren't Texans." Evans fidgeted around on his chair a bit, came to attention sitting down, and straightened the lapels of his uniform. "We're officers and men of the United States Army. We don't do things like that. Tell her we just want to help her find her family."

Jones repeated Evans' justification in Comanche, as he shifted his position on the floor. He could sense her fear and desperation; his questioning could only make it worse. That was the nasty part of being an official interpreter; sometimes you were forced to do things against your conscience.

The orderly came in with some corn bread on a saucer. Jones offered the woman a wedge of bread, inviting her again to sit and talk. Slowly, reluctantly, the woman settled, then took the bread, but would not eat. She held it in her trembling hand and secretly watched the circle of bluecoats around her.

"She's afraid of so many around her," said Jones. "Could you move over to one side? Maybe sit at the other table? A man sitting at a table can't get at his weapons as quick; looks less threatening."

At once, everyone in the room moved to another table.

When the room was quiet, Jones offered a part of his corn bread to the Great Spirit and then took a bite. The woman looked from him to the bread in her hand, and back again, then at the soldiers. Jones touched her arm, urging her to eat. Slowly, she brought the wedge of corn bread to her sweat-covered lips and took a bite. She did not chew, but just gazed at the officers, the wad of corn bread still visible in her quivering mouth, the tears glistening in her blue eyes.

Jones shuffled forward on the floor, took a pinch of her bread, and ate it to show that it was not poisoned. She watched as he swallowed. Then she looked again at the bread, at Jones, at the officers. At last, she started chewing. She looked at Mrs. Evans, who was smiling and nodding. Then she ate rapidly.

Jones spoke in Comanche for a couple of minutes, but the woman refused to respond.

"What's going on, Jones?" asked Captain Evans.

"She's still scared we're going to kill her. She'll come around in a minute." As he spoke, the baby began tugging at the bosom of her mother's dress. The woman unbuttoned her bodice, took out her breast, and allowed her baby to suckle.

"Oh, ain't that nice?" said Mrs. Evans, smiling and cooing. "Such a pretty little girl. Ask her what the baby's name is."

To Jones' inquiry, the woman responded so softly he could hardly hear: "Toh-Tsee-Ah."

"Toh-Tsee-Ah," Jones repeated. "It's a kind of prairie flower. The baby is called 'Prairie Flower Person.' Toh-Tsee-Ah." The woman nodded.

"Prairie Flower," said Mrs. Evans. "Topsannah! What a beautiful name!"

"And what's her name for herself?" asked Captain Palmer.

Jones knew it was impolite to ask such a personal question. But what could he do? The woman would not respond to Jones' question.

"Well, ask her about those boys," offered the sergeant.

That kind of question was more permissible. After some talk, Jones reported: "The boys are named Quanah and Pecos. Quanah means 'Fragrance' or 'Sweet Smell,' you know, like an odor. I never heard the name Pecos before. She says they're the sons of Peta Nocona."

Slowly, Jones got the woman to talk. She had told Nobah Joe repeatedly that they ought to have lookouts posted, but he was settled in his warm nest and didn't want to sit up on a windy ridge. He could have worked as well up there in the sun; then they wouldn't have been surprised.

At the time of the attack, most of their sub-clan had been at a trading meeting with Comancheros, Mexican traders from Santa Fe. The Comanches needed coffee, sugar, matches, needles and other supplies they could not make for themselves. They wanted to lay in a store before winter. It would be getting very cold soon, when no one could travel much.

"Ask her what her name is," said Captain Evans, irritated by all the useless information the woman was relating.

Jones asked the woman not about herself, but about her husband: "What does your husband call you?"

"Náudah."

Jones repeated the name and translated. "It means something like 'She Walks With Dignity and Grace.' She is the wife of Peta Nocona. She only wants to return to the high plains and be with her husband and sons."

"Náh u-dah," said Evans, shaking his head. "Well, I'll be! Wife of Peta Nocona. So she's kind of like a queen, or a princess?"

"Something like that," said Jones, closing his eyes momentarily. "She's head woman of her *Nurhmuhr*, her extended family, possibly fifty or sixty people."

Captain Evans was impatient. "Well, it looks like we're not going to make much headway. Mr. Jones, would you and your wife take this woman to your house and care for her till we've identified her family and relatives?"

"She says she's the wife of Peta Nocona!" exclaimed Jones, astonished.

"I mean her *real* relatives. I'll get in touch with the Parkers over by Fort Worth. In the meantime, will you take charge of her?"

"I'd rather not, Captain."

"But you can speak the language," went on Captain Evans. "She'd be most comfortable with you."

"I still don't want me and my wife to take responsibility for her. She's the same as a wild Indian. She'd be constantly trying to escape, which she'd probably succeed at, because my horses are always tied in the shed room."

Besides, he thought, I'd probably help her. These Americans and Texans could not conceive of the idea that a person might be happy in Indian society.

"You're going to have to lock her up."

"But she's a white woman!"

The story of the Pease River "victory," as told in the *Dallas Weekly Herald* of 2 Jan. 1861, quoted Sul Ross at length. "We thrashed them out," Ross proclaimed to all of Texas. "All my men acquitted themselves with great honor—proving worthy representatives of true Texas valor. Not more than twenty of my men were able to get in the fight, owing to the starved and jaded condition of their horses having had no grass after leaving the vicinity of Belknap."

Captain Cureton's ninety volunteers from Bosque County were bitter. They felt Ross had deliberately cut them out of the battle so he could take the honor himself.

"Well, I was at the Pease River fight," admitted H. B. Rogers, much later, "but I'm not very proud of it. That was not a battle at all, but just a killing of squaws. One or two bucks and sixteen squaws were killed. That's all. Nothing to be puffed up about at all."[1]

1. "B. F. Gholson Recollections," B. F. Gholson Papers, Center for American History, University of Texas, Austin, quoted in Hacker, *Cynthia Ann Parker.*

Late in January 1861, Isaac Parker arrived at Camp Cooper. His white hair cropped close, his face astringent, Parker had been prominent enough in his prime to have Parker County, just west of Fort Worth, named in his honor. Though elderly, he was still the religious and political leader of the family. Through Horace Jones, he tried to talk with the captured woman.

She said she could not remember her original name.

She said she could not remember ever understanding any English.

She could not remember where she came from.

Isaac Parker studied the woman. Except for the blue eyes, there was nothing to remind him of the cute, blonde nine-year-old niece who had been stolen by Comanches in May 1836. This woman was coarse in her movements, not dainty; her hair was dark, not blonde; her hands were gnarled, her body thick. And yet, all the other details fit.

"Tell her," said Parker at last, "tell her that I think I am her uncle, her father's brother, and that I only want what's best for her and her child. I want to reunite her with relatives who love her."

After that, the woman sat immobile lost in profound meditation, oblivious to everything around her.[2] She stared at the floor, biting her lip gently and squeezing the medicine bag under her dress. The baby squirmed in her arms and said a few words in Comanche, but she did not respond.

Images older than her conscious memory began shaping themselves in her inner eye. She saw

> *A woman in a field, a pale woman, with four children. None of them had faces. The mother had a baby in her arms, a small boy about four, a boy about six, and a girl about nine. A man on horseback, a young warrior, came up and demanded the older children be given to him. The mother refused; the horseman lifted his war axe to hit her. She backed off. She gave up her children. She gave away her children. That's what Náudah had remembered before she married Peta Nocona. The mother didn't love her children. She had given them away.*

2. The Galveston Civilian, 5 Feb. 1861. As reported by A. B. Mason, a journalist who had accompanied Parker to Camp Cooper.

Náudah sobbed involuntarily, then quickly closed her eyes tightly to stop the tears and the trembling. She would not look up. She would not respond to questions, though Jones and Parker kept trying. She stared at the floor between her feet, as if lost in some far distant world.

And now Náudah was just like that pale distant woman with no face. The men with six-shooters had taken her away from her two sons. But she loved Quanah and Pecos. She loved them like her own life. There had to be a difference. She loved her sons.

Now and then, the woman would shake with some emotion, which she struggled to suppress. When at last, she released the medicine bag under her dress and looked at Parker, she shuddered and squinted to hold back her tears.

Through Jones, Parker asked her, "Do you remember where you lived when you were a child?"

The woman shook her head and stared at the floor again. Her shoulders quivered, and she put her hand up to steady her cheek.

A big clearing, outside a big palisade. Several warriors were counting coup on a white man who held meat in his hands. Their clubs broke open the white man's skull.

Through Jones, Parker asked again, "Do you remember the house where you lived as a child?"

The dazed woman mumbled something so quietly in Comanche that Jones had to ask her to repeat. She sat still for a long moment, not looking at any of the men around her. Gently, Jones asked her again. And this time, she whispered loud enough for Jones to interpret. "It was a big house. The logs ran up and down. A clearing surrounded the house, but there was a big woods just a short walk away."

"My God!" exclaimed Parker. "That fits the description of Parker's Fort. She must be my niece. Ask her if she remembers anything about her parents."

The woman shook her head.

"Ask her if she remembers a war at that house? At the time she was kidna—when she first went with the Indians?"

Again Jones talked with the woman for some minutes. "Yes," reported Jones, "she remembers when Peta Nocona came and took her."

She straddled the horse behind Peta Nocona and hung on to his waist. They rode away from the woman who did not love her children.

"He was nice to her. It was in the early summer, twenty-four years ago."

"That's only a few months off! Ask her if she remembers her brother, John?"

Through Jones, she said that she remembered the name John, but she didn't know if he was a brother. She didn't know what had happened to him. She thought he died of red spots in one of the white man's epidemics that struck the Comanche people now and then.[3]

"And she doesn't remember anything about her mother and father?"

Jones hesitated. Isaac Parker had no idea how cruel he was being. But it was Jones' job to translate, regardless of what he felt. "She says she once had pale-faced parents, but she cannot now remember even what they looked like."

Isaac Parker turned to the woman directly and spoke in English. "I'm your uncle Isaac, your father's brother. Don't you remember Silas and Lucy? They were the best, the most loving mother and daddy a child could ever have."

But the woman remained silent, glancing at Jones, waiting for him to interpret. She hugged her own shoulders, as if cold and tired.

When Jones had translated, she still remembered nothing about her parents.

"Does she remember her uncle Benjamin at the time of the attack? He went out to take meat to the Indians and talk under a flag of truce. They surrounded him and beat him to death with their tomahawks." She did not remember.

3. What happened to John is something of a mystery. He apparently escaped from the Comanches or was ransomed. (In December 1842, Texas President Sam Houston authorized compensation for his ransom but the money was never spent.) The most reliable story holds that John went to Mexico with a Comanche raiding party, married a Mexican girl, and lived out his life on a ranch in Chihuahua, refusing to cross the Rio Grande to enter Texas and the United States ever again. See *The New Handbook of Texas*, vol. 4, p. 60.

"Does she remember Elizabeth Kellogg, who was taken prisoner at the same time? Or does she remember Rachel Plummer and her little boy, James? They were taken at the same time."

Isaac asked several more questions. To all of them, the woman responded that she did not remember. She had never heard of these people. Parker and Jones had exhausted her memories.

"It must have been a terribly painful experience," said Jones. "Maybe she's forgotten it all on purpose. Maybe that's her heart's way of defending itself."

Isaac was exasperated. "Well, damn me! We're not getting anywhere," he said, turning to Jones, as if getting ready to leave. "If this is my niece, her name is Cynthia Ann."

Before Jones could translate, the woman sprang up, struck herself on the chest with the flat of her hand, and cried out, "Me! Cinsee Ann! Me Cinsee Ann."

"By God! She is! She's my niece, Cynthia Ann Parker!"

Náudah sank to the bench again and hugged Toh-Tsee-Ah, looking away. Her heart was suddenly beating too fast, the muscles in her throat were quivering, and her forearms tingled. Too late, she feared her hasty impulse had just made the worst mistake of her life.

Lost in the Snow

Overnight snow fell, leaving the rut-marked roads icy and smothering the earth in a white envelope that showed no signs of melting. Isaac Parker was put out. The weather meant he and his niece would not be able to start for his home near Fort Worth until it cleared.

In the officers' mess at Camp Cooper, Náudah would hardly eat. She sat on a bench, staring at the floor, lost in some fantasy. When Toh-Tsee-Ah got her attention, she would hug her almost hysterically and cry out to the men around her, "Mis hijos! Mis hijos! Porqué esconden Ustedes mis querridos?" *Why are you hiding my darlings?* Then she would hug Toh-Tsee-Ah too tightly, whispering, "Pobre, pobre hermanos. Tus hermanos perdidos. Perdidos, en la nieve." *Poor, poor brothers. Lost in the snow.*

"Damn her!" cried Isaac Parker, then immediately added for the interpreter, "Don't translate that."

Horace Jones smiled. "She'll hardly need a translation of that. She may not understand the words, but in her heart, she understands what you're trying to do to her. She thinks her boys are lost in the snow."

"Everybody says they weren't there," said Isaac Parker, his stern preacher eyes boring into her. "Tell her again for the fortieth time that they're safe with their father."

When Horace had translated, Náudah asked, "¿Es verdad? ¿Creas que sí?" *Do you really think so?*

"Yes, yes," said Isaac. "They're safe with their father."

Instead of that comforting Náudah, it set her off in another wail. "O, mis hijos! Mis hijos pobres. Mis hijos lloran por me! Mis hijos lloran por me en la nieve."

"She thinks her sons are crying in the snow for her," reported Horace.

Suddenly, Náudah jumped up and ran out of the mess hall, into the snow, pulling Toh-Tsee-Ah in tight against her body so she could run. If she could only get to the corral, maybe she had a chance to get away and find her sons. Several of the men chased after her and caught her in the middle of the parade ground. One of them tackled her, sending Toh-Tsee-Ah rolling ahead in the snow.

First, Náudah hit her tackler hard in the mouth with a strong right fist, knocking him backward; then she ran for the screaming Toh-Tsee-Ah. Several of the men now stood on all sides of her, hemming her in.

Isaac Parker came out in his shirt sleeves.

"Oh, Oncle Isaac," said Cynthia, trying to speak English. She fell on her knees in the snow in front of him and embraced his legs with the now-quiet Toh-Tsee-Ah at her side. Breathing too fast, she poured out a string of mixed Spanish and Comanche. "Por favór, tio mio. Take me to my sons. Tu puedes. You can do it. When Our People see me with you, they won't hurt you. When they see Toh-Tsee-Ah, they will lower their weapons. I won't let them hurt you. Toquet, oncle. You'll be safe. Mea-dro. Kee-mah. You know the way. Please, please, mi querrido uncle, if you have any feeling for a mother's love in tus corazón, please take me to my sons."

Isaac bent over and lifted her by the shoulders. "Look, my dear Cynthia Ann. I understand that you love your sons very much. But it's out of my hands. I don't know where they are."

"Oh, mis hijos! Mis hijos perdidos!"

"Listen," Isaac went on, talking through the interpreter and leading her back to the mess hall. "We'll send out messengers to look for your sons. We'll have them go everywhere. When they find them, if they find them, we'll bring them to Birdville to be with you. I have a big house. We have plenty of space. You, your sons and Topsannah can live in the other part of my house."

When the interpreter had explained that to her, Náudah fell into another of her silences. It was almost as if she had gone into a trance. Toh-Tsee-Ah stood at her feet, waiting. Náudah stared at the strange white man who said he was her uncle.

Horace brushed a forefinger across his nose and wondered if there was other work a man could find. He didn't understand why they wouldn't just let her go back to her husband. Well, yes, he understood with his head; he just couldn't understand with his heart.

He knew that these officers and men—kind-hearted and benevolent though they thought they were—really wanted, deep down to kill what was essential in this woman. In the center of their souls was something their minds didn't even know was there, something with a will and a life of its own—it wanted to kill the Indian in this woman. And he'd have to help. They wanted him to help. They were forcing him to help.

At last, Náudah looked up. "Ha-itska Nocona? Nuh kumah-puh?" she asked Jones—*where is Wanderer, my husband Peta?*

Horace could only shrug.

"I don't have any choice, do I?" she asked Horace in Comanche. "You who understand my language, you can tell me truly. I don't have any choice, do I?"

There was nothing he could do to free her; he might as well try to make her as happy as he could. "These are your family, Preloch," said Horace, using her special Comanche title. "These are blood of your blood, heart of your heart. They will love you, and you will come to love them."

"Do you think so?" asked Náudah, grasping the wooden bench to steady herself. "Do you think I can, when my sons are lost in a brutal world?"

"Your sons aren't lost, Cynthia Ann," said Isaac, after the translation, smiling to reassure her. "When we find them, we'll bring them to Birdville to be with you."

"And you won't kill them?"

"Of course, we won't kill them!" He looked at her earnestly. She turned away her teary eyes. "We're Christians and Texans. We'll love them as we love you, and we'll teach them to be good Christians."

"¿Puedes amar un Comanchito?" *Can you love a Comanche boy?* she asked, not looking at him.

"Of course. They are our relatives, the same as you are. We'll take care of them and protect them, just as we will you."

"Promise?" asked Náudah, doubtfully. She bit her lower lip.

"Promise," said Isaac Parker, taking one of her shoulders in one hand and lifting her chin with the other, so that she had to look at his eyes. "It is my holy covenant to you."

She understood that such a promise was like a treaty. But treaties had not been good for the Comanches. They took away their way of living—would not let them continue to be Indians, free on the high prairies; but the whites would not let the Indians become whites either, for they insisted the Indians live on reservations. Uncle Isaac was putting her in a painful quandry—his treaty would not let her be Comanche, but she doubted if she could ever become white.

Preparations were almost complete for the journey to Fort Worth. "I must have my dress!" cried Náudah in abusive Comanche to Mrs. Evans. "What have you done with my cowrie-shell dress?" She grabbed Mrs. Evans by the wrist and twisted.

"Ouch, you're hurting me."

"You took my sheath," said Náudah in Comanche. "Give it back."

When the interpreter arrived, Mrs. Evans was practically in tears. "I just don't know what to do. She's so strong. And so strong-willed. I'm a little afraid of her."

Horace Jones explained that Náudah wanted her Comanche
dress.

"That old thing!" said Mrs. Evans, putting her palms together. "I thought she'd want to get rid of it. You can't wear that thing in civilization," Mrs. Evans said directly to Náudah. "Why, everybody would stare at you."

"Give me my dress," insisted Náudah, drawing its cowrie shell yoke in the air. "I must have my Comanche dress."

Sheepishly, Mrs. Evans took the garment out of a wooden chest at the foot of her bed. "I just couldn't destroy it," confessed Mrs. Evans. "It's too pretty. I was going to keep it."

"And the leggings," demanded Náudah, indicating there was more. "Where are the leggings?"

But Mrs. Evans had no idea where the deerskin leggings were. They had been lost in the confusion.

"And Toh-Tsee-Ah's antelope-skin shift. Bring out Toh-Tsee-Ah's dress, too."

"Oh, my, my," said Mrs. Evans, taking the little dress out of the chest. "Mr. Jones, can't you talk some sense into her? Clara and I—Mrs. Palmer and I—have fixed her a nice travel frock, as nice as anybody in these parts can get these days." She brought out the full-length, wide-skirted dress, a dark, heavy, wool gown, fitted tight in the bodice and braced to hold up an ample bosom.

"Maybe you could get her to accept both," suggested Horace.

That was a compromise Náudah was willing to agree to. She held up her loose-fitting deerskin sheath with the fringe at the hem and the yoke of cowrie shells on the front. This dress and her medicine bag were almost as important as her soul. The little worn bag contained her mementos of past events, little gifts of medicine-power, as well as a little clay pipe and some sacred tobacco. They would be a little part of her past she could take with her.

Mrs. Evans gave Cynthia Ann a brocade bag to put her and Topsannah's extra change of clothes in. But Náudah refused to wear the tight frock Mrs. Evans had fixed. After some maneuvering, she accepted a loose-fitting, polka-dot blouse and a wide cotton skirt. Furiously, she stuffed the frock into the brocade bag, over her and Toh-Tsee-Ah's leather clothes.

Cynthia Ann and Isaac Parker started the bone-jarring, two-day trip to Fort Worth in a closed coach with a brazier of hot coals at their feet. Náudah had heard descriptions of such fire-buckets from Mexicans at Santa Fe, but she had never seen one. Isaac had to warn her repeatedly, however, to keep her long skirt away from the coals, else they would all be in flames, the whole stagecoach. Toh-Tsee-Ah, too, had to be kept back from the coals for fear her little smock dress with the white diamond prints would ignite.

"¿Tu?" Náudah asked Isaac. "¿Hermano de mi madre?" *Are you my mother's brother?*

"No, no, no. I'm—" He spoke slowly, enunciating each word with care. "I am your father's brother. Hermano de su padre. But Silas is dead. El está muerto. He was killed when you were taken from us. The same blood ran in our veins. The same passions and compassions flowed from our hearts."

Náudah looked away and down, silently. That was an end to the trust she felt growing slowly. If Uncle Isaac were not her mother's brother, he had no responsibility at all for her. He had no obligation and no loyalty. She was alone when she was with him.

Without an interpreter, it was a difficult trip. Isaac was getting better at making signs to communicate what he meant to say, but he was very awkward, and his attempts to remember Spanish phrases often failed. He was intent upon stimulating her memory of her kidnapping twenty-five years before. "You don't remember your cousin, Rachel Plummer? She was the lovely daughter of my brother, James. She and her little son were captured by the barbarians at the same time as you were. The treacherous demons beat her and the baby until they were bleeding to death, then the unspeakable curs forced her to gather buffalo chips for their fires. She was given so little food that she practically starved, and so little clothing that she almost froze to death. She was sold as a slave or concubine to six or seven different people. One old witch of a woman beat her with a club, until Rachel lost her patience, grabbed the club, and began beating the old hag. She expected to be put to death then, but the Comanches approved of her courage, and treated her a little better for a time."

Though Isaac used many Spanish phrases, Náudah understood next to nothing of what he said, though she did discern what the subject was. He seemed to want to impress upon her how cruel the Comanches were and how kind and gentle the Texans were. Neither of those propositions agreed with her experiences among Texans or Comanches.

"After twenty-one months of that horrible and insufferable slavery, her prayers and lamentations were answered, and Rachel was sold to a trader in Santa Fe, who took her to Independence, Missouri. Her brother-in-law Dixon went and redeemed her. Finally, after so many unspeakable horrors, she was restored to her father and husband at Fort Houston. Unfortunately, she died only about a year later."

"She never got her revenge, the way Elizabeth Kellogg did," Isaac went on after a moment of silence. "You remember your grandmother Doty's sister, Elizabeth Kellogg? The demon savages captured her at the same time, but she was ransomed in Kansas soon afterwards. She met James at Fort Houston, and, as they were on the way home, they came across some Comanches who had been captured. This one ugly buck, who had scars on both his arms, was the one who killed Elder John and carried Elizabeth away. She pointed him out, and James summarily killed the scoundrel, saying with a great deal of satisfaction and justification, there was one perfidious murderer that would never kill or scalp another white man."

Náudah tried to sleep to avoid such conversation. When she was awake, she talked with Toh-Tsee-Ah in Comanche, but she kept losing her train of thought. She daydreamed about her husband and sons. Ha-itska Nocona? Ha-itska po-mea? Were they warm beside a bucket of fire? Did they miss her like she missed them? She tried having silent, imaginary conversations with them. Peta Nocona had a way of calling her "Walks-With-Dignity," not as if it were a name, but the sentence her name came from. He made it sound like, "She walks with dignity and grace." Does a prisoner have any dignity? she asked silently. She put one hand over her eyes to wipe away a tear and felt with the other for the comfort of her medicine bag, where, among other things, she kept the small fire opal that Peta Nocona had once given her.

> *He opened his own medicine bag in front of her and took from it an opal amulet, the size of her little fingernail. "I call this the eye of the heavens," he said, holding it in his open palm so that it caught and reflected the fire of the sun. "I took it from the neck of a white woman once, but the little chain is now lost. I want you to have this 'eye of the heavens,' because you are the most important person in the world to me. You are the heavens and the night to me; you are my reason for living."*
>
> *She accepted the opal pebble reverently and held it gently in her own hand. She could feel the heat of it, traveling into her arm, into her bosom, where it warmed her heart. When Peta Nocona looked at her, her heart flashed fire like that opal pebble in the sunlight.*
>
> *She put the opal in her own medicine bag, where it lay against her rib cage.*

She had often taken it from the medicine bag and gazed at it, especially when Nocona was off on a trading expedition or a long hunt. Most of the time, she did not even have to open the bag to know it was there. She could feel its presence. And her awareness of it made her heartbeat ripple like a happy flowing stream.

They stopped each day to eat at crude roadhouses. Ground meat that would have made good pemmican if it had been treated right, loaves of bread that flaked off in crumbs, but she had no appetite. And, even more than the Mexicans at Santa Fe, these whites expected her to pick up her food with a fork. The knives they gave her to eat with would hardly cut off a piece of meat in her mouth. She decided they gave her such dull ones for fear she would stab her uncle and run away. She had thought of that. But she would have to wait for a better opportunity. The soldiers would catch her and Toh-Tsee-Ah quickly, if they tried to run now. She had no horse; she wasn't even sure which way to run.

When Toh-Tsee-Ah wanted to nurse, Náudah simply opened the front of her blouse and let her nurse. At first, Isaac was pleased and amused to see a suckling child, but then he became extremely upset, making gestures, wagging his finger, pointing to Náudah's other breast. At first, she thought he was rudely pointing to her medicine bag, hanging against her rib-cage in the hollow below her arm.

Finally, she realized that he was upset that Toh-Tsee-Ah liked to play with Náudah's other breast while she was nursing on one. She liked to run her little hand over its roundness, to feel the nipple, to fondle the whole thing. Isaac didn't want the child to do that. But she didn't stop Toh-Tsee-Ah from playing with her breast. She was aware that it was an act of defiance. She couldn't stab him with a knife or beat him with a stick, but she could offend his sense of propriety. And, in a curious way, the defiance made her feel a little better.

At Fort Worth, Isaac took them to an itinerant daguerreotypist named A.F. Corning to have Cynthia Ann's image made. It happened that Toh-Tsee-Ah wanted to nurse while Corning was trying to take their picture. Náudah opened her polka-dot blouse and let her.

"Ah! Wonderful! Wonderful! Nursing mother. An artistic shot!" cried Corning, as he rushed to prepare the copper plate. He put it in the camera and uncapped the lens. "We'll call the picture 'Madonna and Child.'"

Toh-Tsee-Ah—at her mother's bosom—peered back in curiosity, trying to see what Corning was doing, her eyes turned to the very corner of her lids. Cynthia Ann stared grimly at the camera through pale eyes, her hair hacked short, her gnarled hands clutching the child. She tried to smile as if wanting to make the best of things she did not understand.

From Fort Worth, it was only a few hours by buggy northeast across blackland prairie and timber to Isaac's farm on the West Fork of the Trinity River. The double log cabin they came to was considered one of the finest in the area.[1] Two twenty-one-foot square structures sat under one roof with a breezeway between them. A ten-foot-wide porch ran the length of both. The whole affair was covered with milled lumber and painted white. Two front doors opened onto the porch and overlooked a meadow with barns at the lower end.

Bess Parker, Isaac's wife, and daughter Anna met them at the door. "Welcome home, Cynthia Ann," said Bess. "We'll make you as comfortable as we can." Making motions of eating and drinking, Bess asked, "Would you like something to eat after the trip? Or something to drink?"

Náudah did not understand the words, but she did grasp the signs. And she understood that this was the matron, the senior wife, of the house. She smiled and made a motion of drinking. Anna brought two glasses of milk for Náudah and Toh-Tsee-Ah.

Isaac, Bess, and Anna escorted Cynthia and Topsannah to the rear cabin. "This is where you'll make your home," Isaac said, knowing that she would not understand the words but hoping that the gestures would communicate his meaning.

There was a stone fireplace in the end wall and small doors in the other three walls, but no windows. Beds stood in two corners and a table and chairs had been arranged near the fireplace. A stuffed armchair next to a little round table—with a vase on a small scarf—completed the furniture. On the mantle and table sat two glass lamps. Anna took a match from a cup on the mantle and lit one of them.

"Peligroso," said Isaac. "Muy peligroso. Very dangerous. You can burn down the whole house." He held up the burned match.

"Sí," said Náudah. "Comprendo. Tenemos palos de fuegos en la Comanchería." *We have sticks of fire on the prairie.*

Bess lit a stack of wood in the fireplace. "Knock the chill off the place," she commented to no one in particular.

Náudah looked closely at a plaited rug on the floor. Though thick, it was smooth to the touch and spongy; she would study how

1. The Parkers' dog-trot-style cabin has been preserved. Amon G. Carter purchased it in the 1920s and moved it to his estate at Lake Worth. In 1959, it was moved again—to "Log Cabin Village," in Fort Worth, where it can be seen today.

it was made. When she returned home, she would make one like this for Peta to lie on.

Isaac pointed to a piece of cloth hanging on the wall above the mantle. Colored threads made words: "Home, Sweet Home." "That's where you are now, my dear Cynthia Ann. At last you are home. You are safe again among those who love you." Isaac reached out to embrace her. Náudah did not understand the words, but she understood the intention. She allowed him to put his arms around her shoulders, and she laid her forehead against his chest. She hardly knew what to say, but knew she had to acknowledge his gesture and agree with it. "Grácias. Muchas grácias."

"That's another thing," said Isaac. "You've got to forget those heathenish tongues and learn English again."

"Eng. . .?" asked Náudah.

"Yes," said Isaac, making the Indian sign for words. "White man talk."

"Tosi-taivo rekwaruh," repeated Náudah.

Náudah and Toh-Tsee-Ah lay down to sleep that night in a featherbed that puffed up around them like water in a warm, shallow stream. Toh-Tsee-Ah crept close to nurse. She was tired but also hungered for the close contact. She fondled her mother's breast and suckled, stopping occasionally to look and listen. "Meadro Quanah"—*Let's go to Quanah*—she said, then went back to nursing.

Náudah bit her lip, but that didn't keep the memories from flooding back, covering her, consuming her like a flash flood in an arroyo. Yes, indeed, let's go to Quanah. And Peta Nocona and Pecos, and all our friends in the Quahada band. Let's eat with them in a warm buffalo-skin tipi, and tell stories of our day's experiences, and lie down in soft buffalo robes. Let's watch the fire burn low and listen as the children drift off to sleep. Let's touch those we love.

She allowed herself to imagine that it was Peta Nocona who was fondling her breast.

"Come to bed, woman," he said. "That moccasin can be mended tomorrow."

She glanced at Quanah and Pecos. They had long since learned to turn their faces away and at least pretend sleep when their parents were privately talking or making love. She drew her doeskin dress over her head and lay it well away from the fire.

He had folded back the buffalo robe to let her in. She lay against him, letting him enclose her, as if she were sinking in warm water. He filled her, as air fills the sky. She could hardly get her breath.

Quanah lay in the grass. His arm had been hacked off with a war-axe, and his legs were strewn along the creek bank. He had been scalped. There was no one to recover his body, no one to bury his bones; his soul would never escape, never be free to go to the Afterworld.

Náudah awoke with a start, aware that her mind was playing tricks on her. The sheet was wet with sweat and tears. Where was she? A small fire still glowed on the hearth, spreading a dim light on a wall and a door. She stood, went to the door and peeked out. A nearly full moon shone on the meadow, making the dry grass look like snow; the light spilled into the room and told Náudah where she was: a white man's cabin. Her white-man uncle, Isaac Parker's home. Quickly, she searched for her medicine bag and relaxed when she found it. Why—why had she ever let him know who she was?

She opened the door and, naked, went out on the porch and watched and listened to the meadow in the moonlight. It was a clear winter night, chilly but not so cold one couldn't stand it. The moonlight made wispy ghosts of the leafless trees. She could not go far in case Toh-Tsee-Ah awoke, but she stepped off the porch and waded into the short grass.

In the moonlight, she could almost forget that she was a prisoner. The sheen of the night was the same everywhere. It turned the familiar strange and the strange familiar. She imagined she was at home, among the spirits of her own land. She lifted her arms to the moon. "O, Kaku-Tohmua, *Oh, Grandmother January Moon,*" she prayed in Comanche, "Oh, Stars of the Grandfather Sky, take me home to my people. Show me the path; light my way; guard my footsteps."

"It's light enough for us to travel, but not light enough for the enemy to track us easily," Peta had said, explaining why the warriors of Our People liked to go on horse stealings or raids on enemy camps during the time of full moon. "We can break into small groups and travel all night the first night, when it is difficult to follow us, because we can see where we are going, but the enemy cannot see the signs to follow. We travel on into the second day. That way, we often escape entirely from the enemy's retaliation."

Náudah raced back to the room, found the brocade bag, and jerked out her doeskin dress. She strapped on her medicine bag and slipped the garment over her head. She could feel the fringe brushing against her legs; so right it felt. She already felt better; a twinge of happiness. Yes, she could, she would escape in the full light of a Comanche moon. She made a sling of the table cloth to put Toh-Tsee-Ah-ne in. She wouldn't bother to dress her baby just now. She slipped on her moccasins, crept to the door again, went out, walked quietly down the porch toward the back end, toward barren trees.

"Cynthia Ann? Is everything all right?" It was Uncle Isaac. He was standing in the shadow of the porch in his nightshirt.

She turned and walked to him. "Oh, tio mio," she said, putting her free arm around his body and pulling him to her. He was shivering with the cold. "Querrido tio, yo estoy el mejor triste. Pido una poca lástima. Deseo ir a mis hijos, a mi familia." Then she shifted over to Comanche. "I am so sad. Nothing looks right to me here. The moon tells me that I should be with my family. Por favór, let me go to my family. I need mis hijos."

She pulled Isaac closer, desperately trying to make him understand. He touched her arm, saying "You're hurting me. You're hugging me too tight." She realized that, if she did not have Toh-Tsee-Ah in her other arm, if she had both arms to her use, she could break his back and run away. But he was family, even if distant. She released her grip.

He took her bare arms in his hands and held her away from him. "Cynthia, my dear Cynthia Ann," he said, "you've got to try to speak English. Use white man's talk."

"Tosi-taivo rekwaruh?" she echoed in Comanche.

"Yes. This is your home now. We will provide for you and your daughter, everything you need. We will buy you proper clothes, feed you wholesome food, help you to love God and all His Creation. Oh, God in Heaven," he broke into prayer, "Help us to make this woman happy. This is our daughter, who was lost and is now found. This is your Lamb; bring her into Your Fold."

Náudah did not understand the words, but she understood that he would not let her go back to the high plains of the Comanchería. He was dooming her to stay here, here where, now, even the moonlight looked strange. She turned away and walked back to her cabin, so that he would not know there were tears on her face or feel the trembling of her heart.

As Isaac called "good night," Náudah heard a prop being put against the outside of the door to lock it. Then, after a moment, the outside latch bars were dropped into place at the other two doors.

She sank to the plaited rug and pulled her baby close. "También nosotros, Toh-Tsee-Ah," she murmured, tears streaming down her face. "También estámos los perdidos. Perdidos en la nieve." *We, too, are among the lost. Lost in the snow.*

Victory Dance at Birdville

Náudah woke when Bess opened the door and found them asleep on the rug. "Goodness!" exclaimed Bess. "You'll catch your death! Aren't you cold?" She hugged her own shoulders and shivered.

"Tengo frío," Náudah admitted.

Bess put a few shavings on the embers in the fireplace, puffed and fanned until they caught fire, then piled on kindling, and finally firewood. The friendly crackle of the fire quickly filled the room. "Bueno, bueno," said Náudah, crowding up close with Toh-Tsee-Ah to catch the heat.

"Would you like some hot coffee?" asked Bess. But Náudah did not understand. Bess brought a cup of steaming coffee anyway and offered it to Cynthia Ann.

"Oh! Too-pah!" Náudah cried with delight and took a sip. Coffee was a great delicacy on the Comanchería, but this was bitter.

"And I brought some hot chocolate for Topsannah," Bess added, smiling.

"¿Azúcar?" Náudah asked.

"Sugar? Sure. I'll get some." Bess came back almost at once with the sugar.

Náudah felt a surge of gratitude for Bess. "Gracias! Thank," she stammered. Bess was the favored wife in this lodge, and she was kind and loving.

"I can see that everything's going to be all right," said Bess. "Everything is going to be right."

But in spite of Bess' optimism, Náudah felt lonely for her husband and sons, and she felt dirty living in a white man's house. There was no explaining it. She admitted that the women kept everything clean, even the rug she and Toh-Tsee-Ah slept on. Something more profound contaminated the Parker house, something built into the very assumptions they lived by. Her Comanche father Paha-yuka had put it simply: "The whites are crazy; they don't think the way we do." And, Náudah knew, their spirit would contaminate her and Toh-Tsee-Ah-ne, too, if it got the chance. She had to protect herself. She must stay pure in soul until she and Toh-Tsee-Ah could get out of here.

In the barnyard, Náudah saw a scissortail—messenger of the Spirits.

"Fly away, brave, bird. Fly away to the Comanchería. Tell all my relations where I am. Tell my family to come and get me and Toh-Tsee-Ah. Tell them to come and kill these Tejanos, and take me home."

She discovered a juniper bush in the corner of the Parker yard. It wasn't cedar, but it was a close substitute. She nipped small twigs and branches from it, made a thatch of it, and lit it at the fireplace, then wafted the smoke over herself. She brushed the smoking thatch up and down, close to her legs, across her head and down her back as far as she could reach. She felt cleansed. Then she smoked Toh-Tsee-Ah-ne the same way.

She felt good, renewed. Paha-yuka had taught her that the ritual was an affirmation of her place in the world. It asserted the individual's version of the partnership every person has with the universe. It tells the hunter that he is never alone, no matter how far away he wanders from this relatives and friends. It guarantees the captive that a world of harmony and good fortune exists, no matter how many restraints prevent one from reaching it.

Náudah refused to wear anything but her deerskin sheath, rejecting all the clothes the white woman tried to force upon her. She put aside the polka-dot and print pinafores and smocks they had given Toh-Tsee-Ah and dressed her in her antelope shift. It was a pitifully small gesture, but it was all she had to maintain their identity and a fragment of their dignity.

"That's all right," said Anna. "She must feel a lot more natural in her own clothes. It won't hurt anything for her to wear them."

"Well, it's all right," said Bess. "For now."

"Yes," said Isaac. "We've got to be patient."

"I just can't see why she wants to go back," said Anna.

"Well, once she learns the conveniences of civilization, she'll forget all about going back," said Isaac.

Bess and Anna repeatedly came into Náudah's room or took her and Toh-Tsee-Ah into the main room of the double cabin, with their sewing baskets and bowls of vegetables to peel. "It's better, we don't have to heat both rooms," Bess explained.

Náudah thought of hiding from them. But they would soon find her; they knew all the hiding places, and then they would watch her even more closely. If she were going to find a chance to get away, she would have to pretend to do what they wanted.

Another storm hit, this one with rain, sleet and wind. "That moist wind just gets into a person's bones," declared Bess. And Náudah admitted it was cozy to sit by a good fire and work. Anna was teaching her to embroider, which she enjoyed. She thought, at times, that maybe she would be happy in such a house. Or rather, that if she could take this house with her to the Comanchería, she would be happy to accept it for her family.

She held the edge of the rug and asked "¿Cómo se heche?" then made motions of weaving.

When Bess realized that Cynthia Ann was asking how the rug

was made, she admitted she didn't know. "Why, we bought that rug from Julian Feild over in Fort Worth. He had to order it from Dallas. We don't know how it's made."

So Náudah lay on the floor and traced the strands of the braid, until she had figured out the method and the pattern. Bess and Anna showed her how to cut old socks and underwear with a pair of scissors to make the strands, and she braided a small rug. She left the ends loose, so that she could add to it when she got more material.

"Look at this!" Bess said, showing the rug to Isaac. "She's real industrious. She figured out how they make those rugs we buy."

"That's wonderful," said Isaac. "I knew it would all work out. She'll fit right in and learn English in no time. All the others of our family that were captured were recovered from the merciless savages before they forgot English. We have to be patient."

But Náudah still felt soiled by life in the Parker house, and she gathered more juniper to smoke herself and Toh-Tsee-Ah. Every time she realized the Parker's spirits were crawling all over her, she had to cleanse herself.

"Tio Isaac," she said. "Tio mio. ¿Cuándo vamanos a la Comanchería? *When will we go to the prairie?* I'm so lonely here. My heart cries all the time for my husband and sons. You said we would go and look for them. When can we start?"

"Soon," he answered. "Soon."

But "soon" was slow in coming. Náudah began to see that, if she and Toh-Tsee-Ah were going to get back to the prairie, she would have to devise the method and the trip herself. "Give me a horse and show me the way?" she asked Isaac. "Toh-Tsee-Ah and I will be all right. I know how to travel and take care of myself on the trail."

But Isaac wouldn't hear of it. "After we've saved you from that long night of suffering, we can't just let you go. Don't you realize those infidels out there would just torture you, the way they do all white women? Those howling demons would beat you, force you to work, let you starve and freeze. And every crude buck that came along would feel free to ravage you. I can't let you go back to that miserable plight."

Then I'll have to find a way on my own, Náudah said to herself.

The first Sunday after church, many people followed the Parker clan back to Isaac's cabin in a parade of buggies and hacks. And people began arriving from other places: women in long gowns whose sleeves were as white and round as mushrooms and whose dark skirts went down to the ground; men came in black coats and white shirts and stood around visiting, smoking cigarettes and sucking on grass stems.

Isaac Parker was clearly the chief. Standing on the porch, he called for attention, and everyone stood silently while he made a little speech. "We are gathered here today to welcome our Cynthia Ann back from perdition and into the fold of her rightful family. I want to thank you all, friends, neighbors, family, for coming here today to wish her and us well. She has suffered long, unprotected and undefended, in ways that none of us can come close to imagining. She has lived in the most despicable of conditions and participated in the most contemptible of practices, forced into diabolical perversities by those miserable, heathen wretches. But she is now—praise be unto the Lord!—restored to those who love her. Let us thank the Lord," he said, breaking into prayer, and all those around obediently bowed their heads.

"Thank thee, Father, for restoring Cynthia Ann to us. In Your wisdom, You looked down and saw what was right. You saw the lamb that was lost, and You restored it to the fold. You saw the child that was hungry, and You showered down the loaves. You saw the soul that was groveling in sin and filth, and You lifted up her eyes to perceive again the glory of Your ways. Lift up our eyes, too, that we may see the Glory of Your Kingdom. And bless all our endeavors. Lead us into the right, that we may do Your will. Lead us into the right, that we may glorify God and all His wonders. Amen."

Náudah did not understand the words, but she recognized the gestures and tones of prayer. Her heart in her throat, she realized that her uncle Isaac had started the Victory Dance. The torture was about to begin.

She had been present at many of these dances. The warriors sent word from some distance outside the camp, so everyone would put on their finest clothes and be ready and waiting when the parade of victors marched slowly into camp, the warriors leading their prisoners with ropes around their necks.

The prisoners were tied to posts in the council ground, and the warriors rode around the posts, recounting how the prisoners had been captured, and how many of the enemy each hero of Our People had killed. Only the most courageous were brought back to camp for slow torture. Some would be slowly dismembered: first a finger would be taken, then a hand, then a foot. As long as the enemy did not cry out in cowardice, his valor became the property of the whole village. The best tortures were those when the enemy never lost the will to live, but called defiantly for the victor to cut off another part. Sometimes, brave people were left to live.

With dread in her breast, Náudah realized they were ready to start her torture. But they would do it differently. Instead of cutting off her hands and arms, they would take one thing after the next from her. They had already taken her freedom; step by step, they would take her dignity, her self-respect, her possibility for happiness, her everything. They were trying to take her name from her. They would even try to take her will to live. But she could not cry out in defeat or protest, for then she would have lost everything and they would have gained all.

Náudah was brought before each one of the strangers and told what the person's name was. They said one, a short man with dusty hair, was her brother. "Here's Silas Junior," said Isaac. "He was only three when you were stolen from us, Cynthia Ann."

With surprise, Náudah realized what they were saying. This was her baby brother, a brother she didn't know she had. Suddenly, she understood an image that had lurked in her mind for years.

A toddler, his fist clenched around a fold in his mother's long dark skirt like a possum clinging to his mother's fur. Had the mother loved him more than the children she let be taken away?

"Orlena isn't here," someone said. She did not recognize the 47
name. Orlena must be the nursing baby in the mother's arms, a
baby sister whom Náudah had forgotten. Could one refuse to love
such relatives? Could she ignore them and love only those real relatives she had known? With a blush of sadness, Náudah realized
that Loves-Horses and Trades-It and many of her other relatives
were dead. Perhaps even her husband and sons were dead. But she
would not cry out in pain. She would not give them the satisfaction
of seeing the torture succeed.

Silas, now in his late twenties, was sandy and slender. His young
wife, Amelia, had small clearly defined eyes and a mouth painted
with precise lines. Kwasinabo nabituh', thought Náudah—*she has
snake eyes.* Silas said something to Náudah, but no one bothered to
translate. Tah-mah kuyanai, thought Náudah—*brother turkey.* She
was determined not to give them her love or recognition.

"Let me hold the baby," said Amelia, reaching for Topsannah.
Náudah pulled back, holding the child tighter.

"Oh, come, Cynthia Ann; viene, viene," said Isaac in broken
Spanish. "Este, su familia. This is your family. We mean you and
Topsannah no harm." He took Toh-Tsee-Ah from her arms, held
her for a moment, then handed her to Amelia.

"Thank you, Uncle Isaac," said Amelia. "We've got to do everything we can to save the child from the demons of barbarianism."

Náudah reached for Toh-Tsee-Ah, but Isaac took hold of her
shoulders and guided her to another couple. "This is your cousin,
Billy Parker, who lives only a few miles south of Birdville, and his
wife, Serena." The couple was young and open. Billy smiled a lot, so
that Náudah almost felt welcomed. She found herself smiling back.

Serena touched her arm, "If there's anything you need, just let
us know." Náudah felt a trust growing, but the captors did not
allow her to pause and get to know them.

There were aunts and cousins, friends and mere acquaintances
who wanted to see the Indian and her papoose.

"Couldn't they get her into some civilized clothes?"

"Bess tells me she still sleeps on the floor. Finds the bed too soft!"
"Ain't that a shame?"

Neighbors Edna Brown and Alice Raymond cooed, "We'll take good care of you, my dear."

Náudah glared down, then looked at the whites. They had formed a big circle around her; they were staring at her. They had no bonfire, and they had not yet brought out their weapons, but she knew they were quietly telling each other the story of how she and Toh-Tsee-Ah had been captured; they were recounting the coup.

Some of the men brought out sawhorses and laid planks across them. Then the women put a cloth over the boards and began arranging food in the spring-like sun. It was a victory celebration, as surely as if they had been singing and dancing in ways that made sense. All that was lacking was the torture ceremony. But Náudah was certain the torture was soon to come. She just didn't know what it would be.

Strange that they had not tied her up. Had not even tied her hands behind her. If she had the opportunity, she could escape. She looked around. Several horses were grazing on the winter grass at the edge of the meadow, their reins dragging on the ground, their saddles still cinched tight. A big gray looked like a suitable mount.

She looked around again. Almost everyone was strolling toward the food table. She was left, untied, at the edge of camp.

Náudah yelled in Comanche, "Get down, Toh-Tsee-Ah. Run to me!" She sprinted to the big gray horse, swung up on its back, and kicked its sides. Her feet did not reach the stirrups.

When Toh-Tsee-Ah saw her mother on the horse, she squirmed out of the woman's arms and toddled across the yard toward the meadow. Náudah grabbed a handful of the horse's mane in one hand, hooked her heel on the cantle of the saddle and leaned low to scoop her daughter up from the ground. Before anyone knew what was happening, Náudah and Toh-Tsee-Ah were racing away, down the road toward the west.

Her heart beat rapidly with excitement and happiness. She was on her way to the Comanchería. If only she could meet a party of Comanches, she would be safe. "Nuhrmuhr-ne!" she called, to attract their attention. "Nuh-nuhrmuhr-ne!" But now she could already hear the Parker men pursuing her.

The one called Billy caught up with her first. As he leaned down to grab her horse's bridle, his back was close enough that she could have stabbed him.

"Lo siento," Billy said, a silly smile on his face. "I didn't want to do this, Cynthia Ann. If it was up to me, I'd let you go."

Then the others came up, several men, on all sides, so there was no way she could kill them all and get away, even if she had weapons. She slumped back in the saddle and felt like vomiting. They had captured her again. Their horses surrounded hers, and they were leading the captives back to camp. This time, it was the torture march.

"That was quite a run you gave us," said Isaac. His horse was a big white stallion, one of the best horses there, one that could run for miles before tiring.

"She's sure a good rider," said young Silas.

"Don't you wish you were as good," said someone in the pack.

"If some of our hands were as good a rider as she is, we'd get a whole hell of a lot more work done," said another.

Náudah understood that they were bragging. Riding on all sides, so that there was no chance for her to escape, they were escorting her back to whatever agony they had planned. Silas let his horse fall back, then came up between Isaac and Náudah. "We just want you to fit in," said Silas. "We want to help you fit in with your friends and relatives."

She trembled uncontrollably, for she understood Silas' words. That was the torture they planned for her: to be loved by these friends and relatives. And she was afraid there was not enough cedar smoke in the universe to protect her.

Ceremonies

In a white woman's frock Isaac had forced on her, Náudah sat on the porch and waited. Waited for nothing. The emptiness in her ached. Except for her images of Peta Nocona, Quanah, and Pecos, her mind had gone blank; she yearned for the others, the grandmothers, the adopted sisters, the elders of tahuh nuhrmuhr-ne, *Our People*. Her sorrows had dried the milk in her breasts; so Toh-Tsee-Ah no longer came to cuddle and fondle. "It's about time that child was weaned, fer pity's sake," said Bess Parker. "How old is she, anyway? Over two, ain't she? Maybe two-and-a-half?"

Náudah did not look up from the floor, partly because she did not understand the English, though, in spite of herself, she was grasping more of the language. "Why are you doing these things to me," she asked in Comanche. "If you love me, why are you doing these things?"

"You'll have to speak English for me to understand," said Bess.

Anna had coaxed Toh-Tsee-Ah to sit with her on the step. She had a book with pictures in it. She was pointing to the pages and saying the names of the animals there. "Dog," she would say, and Toh-Tsee-Ah would repeat, "Dog."

Sitting with Anna and reading, Toh-Tsee-Ah had learned more English than Náudah. Toh-Tsee-Ah knew many of the names of their foods, now, so she could ask for more than bread, butter and jam.

"I'll swear, Cynthia Ann," said Bess, "you've got to do something more than just sit here like a turnip. You'll just dry up." She called Isaac and had him ask Cynthia Ann in his halting Spanish if she would help prepare the food in the kitchen. He touched her forearm and lifted her chin to get her attention.

Náudah nodded and went with Bess.

"Would you wash and scrape these carrots?" Bess asked. But Náudah did not react.

Bess dipped water from the cistern bucket and poured it into a basin. She took a small brush and swished at a carrot. "Wash," she said.

Náudah nodded. "Wash," she repeated.

"Carrot," said Bess, holding the vegetable up.

"Crut," repeated Náudah.

Bess took a dull knife and scraped away the outer skin of the carrot. "Scrape," she said, and Náudah repeated.

"Good," said Bess, pleased that she had gotten some response. "Now, these carrots"—she pointed to the pile of dirty carrots—"wash"—she made the motions in the basin—"and scrape"—she made other motions and pointed to the cleaned carrot.

Náudah nodded and set to work. She worked rapidly, studiously, absorbed in having something to do. She understood cleaning away the dirt particles, because the carrots had been stored in moist sand trays in the root cellar to keep them crisp over the winter, and the dirt made the stew gritty.

These carrots were not much different from some of the roots they ate on the high plains. She saw herself,

scooping out a hollow in the ground and lining it with a buffalo paunch before pouring in the water, meat and roots. Then with forked sticks, she would drop clean, hot stones into the stew, making the water boil. Peta Nocona would comment on the good smell. Pecos would be sitting, watching his chance to sneak a morsel out of the paunch with his buffalo-horn spoon even before the stew was

cooked. She would let him, then complain about his behavior. 53
Nocona would snort that she was the one teaching him such wild
habits by letting him get away with it. Quanah would nod, waiting
with his spoon. Toh-Tsee-Ah, still in her belly, would kick, as if
agreeing with Quanah.

Náudah finished scraping the carrots and stood, staring at the
nothing that was outside the window.

"Wonderful!" Bess exclaimed at Náudah's shoulder. "Thank you,
Cynthia Ann. That was wonderful!"

Náudah slipped the knife into her pocket, then turned and
walked out onto the porch again. Why did everything remind her
of those she had lost? And each time, she was left even emptier
than before. How much, how long, how empty could they make
her? She slumped in the rocker and stared at the nothing on the
porch floor.

She needed a good eagle doctor. The Spirit of the whites was
creeping in and infecting her insides. She could almost feel them.
A good Eagle Doctor would know the songs and have the power to
drive the foreigners out.

Anna, still reading to Toh-Tsee-Ah, reported "Topsannah really
learns fast."

"Maybe we should try it on Cynthia Ann, too," suggested Bess.
"Maybe that would be a way to get through to her."

But Náudah understood their trick and would not participate.
She understood that the book was just part of their puha, *their
power medicine.* A shiver of revulsion and fear that they were trying
to steal her soul ran across her body. That's how they did it, a tiny
step at a time. They got you to do their work, to say their words,
think their thoughts, and then they had your heart. You were no
longer yourself. Your mind would be made out of their ideas—their
book and their words—and you would no longer be free to think
your own thoughts. Your heart would think like their hearts, want
what their hearts wanted.

Náudah sprang up from the rocking chair, almost knocking it
over, and picked up Toh-Tsee-Ah. She carried her out into the
meadow, talking rapidly in Comanche. "This is the sky we were

born under, Toh-Tsee-Ah-ne. Don't forget it. Don't forget how to say the word that means sky, tomoobi. This is not the grass we were born beside, but there on the high plains, we have a home. We have a buffalo-skin lodge where we can sleep and be safe from all enemies. And plenty of cedar smoke to purify ourselves with. Your father is a chief, and I am a princess; they call me Preloch there. We don't have to have books, because we have dogs to look at and play with. We have buffalo to hunt and eat the flesh of. We have horses. Every man and woman has several horses. One of your uncles will give you a pony when it is time for you to learn to ride. He will braid your first bridle and show you how to strap on the surcingle. We don't need these people. We have a life of our own. Oh, I wish we could escape and go back there.

"We will," said Náudah, getting excited. "Like the squirrels, we'll save back things. We can hide bits of food, this knife I took—we'll need matches and some kind of weapon, too. But these people don't have bows and arrows. Maybe we can find something to make a lance of. We'll collect everything we need. And the next time the moon is full, I will break the latch of our prison—I've noticed where the latch-bar is weak—and we'll run away into the night. If we only had a good horse. Maybe we'll be able to steal one from Uncle Isaac or maybe from the next farm.

"Don't forget the color of the Comanche sky, Little One. So big, so clear, so blue, so full of good fortune. And not so many trees and hills to keep you from seeing it. It is better than any book to look at, and it will teach you about the harmony it had in the beginning and how you can keep it in balance."

"Cynthia Ann, my dear." It was Bess on one of her arms and Anna on the other. "You've got to try a little harder. We're your family. Please try." They led her back to the porch and gently sat her again in the rocker. When they looked at her face, tears were streaming down her cheeks. Her mouth was pulled out into a wide grimace of pain.

"No me mate," she said; *don't kill me*. "Pido su lástima. No mate mi corazón, por favór." *I beg your pity; please, don't kill my heart.*

"There now. That's better," said Bess, as Anna again took Topsannah into her arms.

"You've gotten your hem all dirty in the meadow," said Bess. "Let's see if we can't find you something real pretty to wear." In the house, Bess brought out a cotton shirtwaist that had been embroidered across the yoke and along the facing. "Wouldn't you like to wear this?" Bess asked.

And because Bess was the mother in this lodge, Náudah had no way of refusing.

Isaac Parker, also, took his turn. He brought out a book, *Three Years Among the Comanches.*[1] As he read, he put his finger on the words, as if pointing to the paper and ink were an endorsement of the vision written there, an assertion of sublime truth, if not divinity. He read the words slowly and distinctly, translating some to Spanish, trying to make her understand.

"Listen to this, Cynthia Ann," said Isaac, pointing to a page:

> The scene was awful and heart-rending. They had cut and hacked the poor, cold bodies in the most brutal manner; some had their arms and hands chopped off, others were disemboweled, and still others had their tongues drawn out and sharp sticks thrust through them. All the dead were scalped, and the scalps, still fresh, were dangling from the savages' belts.

Náudah caught the gist. "Captain Ross do this, too."

"No, No," insisted Isaac. "This was the savages."

Náudah made motions in the air; she couldn't think of the word "stack." "Lay dead people out . . . lo mismo wood for fire?" she asked.

"Don't you understand?" Isaac asked. "You can't continue to be Indian. This was the work of the savages. The Comanches. They were farther down toward Mexico."

Isaac turned again to the narrative:

1. See Nelson Lee, *Three Years Among the Comanches: The Narrative of Nelson Lee, The Texas Ranger. . . .* (Norman: University of Oklahoma Press, 1957 [oiginally published in 1859]).

They would rush toward us with uplifted tomahawks, stained with blood, as if determined to strike, or grasp us by the hair, flourishing their knives around our heads as though intending to take our scalps.

Náudah understood the gesture if not the words. She thought of the way Kelliher had cocked his pistol and pointed it at her and Toh-Tsee-Ah, and urged his horse to bump hers, every time he thought she might be trying to run away. And the rough way they had handled her in bringing her to Captain Ross. But she was unable to find the words to say that the same things had happened to her and all her relatives on the banks of the Pease River.

"This all happened a few years ago, out west," Isaac went on. "A band of savages led by 'Big Wolf'—Osolo."

"Esa-Lo!" exclaimed Náudah before she could stop herself. She knew the man by reputation, a band leader among the Katsotekas. He had led many a successful raid against both the Tejanos and Mexicanos. He was a man with many feathers in his bonnet.

"The only thing that saved Lee was his pocket watch that had an alarm in it. He would wind it up, set off the alarm, and astonish the simple-minded savages. He made them think there was a god in the watch, and that he was the only one who could get it to sound off. Like he was saying to them, 'You want the watch, you save me.'"

"Esa-Lo?"

"Yes, that was the chief's name, Big Wolf. The savages tortured two of the men to death in front of Lee and a companion. They tied them to a post, hacked them with tomahawks, scratched them with knives, pelted them with rocks for several hours. Finally, they dispatched the poor wretches by splitting their skulls with metal hachets."

Náudah was silent. She knew the ceremony. Everyone in the village would get a chance to posture before the captives, frightening them into crying out in pain and for relief; then finally, the men who had captured the enemies stepped up to show their strength by killing them with one blow. The capture and killing of a brave enemy earned one a feather.

Uncle Isaac was going on and on about how Nelson Lee had lulled his captors into thinking he was content to be with them. He walked short distances from the camp in the evening and returned. He built their confidence by seeming to obey every command and fulfill all his duties with care. But Big Wolf was more or less forced by a stronger chief, Spotted Leopard, to sell him and the watch to Spotted Leopard.

Spotted Leopard was a surly and cruel man. When Lee was caught a little too far from the camp, Spotted Leopard tied him to the floor of a tipi and cut the tendons on one knee, not enough to sever them, but only enough to cripple him.

"That sounds awfully cruel to me, doesn't it to you, Cynthia Ann?"

Náudah shrugged. She did not understand what Isaac was objecting to. If the man had misbehaved, he deserved the punishment. But she also understood that she would have to be especially careful. Was Uncle Isaac warning her that he would cripple her if she tried to escape? Surely, he wouldn't cut her, but he might find some other way, some way even more effective, to cripple her.

Isaac continued to read: "Lee says,

My soul still longed to reach the abodes of civilized man. Though greatly discouraged, I never entirely despaired of sooner or later effecting an escape.

"That must be the way you felt all that time," said Isaac. "Longing to see and be with your loved ones at home."

Náudah did not respond. She did not understand, and Isaac could not conceive of the possibility that a human being could prefer to be Comanche. Nor could he conceive of the possibility that he was not communicating anything at all to his niece.

"Soon," continued Isaac, "Barkis, as they called him, was sold again, this time to a chief named Rolling Thunder. Lee got along with Rolling Thunder much better. They had long discussions in the evenings. Rolling Thunder offered Lee a wife, whose name was Sleek Otter. Then one day, when Rolling Thunder bent to take a drink of water from a stream, Lee grabbed his tomahawk and sank it deeply into the old man's skull. That's how he made his escape and returned to civilization after days alone in the wilderness."

"Rolling Thunder?" asked Náudah.

"Yes," said Isaac, looking at the book again to read. "His Comanche name is Kansaleumko."

With a shock, Náudah realized that she had heard this story before. Heard the true version. Heard of the man who pretended to adopt Comanche ways, who pretended to love a wife and the free life on the high plains. Heard of his treachery in killing Kansaleumko. A surge of disgust made its way up toward her throat. Náudah would never be such a person. She would always be true to what was true in her.

But she just might lead them to believe she was adapting to life with the whites. When their guard was down, she and Toh-Tsee-Ah could escape. She slipped a spoon into her sleeve.

Every night the Parkers locked Náudah and Toh-Tsee-Ah in their room, where she divided the matches in the cup on the mantel and put half of them in her cache of supplies. Every day, Náudah sat on the porch, bound and girdled in her white-woman clothes. She held Toh-Tsee-Ah and her medicine bag closely and cried, the tears streaming down her face. She was in such distress that she did not even talk much to Toh-Tsee-Ah.

Bess and Anna Parker came each day and tried to get her to listen to English. She could not close her ears tight enough nor her attention completely enough. In spite of herself, their barbarous tongue began to sound familiar.

"Please, Cynthia Ann," said Isaac Parker, in his awkward Spanish, repeating each sentence in English. "Won't you please try to learn English? We all know that you have suffered greatly at the hands of the heathens, but you are safe now. You do recognize, don't you, that I am your uncle. I am your father's brother, and these are the family that love you."

"Sí," was all Náudah could say. That was the trouble. She did recognize that these were her white relatives. These were the family of her pale-faced parents whom she could not even remember, the pasty people who had no faces in her mind. She believed these relatives meant well. But if they had really wanted to make her happy, they would at least let her visit her relatives on the high plains, so that she would know for sure whether they were alive or not. She cried because her heart was so empty. She craved the love of her husband and sons to fill that void in her chest, which seemed only to grow with each day.

She sat on the porch, deliberately reconstructing memories of Nocona. She could still see his open palm offering her the little fire opal, the magic and power of it radiating from his love for her. She could still see it glinting with fire, even as she could still see Peta Nocona's heart flashing adoration. Oh, where was Nocona now? Where was the comfort that only he could give her?

She became aware of herself in a rocking chair on the Parker porch. Her head was lying against her knees, and she had wet her skirt with weeping. Why didn't the whites realize how unhappy she was? How could she pretend to please them when heartache so consumed her? Why couldn't Uncle Isaac understand that her heart was now made of sorrow and grief?

K.J. Pearson, the husband of a kinswoman, watched her "ceremonial," as he called it.

Náudah, clothed again in her Comanche dress, carried her medicine bag and a kitchen knife. She went behind the house, to a sandy place, where she thought she would not be seen. She knelt and smoothed off a circular area in the soft dirt. She drew a big cross in a circle in the sand, then gathered several small sticks the size of her finger and slightly larger.

She paused then and looked around, as if to see if she were being watched. Finally, she opened her medicine bag, carefully, reverently.

She placed the opal at the north fork of the crossroads of the universe, the fork of wisdom and insight, for the iridescent gem was the eye of the Great Spirit who looks down on all and guides them.

At the south fork, the fork of daily nurture, she placed the pewter Christopher medal that Peta Nocona had brought her from Santa Fe. He was always going off great distances and returning. It was a comfort to remind herself that the sentence behind his name meant "he travels far and returns." Her breath caught again. Why was she not the one called "she travels far and returns?" She would long since have been on her way home. The medicine power in the name would have helped her escape. Its potency, its puha, would have brought her again to the high plains.

She wiped her eyes and continued. From the bag, she took the cured cottontail's foot from the first rabbit Quanah had killed. She held it a moment, living the moment again in memory. He was such a strong boy—and smart. He was already a leader; she had no doubt that he would one day be a chief. Tenderly, she placed the rabbit's foot at the east fork of the cross, the source of beginnings, the source of the future. She had nothing to represent Pecos. He was always in Quanah's footprint; let him be there with Quanah in the rabbit's foot.

At the west, the gateway to the afterworld, she placed the medicine bag itself, first taking out the straight little pipe and the small clump of sacred tobacco she had managed to save through all her sorrows. She hesitated to lay them down, for they might effect her end, might hurl her at once into death, the transition to life hereafter. Bitterly, she mused, that would be a solution to her problem; but what would happen to Peta Nocona and Quanah and Pecos and Toh-Tsee-Ah? She could not abandon them, not willingly.

She paused and looked around. She needed others to participate in her ritual. She searched the barren trees for one of the sky people; she finally saw a raven. Well, old scavenger, old picker of dead bones, you are hardly an eagle, but you will have to do.

She searched for one of the ground people. The family's old dog had followed her and now lay near her left foot. Yes, he was familiar enough, a member of the family. He would understand her sorrow.

She looked for a burrowing animal, a snake preferably, for their medicine was strongest, or at least a ground squirrel, for their messages were swift. She saw only a beetle who was pushing aside the dirt that had covered him for his winter hibernation. She was disappointed, but she took hope. He was coming to life again, after a long sleep; perhaps it was a good omen that she, too, would come to life again after a wintry sleep.

She looked around for a totem of the All Spirit. She did not want to take the smoke that rose from the Parker chimneys, so she avoided looking in that direction. She did not see any clouds, or vapor, or smoke from any of the other directions. Of course, she chided herself—when she lit her pipe, the sacred tobacco would send up its smoke to participate in her ritual.

She picked up the butcher knife and whittled a few small shavings, which she placed at the crossroads of the circle of the universe. She lit them with a match, the only white-man medicine she was permitting to enter, for Our People had long used palos de fuegos, Mexican matches, on the plains. She carefully stacked small sticks first, then larger sticks on her little fire.

When the fire was burning satisfactorily, she untied the shoulder straps of her doeskin sheath and let it drop, so that her shoulders and chest were bare. She took the knife and cut a gash in her chest, then a diagonal one in each arm. She cupped her hands to catch the blood. She let it drip off her fingers into the fire, where it sputtered, cooked, and evaporated. She leaned over the fire, so the drops of blood from her chest would fall directly into the flames.

Finally, she stuffed the little pipe with a small amount of her sacred tobacco and lit it with a bloody stick from the fire. She puffed the smoke in the four directions, chanting:

Náudah is dead, Great Spirit;
She walks no more in dignity.
"She-Mourns" is her name.
Her source of nurture is gone;
Her beginnings have all ended;
Her soul has already walked to the West.

Let the bone picker clean her corpse,
Let the fire in her lodge burn out,
Let the beetle and the ground squirrel tell all:
Let the sacred smoke go through the world and tell all:
Náudah is dead, Náudah is dead: she weeps no more.
She-Mourns.

2. Letter to John D. Floyd, 3 Feb. 1861, Quanah Parker Files, Fort Sill Archives, Lawton, Oklahoma; quoted in Hacker, *Cynthia Ann Parker*.

The husband of the kinswoman, who was watching, later described her ceremonial to the Great Spirit in a letter.[2] It was a prayer, he thought, to "help her understand and appreciate that she was among relatives and kindred."

6

At the Secession Convention:

Austin

Three moons and more had passed since She-Mourns came to the Parker house, and there was no sign that they would honor any of their promises to her. She sat in a rocking chair on the porch and held Toh-Tsee-Ah tightly, too tightly. The child squirmed, wanting to get down and play. "Don't leave me, Toh-Tsee-Ah," she whispered to the child in Comanche. "You're all I have left. They've taken my husband from me. They've taken my sons. They've taken my clothes from me. They want to take our hearts from us." She-Mourns began to cry, and Toh-Tsee-Ah cried in sympathy, running her fingers along the ric-rac decoration on the cotton dress her mother wore.

"Ah, there you are, Cynthia Ann," said Bess Parker, approaching with a tray in her hands. "Anna and I have brought you some hot bread and jam."

She-Mourns did not understand but saw what they intended. She smiled weakly. This was the third time they had done this. They seemed to think there was something special in slicing their bread while it was still hot from their oven, then spreading butter and strange preserved fruits on it. She took the bread and allowed Toh-Tsee-Ah to get out of her lap to take hers.

Anna had a storybook with her and sweet-talked Topsannah into sitting on the step and reading.

Bess pulled up a straight-backed chair and sat near She-Mourns. "It's a nice day, isn't it?" she said, making a gesture that took in the whole meadow. "It's so sunny, you'd think that spring is coming early this year."

She-Mourns just looked at her.

"Go on. Take a bite," said Bess, urging Cynthia Ann to eat. Bess smoothed her long skirt across her knees.

She-Mourns nibbled at the warm bread. She felt utterly power-less. She felt tears behind her eyelids.

"We want to do right by you, Cynthia Ann," Bess went on, ignoring the tears of She-Mourns. "It's so hard, trying to talk to you, when we never know how much you understand. It's going to be lovely once you fit in again. We're so glad to have you back with us. Thank God you were still alive. I mean, thank God you are alive. And with us." Her voice trailed off. She folded her hands in her lap, not knowing what to do with them.

She-Mourns sat on the porch and cried, while Anna sat on the stoop, reading to Toh-Tsee-Ah from a Sunday-school picture book and teaching the child to repeat verses from scripture in English. The child didn't even know that she was a traitor. And She-Mourns could do nothing about it, bound in gray clothes she hated, eating the bitter charity of those she both loved and hated.

Edna Brown was convinced that life was a continual series of adventures, and she was determined not to miss any of them. If that meant she had to harness her own horse and hitch him to the buggy, why she just made that another adventure. She whizzed through her housework, hard and fast, and maybe a little superfi-cially, so she could get on over to Alice Raymond's. "Come on, Alice," she yelled, without tying her horse's reins or going into the house. "We've got to get over to the Parkers' before it gets dark. I've got just the idea to pull that unfortunate girl out of her dumps."

Alice came to the door, wiping her hands on a dish towel. "Now, Edna, that's none of our business. We oughtn't to go butting in where we haven't been invited. It's just none of our affair. That family has its own ideas of what's proper, and what ain't."

"Ah, come on, Alice. That poor ole Isaac Parker is grasping at straws for someone to come along and solve his problem. We're going to do it. We're going to take that woman over for a while."

"We can't—we can't just barge in and—why, neither of us has any room to take care of her. And her all the time trying to get away."

"We aren't going to take her in. We're going to take her on a trip."

"Law—do you know what trouble you're getting yourself into, Edna?"

"Pshaw! Trouble is my middle name. Come on, and I'll tell you about it on the way over there."

Alice lay aside her dish towel and untied her apron. "Jist let me run a comb through my hair."

"You'll jist have to do it again, when we get there," Edna yelled after her.

Edna really liked to take Alice with her. Alice was level-headed and sensible. She was a good check on Edna's enthusiasm. But, sometimes, she needed to be shocked out of the mire she was in. Besides, Edna really enjoyed Alice's capacity to be awestruck; to Alice, every new experience was a miracle.

She had the horse going at a good trot—wind in their faces— before she told Alice they were going to take Cynthia Ann to Austin.

"Austin?" Alice screamed, losing hold of the scarf she held around her hair. She turned in her seat, trying to catch the scarf, turned back as quickly at the shock of Edna's new scheme. "To Austin? We can't! Stop, Edna, Stop! I lost my head rag."

"We'll pick it up on the way back. It's right there at McDonald's corner."

"But, my hair—"

"Oh, pull on a pair of dry panties and listen. The legislature is going to be voting on secession next week. I wouldn't miss that for a brass monkey with a copper tail. And we're going to take that girl along so she'll see another part of the world. Her sitting around all the time, mooning about them heathens on the plains, ain't doing her any good. We're going to take her to the city and show her the sights."

"But—but, how in the world will we get there?"

"Take the Parkers' coach, silly. It ain't like nobody has never been there before. There *is* a road, you know."

The news was out in a matter of hours. Anna Parker was going along to help take care of Topsannah, and Boyd Jones's daughter, Ellen, was going along so Anna would have somebody her own age to talk to. They'd be leaving in two days. That just barely gave everybody time to cook up a bunch of food to send along, or find some unused article of clothing in a chifferobe or a trunk to send with Cynthia Ann. Everybody wanted her to be dressed in neat garments, if not clothed in robes of glory.

About noon, the day before departure, the neighbors started arriving in buggies and hacks with baskets of food or clothing. "I'll bet they's still chilly nights in Austin," said Marge Whitman, shaking out a cloak, "so I got jist the thang for Cynthia Ann. None of us has had a chance to wear this here cape in years, but it's a perfectly good cape. They's jist one button on the facing missing, but you'd hardly notice. Here, Cynthia Ann, try it on."

She-Mourns glanced up and allowed the cape to be draped across her shoulders. It had a lacy round white collar, which they fastened with a clip. It was too tight for her. These skinny little white women had never done any work, so they didn't have any shoulders. "It's perfect," said Marge. "A little tight, but you don't have to keep it fastened all the time."

She-Mourns had to admit it was pretty—a rich brown cloth, with leather facings and a chenille piping along the seams between the cloak and the facing. It felt good to touch leather again. She allowed herself to stroke it and smiled at the woman.

"That's all settled then!" said Marge, too loudly, proud to see that her offering had been accepted.

Another woman offered a skirt with vertical stripes, which She-Mourns liked moderately.

Another gave her a dark blouse with tiny white arrowheads in rows, the points in alternate courses turned opposing directions. She-Mourns stared at the blouse, silently.

> Where the cap rock broke up and tumbled into Palo Duro Canyon, the old men sat in lookout spots where they could watch the distance while they flaked arrow points or lance blades. There were a hundred, a thousand places where flint shards lay in alternating patterns. When she was a teenager, she used to take water in a cured antelope paunch up to a favorite uncle. He would tell her the story of flint and how the people acquired it. He made her a bow and arrows, even though she was a girl, and taught her to shoot. Later, he made her a small lance with a flint blade. She was as proud as any warrior.

She bit her lower lip to hold back the tears. So little—it took so little, to bring back the sky above the high plains and life along Prairie Dog Fork. Were they trying to be mean? Did they intend to hurt her?

"Go on, try it on," urged the woman.

The blouse was too tight across She-Mourns' breasts; each breath pulled open a little gap between the buttons, but She-Mourns had already decided to take it. While all the others were talking about things—things she could not understand and would not be interested in if she did—She-Mourns could look at the little rows of opposing arrowheads and dream of home.

"Well, take it off and save it for the trip," said Edna Brown.

She-Mourns changed back into the heavy dress and many petticoats the Parker women had given her to wear.

"February is a little early for ice cream," Isaac Parker announced from the porch, exuberant for the first time in weeks, "but Bess and Anna have baked a chocolate cake and made some good coffee. Gather around everbody, and have a bite."

"What in the world will we do with all this food?" asked Edna Brown. "I'm afraid some of it will go bad."

"That's why I made cheese and brown crackers," said Ella Jones. "Jist when everbody else's food is spoiling, mine'll be jist ripe to eat. And it'll keep for a month if you want to hang on to it."

She-Mourns sat mutely on the porch, eating cake and drinking coffee with the talkative women. The men gave advice on hotels and livery stables and routes to take. She-Mourns understood their meaning, without understanding each word. But the clothes were uncomfortable; too tight. She longed for her doeskin sheath with its open shoulders and loose bodice. A person could be at home in it. In these white-woman clothes, she felt like a prisoner, tied at the edge of camp, before a sacrifice. Impulsively, she grabbed her dress at the knees and ripped apart the skirt and several petticoats.

"Now, look what you've done," Bess Parker chided her, trying not to be angry and holding a towel to cover her nakedness.

Something bothered She-Mourns the whole trip. At the end of each day, she was exhausted with the anxiety brought on by galloping headlong into new experiences, into the unknown. She was constantly surprised by new turns in the road, new sights, new happenings. And she had no cedar to smoke herself with. But more than that, She-Mourns felt a dread, a foreboding, that they were plunging into some terrifying danger, something she had no way of defending herself against. They were going farther and deeper into the strongholds of Texas, where no warrior, no army could possibly penetrate to rescue her. She felt she was being transported to her doom.

Our People hated Tejanos from the beginning. Tejanos had come first to the edge of Our People's territory and wanted to trade; next, they wanted to scratch the ground and build cabins and bring their women; soon, they insisted on building forts and bringing in armies to fight the warriors. They wanted to destroy Our People completely, so they could steal the land.

For a long time, Our People had accepted that challenge as a kind of game. Comanches were the most numerous and powerful tribe of Texas, maybe of all the Great Plains, and the warriors needed a new enemy to kill, a new opponent who would bring honor and status to victorious warriors.

But the Tejanos had longer, better rifles, and there seemed to be so many of them. You could kill a hundred one summer, and the next summer there would be a thousand. And all of that thousand would be bent on revenge ten-fold for each of that hundred. And such butchery! Our People took a death for a death. If the Tejanos killed twenty-three of Our People, then the revenge party went out after twenty-three. And came home when they had gotten them. The Tejanos just didn't know how to make war. They were more interested in chicanery and deceit and destruction. After they got the despised Tonkawa, Our People's traditional enemies, to join them, they seemed interested only in butchery.

And that's what bothered She-Mourns. Each time one of the women took out a knife to cut bread, she expected one of them to lop off one of She-Mourns' ears, or start cutting off her toes, one at a time, the way a Tonkawa would. This trip and their smiling friendliness were just ruses; they had something terrible planned for She-Mourns. And she had no idea what it was.

"Well, first, we'll settle in at a hotel," said Edna Brown. "Then we'll get out and find a good photographer and have your likeness made. Then we'll call on the newspaper; they can let everybody know that you're here."

Cynthia Ann relented and posed worrying, unsmiling, her hands are clasped tensely at her waist in her arrowhead blouse and traveling cape.[1]

The newspapers, noting the scars on her chest and arms, reported that her body "bears the marks of having been cruelly treated."[2] Some reporters wrote that she had been whipped unmercifully and was now glad to be in the bosom of her friends and family. None of

1. In the tintype, her dark hair had grown out some since she cut it at Camp Cooper in December, but it is still short in the image. She-Mourns is leaning forward slightly, as if ready to run. The tintype is owned by Lawrence T. Jones, III, of Austin.

2. *Clarksville* (Texas) *Northern Standard*, 6 Apr. 1861.

them mentioned that she longed most to return to her husband and sons on the high plains; no Texan in 1861 could have conceived of such an idea. To them, it was clear that she had been saved, most propitiously, from "a long night of suffering and woe,"[3] from a despairing existence among a savage and heathen people.

3. *Dallas Herald*, 14 Apr. 1861.

Dozens of people came to see She-Mourns at the hotel. Some were middle-aged bachelors or widowers with small children offering marriage. Some were Christian fundamentalist women who wanted to be assured—or rather wanted to reassure themselves—that God had done the right thing in redeeming this unfortunate woman. Some were simply curious gossips, who would later claim they had known Cynthia Ann Parker well, for she had already, in her short, unhappy life, become a legend.

"Hurry, hurry," scolded Edna Brown, shooing them like a flock of baby chicks, "we've got seats to hear this session of the house of representatives. We don't want to be late for that!"

"But Edna," chided Alice Raymond, "we have plenty of time. No use getting there and having to wait hours for things to start."

"That's just it!" said Edna. "I don't want to miss any of the representatives as they're coming in. Don't you want to see them before they sit down?"

"They're just men, like any other men. Why, we even know a couple of them from our district and near to home."

"We'll let Cynthia Ann decide. What do you say, Cynthia Ann? Shouldn't we get started now?"

"No comprend—I no *understand*," said She-Mourns, looking away.

"Well, this is a big honor. Not many people get tickets. We wouldn't have gotten any, if it hadn't been for you and the stir the papers have made. Honor. You understand 'honor'?"

"Honor?" said She-Mourns doubtfully. "¿Honra?" But, finally, she did understand—that there was honor in the visit, whose she didn't grasp.

"Well, come on," said Edna, "Cynthia Ann and I and Topsannah are going; the rest of you can come or stay as you like."

The room they entered was huge, larger than any She-Mourns had ever seen. These whites had powerful medicine to make such a big roof stay up. In the main part of the room were dozens of tables and chairs lined up in rows. Around the sides, a raised section contained two rows of chairs behind a little fence. At the doors, men in uniforms prevented the wrong people from entering.

The doors were so small—and there were so few of them. She-Mourns looked around, trying to find a way out. For she now remembered a beastly part of the tribe's history. In 1840, the Tejanos invited all the principal leaders of the Penateka Band to the council house at San Antonio to talk peace and receive presents. They came under a white flag, but, once inside the big room, a council house just like this one, they were told they were hostages. They were the Tejanos' prisoners.

Edna and Alice, her guards, sat on either side of her, preventing escape. Maybe—if she had to—she could jump over one of them. Beyond Alice, Anna Parker held Toh-Tsee-Ah loosely in her lap; it wouldn't be too hard to jump over Alice, grab her daughter, and run for the little door behind the row of chairs. She set her feet for the jump, to see if she had room.

"Can't you stop fidgeting, Cynthia Ann?" said Edna.

"She's just a little uncomfortable," said Alice. "I must say, I'm a little uncomfortable myself."

She-Mourns leaned forward to look more closely at the little fence in front of them. Could she jump over it and have a better chance of getting away? But there was a soldier at each door, just like in the stories of the council-house massacre. And each of them carried a rifle. She-Mourns turned to look directly behind her. There was no escape there.

Men in dark suits and white shirts and ruffled cravats began sauntering into the room and laying papers on the tables. They stood, chatting with each other and with people in the audience.

"These are our representatives," said Edna.

"Re senta taivos?" asked She-Mourns, trying to understand the English.

"No, no," said Edna, "rep-re-sen-ta-tives. These are our leaders."

"No compr—I no understand," said She-Mourns, remembering that she had to try to use English.

"These are the men that make our decisions. Our representatives. Our leaders."

She-Mourns still did not understand.

"Our chiefs," said Edna, perturbed that she had to resort to an Indian idea. "Our chiefs in council. These are our big chiefs."

"Oh, now Edna," said Alice, "They're not all that important. Why, they're men, just like our husbands."

Suddenly, She-Mourns understood. It was the same as at Béxar in 1840. The Tejanos chiefs at Béxar had invited the head men of the Penateka and Yamparika bands of Comanches to make peace under a white flag and release white captives. Then the Comanches themselves were captives. Someone started shooting. Chief Maguar killed three soldiers before they killed him. In a few minutes, forty of the Comanche leaders lay dead in the council house. The incident became known among Our People as the "council-house massacre."

As the smoke cleared, she began to see the destruction. Peta Nocona lay in a pool of blood, his chest blown open. Quanah and Pecos lay beside him. Beyond, under a broken chair, lay Toh-Tsee-Ah and Náudah herself.

"No me mate," cried She-Mourns, springing up and trying to cross in front of Edna Brown. "Por favór. No me mate."

Edna sprang up, too, and grabbed Cynthia Ann by the shoulders. "What's the matter with you?" Then: "Help me, Alice. She's so strong, I can't hold her by myself." Alice helped Edna pull She-Mourns back into her chair.

"No me mate, no me mate," She-Mourns cried. Then remembering she was supposed to speak English, she repeated, "No me kill. No me kill."

"What in the world are you talking about?"

"No me mate. *No me kill.*" She sank back in her chair, crying for the first time on the trip.

"Nobody is going to kill you," said Edna, soothing her shoulder. "Here, dry those tears," she went on, handing Cynthia Ann a handkerchief, "They make you look puny. You don't want to look puny in front of all these men."

"Chiefs," said She-Mourns, motioning toward the men on the main floor. "Talk? Council?"

"Yes," said Edna. "They talk. Make council."

"Talk," said She-Mourns again. "Talk. Kill me. Talk how kill me."

"Why, she thinks she's on trial," said Alice, suddenly understanding. "She thinks the legislature is meeting to decide her fate."

She-Mourns felt the pressure in her bladder; she needed terribly to urinate. But they would kill her before she could find a place.

"Cynthia Ann," said Edna, turning Cynthia Ann's shoulders to face them. "They're your friends. They're not going to hurt you. What ever gave you that idea?"

She-Mourns tried again to cross in front of Edna, but again Edna restrained her.

"Please be sensible, Cynthia Ann," said Edna.

"Oh, Edna. Don't be so hard on her. She thinks they're going hold a trial and decide how to kill her. Can't you see she's frightened to death?"

"Tejanos. Chiefs," said She-Mourns, panting. "Talk. Kill me."

"No, no," said Edna, soothing her shoulder again. "They're not concerned with you. They're going to talk about seceding from the Yankees. South Carolina has voted to secede from the Yankees, and these men are going to talk about our joining a southern government."

"No me kill?" asked She-Mourns, doubtfully. "No talk. Me Kill?"

"No, of course not. These are your friends."

Toh-Tsee-Ah had gotten down from Anna's lap, crossed in front of Alice, and crawled up onto her mother's legs. "Toquet, pia," she said. *It's okay, mama.*

Then all the men on the main floor sat down, except one who stood on a little platform at one end of the room. He shuffled the papers in his hand, hit the table with a gavel, then spoke in an extraordinarily loud voice.

"Gentlemen, I have the honor and privilege to introduce to you a couple of very special guests. Miss Cynthia Ann Parker and her daughter, Topsannah." He gestured in She-Mourns' direction.

As one, the council chiefs of the Tejanos turned their heads to gaze at She-Mourns. Then, at once, starting in the middle and rippling out like a stone's wave in still water, they stood. They all looked at her and all bowed slightly, stiff from the waist.

She-Mourns felt the hot sting of urine on her groin and legs. The seat of her skirt was wet. She let out a wail and tears streamed down her face. Toh-Tsee-Ah put her arms around her mother's neck and said, "Toquet, pia. *It's okay, mama,*" speaking both Comanche and English, so that her little voice rang through the council hall. "Ka taikay. *Don't cry.*"

All She-Mourns could do was wait. Wait for whatever doom the Tejanos had planned for her.

"Welcome to the Texas House of representatives," said the Speaker. Then he turned toward the assembled council and said, "Gentlemen, the Republic of Texas owes this little lady something special."

"Damned right." "Sure enough." Even "Hear! Hear!" and "Ja Wohl" rang through the hall, as the representatives took their seats.

Within minutes, the Texas legislature had voted Cynthia Ann Parker a pension of $100 per year for five years and had given her a grant of a league of land to be located and improved by Isaac and Benjamin Parker as her guardians.

She-Mourns understood vaguely that they were making a place for her. They were telling her that they would never let her go back to Our People. That was her doom, her torture, her punishment. She was condemned to spend the rest of her life in a strange and uncomfortable place, amid well-meaning savages who did not love or understand her.

She wailed again, her mouth contorted in pain, tears streaming down her face as Toh-Tsee-Ah's little voice rang out again, "Don't cry, Mama. Don't cry."

House of No Escape

"I'll swear," Isaac muttered on the porch stoop. "I'll swear."

They no longer let She-Mourns out of sight of some family member except when they locked her in at night. The words registered in She-Mourns' mind, her brain understanding the English words without noting them or the meaning.

"Something different has got to be done," Isaac added.

"Well, we just have to talk with her," countered Bess.

Isaac went into the house and came back, carrying a tray with coffee and cups. Listlessly, She-Mourns accepted the cup of coffee Isaac offered and poured in two spoons full of sugar.

"We recognize that you are unhappy here with us, Cynthia Ann. That makes us very sorry." He paused, looking out across the meadow. The buds on the trees were still dormant.

"We don't understand why you would want to go back to those—to that—" He was at a loss for words, but She-Mourns understood his intention.

"Son mi familia," she said simply. "Mi esposo y mis hijos." Then she repeated it in English: "*my husband and my sons.*"

"Yeah," he said, hesitating. "Well—" he searched for the right words—"we want to make a deal with you. You've exhausted us with all your sadness. We're all tired; we're at our wit's end. We've talked this over, and we're ready to make a bargain."

She-Mourns did not understand the word.

"Bargain. Deal. It's sort of like a treaty. You work harder at trying to fit in, you try to learn English again, you make a better effort to conform to our ways," he paused, as if checking in his mind that he had got it all. "And, in the Summer, when it's easier to travel. . . . In the Summer, I'll take you . . . I'll get up a party and we'll take you . . . back to the high plains and see if we can't find your Comanche friends."

She-Mourns could hardly believe she understood correctly. She dared not let herself get excited. Tentatively, she asked in Spanish, "You'll let me go back to my husband and sons?"

"Yeah, well—I'll, we'll take you. We'll take you out there and see if we can make contact."

She-Mourns put the coffee cup down so fast it overturned. She fell on her knees and hugged Isaac's legs. "Grácias, grácias, tio mio." Then she caught herself and tried to speak English. "Oh, thank oncle. Thank. I try. I try. Yo probaría."

"Yeah, well, you see, these are troubled times. The Yankees are making more and more trouble. Everybody is talking about war. If we have to go to war, we'll . . . have to go to war. And that may change everything."

She-Mourns did not understand. "I try," she repeated. "I try English." But then her English would not let her say how much she wanted to go back to Peta Nocona and her sons.

"This I'll promise," said Isaac. "If you'll make a better effort to learn English again and conform, I'll do my best to help you visit your Comanche friends."

But the time of their departure was always in the future. One week, they couldn't go because the Comanches were raiding, right up to the edge of Weatherford. Another week, it had rained in the west and the Brazos River was flooding. Another week, Isaac was busy supervising his Negroes as they planted the cotton, corn, gardens and horsefeed. There was always someone's birthday, or someone's visit. Or the Yankees had cut off some supply route. "Maybe we can go next week."

And often her response was, "I lie down. Sleep." Every time they broke another promise, she seemed to need sleep.

She-Mourns wore their funny clothes and repeated words from their picture books. More cousins and people who were married to cousins came by. They all gazed at her and smiled. She tried to repeat their phrases in English; that was, after all, part of the agreement.

But Uncle Isaac did not seem to understand her desperation. If he had been her clansman, she could have told him what was in her heart. If he were her mother's brother, she could have shared her secrets with him and have known that they were safe.

She grew progressively more and more despondent, but she could not weep; she seemed to have cried out all her tears. She began to see that they had no intention of keeping their part of the bargain. It was another broken promise. No one was going to take her to the high plains of the Comanchería. She felt terribly tired. She felt empty. She was so exhausted and depressed that she didn't even notice that she felt no great anger.

She needed a good Eagle Doctor more than ever. Oh, why hadn't she listened more closely when the shaman sang over her? Why hadn't she learned the songs? But, she realized with a sinking heart, that to know the songs without having been chosen by the Power behind the songs would be useless. It was the Puha, *the Medicine Power,* that did the work, not the songs or the herbs that went with them.

Each night, Náudah lay awake in the dark, remembering what a Comanche night sounded like: the far-off howl of a coyote or a wolf; the screech of a night owl; the gurgling of the stream nearby; the snuffling of the horses in the remuda; the quiet sounds of the sentinels tending the night fires. Here at Birdville, she heard only the crickets calling to their mates and the scurrying of mice. Grandmother Moon seemed to sigh like a stick drawn across a rough rock.

When the moon came full again, Escapes-Now had not collected nearly all the supplies she and Toh-Tsee-Ah would need for a successful flight, but she determined to go anyway. She could not stand another day, here in the white-man's love among a family that could not comprehend her sorrow.

When she was sure the family was asleep, she dressed herself and Toh-Tsee-Ah in their Comanche clothes. With the iron poker from the fireplace, she broke the latch on the back door of their cabin and crept out. Toh-Tsee-Ah did not even have to be told to be quiet; her training as a Comanche had long since taught her that children should not make noise in times of stealth or attack.

A short distance from the Isaac Parker cabin, Escapes-Now whispered to Toh-Tsee-Ah, "We will not take one of their horses. Maybe they will think we are still in this area. We will find a horse along the way. Maybe at one of the neighbors' houses." She knew there was no profit in telling her daughter what they were doing, but the sound of the Comanche words reassured her. It slowed her heartbeat. The words made her feel that escape was possible. "We are out of their camp, little one; now if only we can keep them from tracking us in the moonlight."

At the first neighbor's farm, Escapes-Now crept along the double-rail fence toward the barn. She could hear horses stamping in their stalls. But when she opened the gate a big cur dog began barking and growling with bared teeth. Almost at once, a man came to the door and looked out. She crouched low behind weeds growing in the fence row.

In a moment, the man returned with a lantern. "Whatcha got, Fritz?" Luckily for Escapes-Now, the lantern blinded him so he couldn't see in the bright moonlight. The dog stopped barking and began wagging its tail when his master approached. "You got a spooky imagination, Fritz," the man concluded, and he went back to the house.

After a while, Escapes-Now crept out of hiding and left, for the dog was growling again and she was afraid he would bark if she tried to get closer to the barn.

At the next farm, she got to the barn without being detected; no dog barked, but there were no horses in the shed; they were all out in a pasture. She went out into the meadow, walking slowly, but the horses snorted and bolted away. She put Toh-Tsee-Ah under a tree, and, running after them, tried to catch one. Maybe one would get curious, stop and look back. If she could just get her hand on a mane, the horse would be hers. But she could not get close enough. Disappointed and breathless, she returned to Toh-Tsee-Ah, who had gone to sleep quietly. Both were tired, but they had to go on.

They worked their way north and west for several hours. When it began to get light in the east, Escapes-Now decided they would have to hide. She turned toward the creek; they would have to find a safe place in the thickets. About daylight, she found a hollow among medium-sized trees where wild grape vines grew overhead, cutting out even the sun. Though the fruit was sour, she and Toh-Tsee-Ah ate some of the shriveled grapes. She broke branches and covered the entrance to their little cove in the vines. Exhausted, they slept. Maybe they could find some game or roots to eat during the day. Tomorrow night, they would continue their escape in the full moonlight.

At breakfast time, the Parkers discovered that Cynthia Ann and Topsannah were gone. Isaac saddled his white horse and went looking. He couldn't find any traces; so he stopped at all the neighboring farmhouses to ask.

"That must've been what Fritz was barking at last night. Middle of the night," said the first man. "I didn't see anything; so I thought he was just wishing he was on a coon hunt."

"There's a man in Birdville who has a bloodhound," said Isaac. "I'm going in and borrow that dog."

"You're welcome to use Fritz, too. He does get a little excited when we catch up with the coon, and he sometimes tears 'em up pretty bad before we can get him off. But he's a good hound."

"No, no," said Isaac. "Thanks, Kurt, but we don't want to hurt my niece."

"Well, he won't follow a Indian trail anyway," admitted Kurt. "He's pretty good once he gets on a coon's trail, but I never knowed him to follow anything else."

"The bloodhound will be quite enough," said Isaac, turning toward Birdville. "And he'll be as friendly as a pup if and when he brings her to bay."

When he returned from the village with the bloodhound, several of his neighbors and their dogs were waiting at his house, including Kurt and Fritz. "We've come to help you find that girl," said his third neighbor down, a man in overalls.

"Thanks," said Isaac. "Thank you from the bottom of my heart, but I really don't think I need your help. I'll be able to follow her with this hound."

"Well, we ain't got much to do anyway. We'll jist tag along." Several of the men were carrying shotguns.

"And we surely won't need any guns," said Isaac. "Please leave them behind."

"Awww, they ain't no problem with guns," said another neighbor. "Guns only go off when you want 'em to."

"You're asking for trouble," said Isaac. "I'd feel a lot better if we didn't have any guns, none of us."

"Well, o' course," said another neighbor, crestfallen. "If'n y' don't trust us. . . ." He let his voice trail off.

"We's jist tryin to hep," said a white-haired neighbor.

In the end, Isaac found it impossible to refuse their help and still be neighborly. "For God's sake, men. Be careful! We don't want to hurt my niece; we just want to find her."

"Dog'll hep us do thet," said a white-haired friend.

"B'side," said the man in overalls, "the dogs ain't had a work-out in quite a spell. Do 'em good to get out and howl on a trail."

"Just keep 'em all on a tight leash," pleaded Isaac, "especially Fritz and any other dogs that have shown any sign of viciousness. We're not hunting an animal; we're just tracking my niece."

Isaac took the bloodhound to Cynthia Ann and Topsannah's room and let him sniff around for a while. Then he mounted, holding the dog on a long leash from horseback, and started searching.

Once on the trail, most of the dogs did not know what to do.
They found no scent familiar to them, no direction to go, so they milled around, howling, sniffing, following the bloodhound. But Fritz still had the scent of this prey from last night. He broke loose and sprinted on ahead.

"Stop him," screamed Isaac. "Stop him, Kurt! He'll tear her to pieces." He threw down the bloodhound's leash and spurred his horse after the dog.

Kurt and Isaac dashed after Fritz, Kurt yelling for the cur to heel, to stop, everything he could think of, but the dog didn't respond to anything but the excitement of the hunt.

Fritz raced along the trail of the scent as fast as his nose would let him, with the horsemen following, smashing through under-brush, leaping over fallen logs and small streams. All the other dogs were right behind them, caught up now in the excitement of a chase, and the other horsemen brought up the rear.

Escapes-Now heard the commotion and figured out what was happening when the dogs were still a quarter of a mile away. She broke cover and ran for a small tree, leaving her bundle of supplies. She put Toh-Tsee-Ah up as high as she could, saying, "Hold on to the branches, little one. Hold on!"

She too was trying to climb the tree when Fritz hit her a glanc-ing blow on the hip. If she had not been wearing leather, he could have torn a wad of flesh from her leg. The blow caused her to fall on top of the dog, bringing down a limb the size of her wrist with her.

The dog was up at once, but so was Escapes-Now. She held the branch by the small end and shoved the brushy end into the dog's face. He growled and gnashed at the leaves, but was unable to get forward. He lunged again. She managed to keep the branch between herself and the animal. He lunged again. The impact car-ried her backwards into the tree trunk, and she half lost hold of the branch. Many other dogs were around her now, some nipping at her, some confused by the presence of a human being and just waiting to be petted. The big dog was coming at her again, snarling.

Something white hit the big dog and pushed him aside. At the same time, the man on the white horse leaned down, grabbed her under her shoulder blades, and swept her up onto the white horse. Only then did she realize that it was Uncle Isaac. He had saved her.

When the other men rode up, they dismounted and reluctantly leashed their curs. Then came the bloodhound, baying because the scent was strongest. Isaac rode out of the melee, carrying Cynthia Ann on his hip. She squirmed and yelled. Her heart was beating against her ribs like a frenetic dance drum. "Toh-Tsee-Ah!" she screamed in Isaac's ear. "Toh-Tsee-Ah!"

Isaac looked back, saw some of the dogs straining toward the lower limbs of the small tree, and guessed where Topsannah was. He wheeled his horse and rode back into the howling mass. By that time, Náudah had managed to straddle the horse behind the saddle. As Issac was fending off dogs, she reached up and took her daughter from the tree. The baby had not cried until she was in her mother's arms again; then she let out a wail that rivaled the noise the dogs were making.

Someone fired a shotgun into the air, thinking it would quiet the dogs, it being a signal that the hunt was over. But the noise only started them again. Some of the horses were startled by the shot and began neighing and prancing about; one or two even bucked a jump or two, but their riders held on.

Then it was quiet, except for the crying of the baby and the beating of hearts and the huffing to catch breath.

"Hoooo-eeee," said the white-haired neighbor. "They ain't nothing quite like a good chase, is thar?"

Isaac saw that the men had control of their dogs now; so he let Cynthia Ann down and dismounted too.

She looked at him with wonder and dismay. The hounds had howled and bayed and had come right through the woods to Little Bear Creek where there was no trail, right to the hiding place which Escapes-Now had thought was undetectable. Their white-man puha, *their power-medicine* was strong. Was there no way a Comanche could escape it?

dozen Pawnee arrows in him and several bullet wounds.

"Don't you understand, Cynthia Ann?" he asked. "We're your family. We love you."

With a jerk of her chest, Escapes-Now realized that she understood the English. Unsteady and slightly dizzy, she believed him; she had no doubt about his smothering honesty. She could see his love as something physical—about the size of a pile of Potsana-kwita, *buffalo droppings.* No water in it, no source of sustenance.

She felt, at the same time, the Comanches' love for her—almost as big as the sky itself, as big as a prairie with waving grass.

Up through the grass at the edge of an arroyo came her two boys. Quanah was holding up a cottontail, an arrow sticking through its rib cage. "I got it with one shot," Quanah was shouting. "I saw him before he started to run, and I knew just where he would dart. I shot there and I hit him. It took only one arrow!" He was as proud as a warrior returning from a successful raid.

The boys had come up to her now, Quanah already as tall as her shoulder, Pecos a head shorter. She took the rabbit from his hands, dipped her forefinger in the blood, and drew a line in blood from the bridge of Quanah's nose, down and back to the turn of his jaw bone under his ear. He was trying not to show how pleased he was, but his astonishing gray eyes beamed at her gesture.

She almost cried. Too soon, he would leave the rabbit wars and go with his father on real raids. So many had not come back from those raids. She abhorred the idea of Quanah racing into war; at the same time, she was so proud she could hardly wait. The warmth of her heart swelled like air; it went out into the sky around her boys. And she felt nourished. The warmth that had left her returned and filled her, too.

"Pecos hit one, too," said Quanah, taking the rabbit from Náudah's hand and painting a similar line on Pecos' face. "The trouble is, his bow is so little, it was not strong enough to drive the arrow in. We must ask grandfather Paha-yuka to make him a

stronger bow. Then we will practice and go hunting again. We each will take only one arrow. 'One-arrow-hunters' they will call us through all the villages."

Náudah looked at her younger son. He brushed his coarse black hair back, as if to brush away such talk, but his smile was as big as the sunset.

Something was pressing her shoulders. It was Uncle Isaac. "You do understand, don't you?" he was asking.

In spite of herself, a tear formed in her eye and she pulled herself in tight against his lapel.

Isaac Parker put his arm around her shoulder. "It will all work out. I hope it will all work out," he said, leading her back toward the house of no escape. "Here," said Isaac, reaching for Toh-Tsee-Ah, "Let me carry Topsannah."

"Lo siento, lo siento," she mumbled into his shirt front. And she truly was sorry; doubly sorry that she could not love him and the prairies at the same time.

8

The Cowrie-Shell Dress

"You may not wear that dress around here, Cynthia Ann," said Amelia Parker, indicating her Comanche sheath with the cowrie shell decorations. "I won't have it. Maybe Uncle Isaac couldn't scrub your heathenish ways out of you, but I certainly will."

Amelia stood in the doorway of their small white, wood-frame house with green trim. To her right was the rectangular, two-story cracker-box house so common to frontier homesteads; to her left was the one-story kitchen area with a front porch furnished by a two-seat swing. Two small girls clung to Amelia's skirt, their eyes as big as coat buttons, staring at the wild Indian.

She-Mourns looked down at her dress. She did not understand her snake-eyed sister-in-law's words so much as she understood her challenge. She touched one of the cowrie shells that ringed the neck like a big yoke. This was a handsome garment, the dress of the wife of an important leader, a badge of distinction. When she wore this dress, she was called Preloch among people of the Noconi band, a name-title of honor and position.

"But we won't go into that now," Amelia continued, detaching herself from the two clinging children. "I know you must be tired after the trip. Not that Van Zandt County is at the end of the world, but still, being shaken around in a coach for a couple of days leaves one needing a bath and some rest. Come along," she went on, making a motion of invitation, "we'll heat some water, so you and Topsannah can have a bath."

She-Mourns gazed after her a moment but did not follow. She did not quite know how to act or what was expected of her. Uncle Isaac had declared that he and Bess were too old to continue taking care of Cynthia Ann. So he hired an escort to take her and her baby to live with her brother, Silas, in Van Zandt County. A new house, new people, new demands—it was all very confusing to one who mourned the loss of so much.

Amelia Parker, the one She-Mourns called Kwasinado nabituh, *Snake Eyes*, was a thin, wiry woman in her mid-twenties, wearing a white, puffy blouse and a long, straight dark skirt. She and Silas had three children of their own and looked after Amelia's sixteen-year-old sister, Elizabeth, who had lived with them since she was ten.

Elizabeth, also fashionably dressed in a white puffy blouse and long straight skirt, came out to meet Cynthia Ann. Both women had long, dark, luxuriant hair that balled out in a thick bouffant, then swept up to be tied atop their heads. She-Mourns noticed that Elizabeth had larger breasts than her sister and thicker, healthier arms. She looked ready to make some man a willing wife.

Elizabeth smiled at Cynthia Ann, said "bienvenidos," and offered to take Topsannah in her arms. "I don't really speak Spanish," she went on, "but I know a few words. I'd heard that you know more Spanish than English, so I asked a friend how to say 'welcome.' I do hope you're happy here, Cynthia Ann. I'll try to be your friend."

She-Mourns liked the girl at once. She had understood enough of her words to catch the thrust of what she said.

"You, me," Elizabeth continued, pointing to Cynthia Ann, then to herself, "amigos. Okay?"

"Amigos," agreed She-Mourns, and she allowed Elizabeth to take Toh-Tsee-Ah into her arms.

"Oh, you're getting to be a big girl, aren't you?" Elizabeth cooed to Topsannah, who held up three fingers to indicate her age.

Silas and his oldest child, Elijah, a boy of nine, came in behind She-Mourns, after putting the horses away. "Welcome, Sis. We all hope you'll be happy with us here."

"Come, Cynthia Ann," said Elizabeth, "you must be thirsty, after eating all that dust on the road. Maybe you'd like a drink of water?"

She-Mourns looked at her questioningly.

"Agua?" said Elizabeth, with a drinking motion. "Para tomar."

She-Mourns nodded. She was parched. How thoughtful of the girl. She followed Elizabeth and the small children into the kitchen, where Elizabeth was already dipping water from an oak bucket and pouring it into two tumblers. One she gave to Cynthia, the other she held up to Topsannah's mouth.

"Gráci—Thank. I thank," said She-Mourns.

"Good for you," said Elizabeth, winking. "You're going to be talking as well as the rest of us in no time at all. All you need is a little practice, and it will all come back."

Elizabeth opened the cupboard to display the dishes. "I'll give you a little hint on how to get along," she said. "See these dishes— all the same size and design in a stack by themselves, all the stacks lined up. Be careful when you put the dishes away. She . . . gets pretty frantic if she opens the cupboards and the dishes don't salute."

"There you are," said Amelia, coming into the room. "Come this way, Cynthia Ann, and we'll get you cleaned up a bit. Lord knows, you can use it."

She-Mourns looked at Elizabeth.

"Un baño," said Elizabeth, nodding toward the door where Amelia waited. "I'll take care of Topsannah."

She-Mourns smiled at her and went with Amelia.

"This will be your and Topsannah's room, Cynthia Ann," Amelia said, making a small gesture with her hand, palm up, her elbow in tight against her waist.

The room was small: a bed in one corner, a table in the other, under a shuttered window. Behind them a door opened to the kitchen and, to the left, another door led to another bedroom. On the floor between the doors sat a large galvanized tub with a few inches of water in it.

"Thank. I thank," said She-Mourns.

"No need to thank us. We aren't doing this for gratitude but out of duty. And the sooner you understand that, the better off we'll all be. Here's your bath." Amelia gestured toward the tub.

She-Mourns nodded and pulled her dress over her head at once.

"Stop!" cried Amelia, as she ran to close the door behind them. "Silas is in the kitchen!"

She-Mourns did not understand. She glanced into the kitchen. Silas was standing with his arm across Elizabeth's shoulder.

Amelia slammed the door. "Okay, now, get in the tub. Wash."

She-Mourns laid her dress across the foot of the bed, then stepped into the water. It was as warm as a still pool in late summer. She picked up the wash cloth, remembering Mrs. Evans at Camp Cooper teaching her to dip it in the water and rub her face.

"I'll take care of this," said Amelia, snatching up the doeskin dress. "Ugh, it needs it. Smells like a herd of work horses. How can you wear such filth?"

She-Mourns did not understand, so she smiled, thinking she would try to be friendly. If she were going to have to stay with Silas and Amelia, she wanted to get started right.

Amelia swept out of the room, swinging her own skirt and the doeskin sheath in her haste.

She-Mourns took off her medicine bag, laid it on the floor beside the tub, dipped up water with the wash-cloth, and let it run over her arms. The rivulets cut clear paths through the dust. Snake Eyes was right about that, at least. She-Mourns needed a bath.

Why couldn't she understand Amelia as well as she understood Elizabeth? Maybe it was just that She-Mourns didn't grasp the words, and that made Amelia sound gruff and impatient. Maybe she was silly to feel uneasy. Maybe Amelia meant well. Amelia was her brother's wife; surely, they would support each other like sisters.

After a time, Amelia came back into the room. "Here are some decent clothes for you, Cynthia Ann. I just hope the chemise is big enough. And here is a towel to dry off with."

She-Mourns smiled and nodded. She recognized what they meant by towel, and she had seen plenty, far too many, of their tight, uncomfortable clothes.

"When you're dressed," added Amelia, "come on out to the kitchen. Silas is hungry, so we'll eat soon."

When She-Mourns finished her bath, she stepped out of the tub and wiped with the towel until she was no longer dripping. She pulled on her medicine bag and the underpants that went down to a ruffle at her knees, then the straight skirt. The chemise, she didn't know what to do with, so she put on the blouse without it. The blouse was really too tight for her, but to please Amelia she wore it anyway.

When she came out, her hair still wet and slicked back against her head, the thin blouse was wet and plastered against her breasts.

"Cynthia Ann," scolded Amelia, her hands on her hips. "You can't run around like that, half-dressed. Get in there and put on the chemise!"

She-Mourns understood that she had done something wrong, but she didn't know what it was.

"Momma! Pia!" shouted Toh-Tsee-Ah, running to She-Mourns. "Lizbuff give me bath. We splash." She was wearing a short, print dress, and held up one foot so She-Mourns could see the little, black shoes on her stockinged feet. Silas and Amelia's little girl stood with Toh-Tsee-Ah; She-Mourns saw at once where the clothes came from.

"Go on!" shouted Amelia, lifting a peremptory arm and pointing toward the bedroom. "Get back in there, and don't come out until you're decently dressed!"

"No comprendo," said She-Mourns, looking from one of them to the other. The children were all gazing at her now, the men staring at her bosom. Elizabeth quickly undid the top button of her blouse and tugged at her own chemise. "Like this, Cynthia Ann. Like this."

"Elizabeth!" growled Amelia. "Don't undress in front of Silas and Elijah."

"Oh," said She-Mourns, understanding. She quickly went back

to the bedroom and tried to pull on the chemise. She came back in a moment, holding the lapels of the blouse together with one hand and holding the split chemise in the other.

"Lo siento," she said, near tears. "Lo siento."

"Honestly, Cynthia Ann," shouted Amelia. "You can't come in here like that. Have you no sense of decency?"

She-Mourns understood that the problem was the way she was dressed. "Mi vestida?" she asked. "Donde está mi vestida?" She made motions to imitate the cowrie shells on her doeskin dress.

"Oh, that old thing," said Amelia, suddenly calm and smug. "That's already gone up in ashes."

Silas and Elizabeth turned toward her at once and cried out simultaneously, "You didn't?"

"Yes, I did," said Amelia. "I burned that filthy piece of garbage."

9

Preloch, The Queen

As soon as Preloch realized what had happened to her doe-skin dress—and Toh-Tsee-Ah-ne's little antelope shift, too—she came out of her dutiful quiescence, and she was far from silent. She lunged at Amelia and hit her chest with a clenched fist, knocking the breath out of her. "You—you—" She could not get any words out. Silas and Elizabeth had to each grab one of Preloch's arm, to keep her from beating Amelia unmercifully. "Calm down, Sis," said Silas. "We can't be fighting like this in the family."

Amelia lay on the floor, gasping for breath. "Get her out of here," she whispered. "And that little barbarian, too."

Elizabeth led Preloch into the other room. "Peace," she muttered. "We make peace now. Okay?"

Preloch nodded reluctantly, looking back to where Silas was helping his wife up from the floor. She felt a surge of great shame that she, a civilized person whom the tribe had taught the correct way to live, had lashed out blindly, the way a mother bear would.

Preloch simply withdrew. She sat on her bed or in the swing on the front porch, holding Toh-Tsee-Ah-ne and talking constantly in Comanche.

"They are trying to kill us, Toh-Tsee-Ah-ne. Not with lances and war clubs or bullets but with sweet talk. They want us to take their words as our own, because they think we will then forget our own voices. They think we will forget the puha of the plains and the Palo Duro at Prairie Dog Fork. Then we will be theirs. They will have captured us completely. Then we won't know anything about Nuhrmuhr-ne, or about where we lived, or how we acted. When Our People are gone from our minds, they will have killed the Comanche in us.

"We can't let that happen. We have to remember. We have to talk the language of Our People. We have to refuse to listen to their sugar talk. We have to refuse to understand. They are world destroyers. And, worse, they do not even recognize that about themselves. They read their black book and convince themselves that they are the only people who deserve to live. All the rest are less than animals. And that gives them the right to kill everyone and everything in sight. They are trying to kill us. We must fight back; we must shield everything about us from them.

"Your father is leader of the Noconis. They are the smallest but the fiercest band. When all the Quahada get together, Peta Nocona's voice is strongest in council. He is a great leader. He has many honors. I will tell you about them, so that you won't forget that you are a Comanche and know that you have a right to live with freedom and honor and integrity.

"And your brothers. Remember them, too. Quanah is sixteen now; he has gone on his first raid. Perhaps he has counted coup and taken hair. Perhaps he has come home to the victory dance with a scalp hanging from his lance.

"I wish we could go to them. These people can't hold us captive forever, can they? Surely, someone will come and ransom us, or raid this farm, kill all the Parkers, and take us back to Prairie Dog Fork. They've moved us so many times, I am now lost. I thought I could find my way home from Uncle Isaac's, but I was wrong. I need a guide. They have blinded my eyes and turned me around so many times, I don't know where I am.

"But I know what I am. I am Preloch, the wife of the leader. And you are a princess. We are both princesses. We are Comanches. We can be proud of that. We do not have to listen to their talk. We do not have to smile to them. We have our own path and do not have to set foot in the white man's road."

When Amelia found them speaking Comanche, she scolded them. "I've told you and told you, Cynthia Ann. You *may* not speak that barbarous language. You've got to learn English. You're a white woman. You've got to talk like one."

And Preloch would protest, "No! No!" both because she wanted-ed to resist what Snake Eyes demanded and to protest the actions of her own mind. In spite of herself, she now understood more and more of their words. She pulled sticks from the picket fence and broke them across her knee.

In time, Preloch and Silas Parker's family reached an uneasy truce—one that depended upon everyone acting as if the con-frontation had never happened. As long as everyone pretended, the surface of the peace held, like a thin layer of oil.

A warm fall rain kept everyone in the house except the children. Toh-Tsee-Ah and Amelia's girls had gotten wet and muddy in the puddles. On the high prairies, Preloch would have taken off all the little girls' clothing and let them play naked, but Amelia had insist-ed the children go dressed. They were all drenched and dirty. Preloch went to her room to get Toh-Tsee-Ah clean clothes.

Silas and Elizabeth were naked making love on top of her bed. Silas stopped bucking, and they lay silent, though their breathing was still loud. Preloch pretended to ignore them, as was only polite, as she had been taught on the high prairie. But her heart leaped a little with joy. Silas had taken his wife's younger sister as a second wife. With so many of the young men away at the war, that was almost a duty. It explained why Elizabeth was in no hurry to leave this house. Loves-Horses had married a man from the Quahada band, who agreed cheerfully to take Trades-It along as assistant wife. That was as it should be; a good man took care of his wife's younger sisters. Preloch got Toh-Tsee-Ah's clothes and turned to leave.

Amelia was in the doorway, scanning the room. Silas and Elizabeth were scrambling to pull up a quilt and cover their nakedness. "Cynthia, Cynthia," Amelia said, turning away, "you've got to do some of the work around here. There's a kitchen floor out here to scrub. You're not a lady of leisure. You've got to do your part."

As Preloch pulled the door closed, she noticed a sparkle off Elizabeth's nipple. Preloch smiled, inwardly; her own nipples got moist when she was aroused. Elizabeth's must do the same. It made her feel like a sister to Elizabeth. With a flip-flop in her heart, she turned to do the work of old Snake Eyes, who acted exactly like a senior wife among several.

Preloch was not lazy. She preferred work to idleness. But the kinds of work Amelia gave her were things she did not understand: mopping floors, washing dishes, hanging out laundry.

"I'll swear, she's a baby," Amelia would tell others. "You have to start with her right at the bottom and teach her the simplest things, like how to mop in all the corners of a floor. They must have lived in utter squalor out there with those disgusting savages."

Sometimes, Preloch went out to the barns where Silas was working. If he was making or repairing harness, she was a good helper. She knew how to cut leather into strips, plait ropes, repair cinches, clean leather saddles so that they were soft and supple. Elijah hovered close by, anxious to learn.

"You know that old cinch I was about to throw away?" Silas would report off-handedly to Amelia and Elizabeth. "Well, Cynthia Ann repaired it. Gathered horse hair from the fence, worked it into the braid, and tied it all back together. It's as good as new, now. Better than new; you can't get a good horsehair cinch that's not full of prickly ends."

Preloch found a calf skin, which had simply been thrown across a fence to dry. She took it down, soaked it, pegged it out on the ground behind the barn and scraped away the meaty parts and inner striffen. She took Toh-Tsee-Ah with her, so her daughter could watch and learn.

For a while, scraping the dried membranes from the calf skin, she thought she had made a mistake. Even if she was using a butcher knife with a curved blade, everything about life on the plains leaped back into her mind. She was with Loves-Horses, Trades-It, and the other women, pegging out hides on the banks of the Pease River or along Prairie Dog Fork. And they were chatting as they worked. They knew what their husbands and families would use these hides for.

"This little calf skin would be too soft for a man's use," she told Toh-Tsee-Ah. "It would make a child's dress or a blanket to wrap a baby in. But the men need a stronger leather to withstand time and thorns on the trails. A shirt made of such soft leather would go to pieces on a raid to Mexico. But the husband would be proud of his wife, too, for making such a fluffy skin. He would carry the pelt to other men, get them to feel the texture, and brag about how downy it was. He'd never say so, right out in words, but he always meant that the other wives could not make a skin so delicate."

The memory made Preloch feel hollow, empty, and she stopped talking. She longed to be at home again. It was heartbreaking how something as simple as a calf skin could bring memories like a sudden rainstorm. It didn't give her a chance to protect herself. It flooded her with sorrow and made her aware that she was doomed to always remember her losses, her grief.

Then she was glad for her pain and grief. It meant she had not forgotten. How could she forget? Everything she knew and loved was there on the high plains, and she was captive among strangers in a land where she did not know the directions. She was glad that the memory wounded. So much of the time with Silas's family, she felt nothing at all. At least, remembering the misery, feeling again the ache, savoring the sorrow, told her that she was still alive. She had not forgotten how to hurt.

The day after she had finished scraping the skin clean, she treated it with ashes from the fireplace and old grease from the cooking, mixing them in such a way that they became a kind of soap and washed out the animal fats. Elijah and the little girls stood around watching. When she was finished, the calf skin was as soft as velvet. She presented it to Silas.

"Gollee, Sis. I don't know quite what to say."

She waited for him to show it to Amelia and Elizabeth. She waited for him to exclaim something like "And look! the hair is still on it!" for the whites always scraped the hair away before they tanned their leather. She waited for him to suggest that the white and red markings in the calf's withers would make a perfect back for a leather shirt. Or at least a vest, for this calf skin was not large enough to make sleeves also.

But he said none of these things. He put it on a shelf in the barn, saying "I don't know what we'll use anything that soft for. For harness, you need horsehide or bull hide." Elijah was standing nearby, and Silas ran his hand through the boy's loose hair.

Peeling potatoes in the kitchen, alone with her daughter, Preloch asked the ceiling, "Ha-itska Noconi? Ha-itska Peta Nocona?" *Where are the Wanderers? Where is Peta Nocona.*

"Ka taikay, Pia," said Toh-Tsee-Ah. *Don't cry, mother.* "Toquet, Pia." *It will be alright.*

"Here, here," scolded Amelia, coming into the kitchen and taking Topsannah into her arms. "I've told you both a dozen times, you can't speak that foul language around here. You've got to speak English. I won't have you carrying on all those bad habits you learned from the savages. I'm going to have to wash your mouth out with soap."

"*Pia, don't let her take me,*" screamed Toh-Tsee-Ah in Comanche. "*She's a bad woman. Don't let her take me.*" Toh-Tsee-Ah was squirming, trying to get out of Amelia's arms.

"I said don't speak that language," shrieked Amelia, and she spanked Topsannah on the butt and legs.

"No! No!" howled Preloch, springing at Amelia and grabbing Toh-Tsee-Ah from her grasp. "No hit. No hit Toh-Tsee-Ah!" She restrained herself from hitting Amelia. She burst into a string of

Comanche, explaining that Our People never hit children. They told them what was right and then disapproved when they did wrong, but they never hit a child.

Elizabeth and Silas came in from the bedroom and stood in the doorway, watching.

Preloch sat Toh-Tsee-Ah in a chair and went on, talking rapidly to her daughter in Comanche. "See, I told you, Princess. These whites don't know how to live. They're barbarians. Savages."

"Silas," yelled Amelia. "This can't go on. I don't care if she is your sister, this can't go on. You've got to take my side. When I try to correct her and the child, you've got to take my side."

Silas rubbed his forehead. "We've got to make a go of it, Amelia," he said at last. "There's no where else for her to go."

"Send her back to those savages she loves so much!" cried Amelia.

"You know we can't do that, Honey. After we've saved her from her long night of suffering, we can't do that. Uncle Isaac can't take her, nor Uncle James. And just about everyone else has gone to the war. We've got to make a go of it. Try to have more patience."

"Well, I'm going to spank her every time she calls Cynthia Ann 'Preloch,' or calls herself a princess. Do you hear? If I have to, I'm going to beat it out of them."

"Kwasinabo nabituh," yelled Preloch. *Snake eyes!*

"You witch!" yelled Amelia. "I've told you, you may not use that savage language in this house." She drew back her hand, ready to slap Preloch.

But Preloch saw the gesture and swept up a knife from the kitchen work, ready to meet the blow. "No, you listen," she went on in Comanche. "You are an evil woman. You are the enemy. I will not give up. You were trying to kill me and Toh-Tsee-Ah, but I will not let you."

Amelia backed away, fear expanding her eyes, which never left the knife blade.

It didn't matter to Preloch that no one but Toh-Tsee-Ah could understand what she said. It was encouragement to herself to hear it. "I will not let you kill us. I will fight. And if I ever see you touch

Toh-Tsee-Ah again, I will slit your throat. You thought you had us, lying bloody and still on the battlefield, but you were wrong. We are strong. We will fight."

"Silas," said Amelia, urgently, scrambling to get a straight-backed chair between her and Preloch. "Get her out of here. Get her out of my house."

"Amelia, I can't," said Silas, quietly. "There's no place to send her. Maybe if you just eased off a little. Maybe if we go slower, she'll . . ."

"Well, I—" Amelia, at a loss for words, turned and stalked out of the room, taking the small children with her.

10

Fighting Amelia,
Winter 1861

When cold weather came and it was time to slaughter hogs and cure the meat, Preloch pitched in and helped. No one asked her to, but she saw work that needed to be done, so she rolled up her sleeves, took a knife, and got right into the necessary work. She could skin a carcass as well as any of the men and separate the hams and shoulders at the joints.

"Golly, Sis," Silas would say. "You're sure good at this."

And Preloch would look away modestly, even though she had learned to look Silas in the eye.

"You'd make some man a good wife," Silas added, and he introduced her to the neighbor men who had come to help with the hog killing, especially one shy bachelor. The bachelor came and wanted to walk with Cynthia Ann in the garden at twilight. Preloch understood what he meant by the visit, but she could not understand his drawl, and she refused to look at his face, for fear he would think she recognized his existence and was encouraging his courtship.

She remembered when Paha-yuka had announced that Peta Nocona of the Quahada band was sleeping in their visitors' tipi.

She had known Peta Nocona as a kind of uncle since her memories began; he had taught her to use her first knife; he had given her her first pony. She had been shocked into confusion the day before by Peta Nocona stepping in front of her on the path to the water hole, thus announcing his courtship. Paha-yuka's disclosure put something new in the relationship: it meant he approved the courtship.

It was true she was well past the start of her woman-bleeding, but she was still hardly more than a girl—a shy little slip of a thing, hardly thicker than a lance shaft. Was she ready to be held in some warrior's hand?

"Though it is the custom that I can do whatever I like," said Paha-yuka, "I will not accept the gift of any warrior whom you, yourself, have not chosen."

That was more confusion. Paha-yuka was chief of the entire Tenawish band; no one would dare even suggest such a thing to him. He had been a good and loving father, but she hardly expected such special treatment. She kept her eyes averted and tended the fire in Paha-yuka's tipi, although it did not need tending.

"I have watched you at our bath," Paha-yuka went on. "You have grown into a beautiful young woman. Many warriors will come to my lodge while you are here; you may choose whichever one you like."

Her heart almost burst with pride that he had noticed her; and it overflowed with love for her father. She took a grass cake from a storage basket and handed it to Paha-yuka. She allowed her fingers to rest on his hand a moment, glanced quickly at his eyes, and smiled the tiniest of smiles. She was the happiest daughter in the world.

But in these hard times with the Parkers, such thoughts only made her more unhappy. She preferred to keep her mind on the work to be done. Smoking the bacon was familiar to her, not too different from what they did with meat at home. Salting or sugar curing the hams was new to her, but she watched, asked questions, tasted the result, and pronounced it "good medicine." She made a note to remember the technique when she went home.

When she went home. . . . There she was, again, dreaming of life

on the high plains. It took so little to remind her: a piece of bloody
meat, the smell of meat smoking.

Making sausage was a reminder, too. The women had made
white, cotton broadcloth sleeves to stuff the ground meat and spice
mixture into, instead of using the intestines that the animal had
supplied. She was so swift and efficient that even Amelia commented, "You must have done this somewhere before, Cynthia
Ann."

Yes, the process was so similar to putting away pemmican for the
winter, that she found herself alternately crying and daydreaming.

"¿Vamanos a la Comanchería? *We go Comancheria, no?*" she
asked Silas. "*I so crying.*"

"Oh, I'm sorry, Sis," said Silas, looking up from the sausage mill
he was turning. "I know Uncle Isaac promised you we'd try to take
you on a visit, but we can't right now. Times are so tough. So many
men away at the war, and the Yankees have so much of the world
blockaded.

"And there's been so much trouble out that way. The Indians are
still marauding everywhere. There's hardly a full moon goes by, but
what they strike somewhere. Folks are calling the full moon 'a
Comanche moon.' The Comanches have killed over a hundred
people this year. They even stole a negro man within sight of the
town of Palo Pinto. It'd be too dangerous for us to go out there. I
read in The White Man[1] that the roads are lined with people moving away from the frontier, heading back to some settlement where
they think they'll be safe." Preloch was surprised and pleased to
hear that the Comanches had continued killing Texans. It was
news the Parker family had kept from her. She wanted to ask for
details.

"The Confederacy has just made a treaty with the Comanches,"
Silas went on. "Maybe it will settle things down a little."

"Sweet talk?" asked Preloch.

"Yeah, I've heard you call it 'sweet talk.' The Confederate government has agreed to give the Comanches plenty of cattle and
seeds and plows, to give them a start. Maybe, if things calm down,
we can try going out there in a couple of months."

"Sweet talk?" she asked again. "All Comanches sweet talk?"

1. *The White Man*, a racist journal, published for a time in Weatherford, Parker County, Texas. It openly advocated the extermination of all Indians, the expulsion of all Mexicans, and the continued subjugation of all blacks.

"All but one band," said Silas. "Nine bands signed the treaty. All but the Quohadis."

"Quahada?" cried Preloch, with delight. "Quahada es mi país y mi gente! Nu nurhmuhr-ne! Toh-Tsee-Ah! Toh-Tsee-Ah," she called, "Tu papá! Tu papá!" Then she switched to Comanche. "Your father hasn't given up. He's still fighting the Texans. He's killed over a hundred of them this year. He's fighting! He's fighting! Oh, it makes my heart so glad to hear that he is still fighting!"

The warriors would send word ahead when they were return-ing, so that the whole village could be out to watch the parade of men with blood and hair on their lances. And many a wife would be glad to have her man in their bed again that night. Even young girls, if they could slip away and if they dared, would meet special friends in the bushes and give them a warrior's welcome home.

Peta Nocona led the procession with Isaac Parker's gray hair on his lance point. It made her the proudest of wives. She could already feel him inside her, filling her, rewarding her, even as she honored him.

Preloch burst into tears and pulled Toh-Tsee-Ah to her so hard that the little girl cried out, "You're hurting me, Mother."

Silas looked at his sister, wondering if something was wrong with her mind, when she could be so gloriously happy in one second and so miserable in the next.

Through the winter, Preloch did woman's work in Silas Parker's house—darning socks, spinning yarn, or making clothes. With Elizabeth as tutor, she learned to sew with a steel needle, to wash and iron clothes, to spin and weave, at which she rapidly became skillful. She submitted to wearing the white-woman clothes they gave her, and—in an effort to prevent open conflict with Amelia—refrained from speaking Comanche to Toh-Tsee-Ah, except in their own room. Topsannah, for her part, rapidly became fluent in

English. She loved playing with the small children and soon spoke as well as they.

Every day, someone talked about the war. They read every newspaper they could and anxiously awaited letters from relatives. In one letter from Uncle Isaac, which Silas read by oil lamp at the kitchen table, they learned that cousin Billy Parker had been wounded. "It says he got shot in the leg, or something blew up," said Silas. "They're not sure, but he's in the hospital."

Preloch put on a Billy Parker smile and mimicked Billy.

"Yeah," said Silas, "that's the one."

"Bad?" asked Preloch, leaning forward to look at the letter as if she could see for herself.

"Yeah, it sure is bad," said Silas, not realizing that Preloch was asking how badly Billy was wounded. "But Uncle Isaac thinks he'll be coming home on furlough. Sort of get a chance to heal."

Peta Nocona was down in battle—no, it was Quanah. He had been hit by a nearly spent bullet and was knocked unconscious. There was blood all over him, but it was not his own. He lay behind a dead horse, which protected him from the swarm of bullets. While the white men behind the adobe walls were reloading their buffalo guns, another warrior raced to Quanah and, without stopping or dismounting, reached down, grabbed Quanah's arm, and swung him up on the horse's rump. Quanah was only conscious enough to clutch the horse's shaggy hair instinctively. They raced away, to fight again.

When spring came, Preloch helped Silas with the planting. She knew horses well, could almost speak the secret language of horses, so she quickly learned to plow. With a lack of male hands, Silas was glad to have the help. Amelia was glad to have Cynthia out of the house. The heathen seemed to like rolling up her sleeves and getting sunburned. And just when they had almost gotten her bleached out like a white woman again.

Elizabeth tried to stay out of the conflict. She liked Cynthia Ann very much, but she still had to live in her sister's house. If only a man would come along and ask her to marry, she could get out of this mess. But, then, she reasoned, to marry the first man that comes along, just to escape from a fight at home, wasn't a very good way to start a successful marriage. Still, Elizabeth often wondered what it would be like to have a husband and family of her own.

When Amelia was not around, or when she was in a good mood, Elizabeth would sit and talk with Cynthia Ann. She asked Cynthia Ann to tell about her husband, her sons and her life on the plains. Preloch, for her part, glanced from the corner of her eye at Amelia, and spoke softly, briefly, so as not to open a new fight.

When the crops were put in and had been cultivated, there was no more work until harvest time. And the heat of the summer came. Swaddled in petticoats and bound in tight bodices, Preloch sat on the porch and sweated. She wished again for her deerskin sheath. It was loose enough to let air in; if you kept moving, a leather dress was cooler than these cotton clothes.

Amelia seemed unconscious of the heat. She wore thinner blouses, to be sure, and carried a parasol to protect her skin and hair from the sun, but she cheerfully wore layer upon layer of clothes.

There had been no open hostility between Preloch and Amelia for some time; so Preloch decided to apologize. She still hoped she would soon be permitted to leave this house, to return to the prairie, but the possibility looked dimmer. The war with the Yankees was not going well, and it took more and more of the men and the whole attention of the white people. The Confederacy had not been able to make good on the promises to the Comanches in the treaty of last fall, so the Comanches had started marauding again. It looked to Preloch like they were stuck, so she wanted to make peace.

"I sorry," she told Amelia. "I try." She pointed to Amelia, then to herself: "You, me: friends?"

"All right," said Amelia. "We can try it again. But you've got to understand one thing. We'll go by my rules. And the first rule is, speak only English."

11

Gathering at the River,
Summer 1862

One Sunday after church on a sweltering day when they had decided not to visit anyone, and no one had decided to visit them, they sat around the porch after lunch, humming the morning's hymn: "Shall We Gather at the River?"

"I know," said Silas. "Let's go down to the river, where it's shady and moist." Amelia and Elizabeth quickly agreed.

Silas drove the hack around to the front of the house. Amelia, Silas, and Elijah sat on the front seat; Elizabeth, Cynthia Ann, Topsannah, and the two little girls on the back. It was crowded, and Preloch was still uncomfortable in all the clothes they had put on her. Topsannah was sweating in a layered ruffled dress. Preloch wondered if she would ever get used to wearing so many clothes.

Silas clicked his tongue at the horses and gave the reins a shake, causing them to break into a little trot. Thank goodness, that made a little breeze. Preloch loosened her collar to try to get some relief. This was no time to be out where the sun could hit you with his first lance. This was a time to be in the shade, grinding corn or plaiting rope or beading a dress, not sitting in the open, idly, in a hot wagon, with a crowd of hot people. Toh-Tsee-Ah tugged at her dress.

Elizabeth—young and lithe and vibrant—sat at the other end of the back seat. Over a white blouse, she wore a little jumper which she could open, but hadn't. On her head was a little pillbox hat with a wide brim. She noticed Cynthia Ann studying her and smiled. She was good with children; they sat quietly on her lap, waiting.

It's good that she has Silas, thought Preloch. On the prairie, as skinny as she was, she might not find a man who would take her, much less give good ponies for her.

Then she remembered how skinny she was when Peta Nocona led a string of horses to Paha-yuka's lodge.

Twenty-eight horses; no one had seen such a long string of horses offered as a dowry. Paha-yuka walked along the string, looking at each horse; they were all good horses, fit for a chief. Náudah, lying on her belly and peeking under the skin of the lodge, saw Paha-yuka glance back toward her, over and over again.

Once when he was close and they made eyecontact, she smiled.

"Fine horses," said Paha-yuka, "One for each day of the moon." He took the rope from Peta Nocona and led the horses away. That meant that Peta Nocona could then lead Náudah away to his lodge, the wedding lodge which the women of his family would prepare.

Silas wound through many trees. So many trees. Preloch wondered if she would ever get used to that. So many places for enemies to hide, so many opportunities for ambush. She felt better when they passed a field of cotton or corn. She liked their openness. In a field, you could at least see far enough to know when someone was approaching you. And you could hear things without confusion.

But then Silas guided the horses into deeper woods. Taller trees, too many kinds of trees, thick with bushes underneath. She looked at Elizabeth to see if it was all right. Should they be trotting so blithely into such a thick woods? They didn't even have any weapons with them.

Elizabeth smiled at her. "We're going for a ride, down to the river," she assured Cynthia Ann. "Isn't everything just lovely?"

Preloch understood the intention, if not the words, and tried to smile. Here in the deep woods, the trees almost joined overhead, closing out the sun and air. It was thick and still and humid in the woods. No breeze, not even a little one made by their movement along the lane. And so many clothes. Preloch felt sweat rolling down her backbone and between her breasts. She could hardly get her breath. She loosened the top buttons of her blouse to let the air in.

"Oh, look, Mother," cried Toh-Tsee-Ah in Comanche. "A river."

"I told you not to let that child jabber that language!" Amelia reprimanded, turning in the front seat to scowl at Topsannah.

They had come to an open place. A grassy bank sloped down to the river, which looked wide and deep but still.

Silas pulled the horses to a stop and looked back at Cynthia. "This is the old swimming hole, Sis. Folks around here used to come down here as kids all the time and swim."

"Swim?" asked Cynthia.

"Yep, you know. Take off your clothes and swim." He made paddling motions with his hands.

"Swim?" she asked to see if she got the word right. "We go? Swim?"

"Oh, no. We can't go today. We didn't bring bathing suits. Maybe anoth—"

"Oh, please, little brother. We swim?" Then she burst into Comanche. "Please, big protector brother. It's so hot. And we have to wear so many clothes. That water looks cool. Please, can't we go and swim?"

"Honestly, Cynthia!" scolded Amelia. "How many times do we have to tell you, don't speak that awful language. You're American. Speak English."

Preloch picked up Toh-Tsee-Ah and jumped out of the hack. She ran toward the water. As soon as she put the child down, she began taking off her clothes. She opened her blouse and threw it away, helped Toh-Tsee-Ah slip her dress over her head, then struggled with her own long skirt. Why did these Tejanos make it so hard to get your clothes off? A loose sheath lets air in, and it was easy to just fling it up over your head.

Preloch had finally gotten the skirt and her underthings off. She looked back at her brother and his family. They were staring, wide-eyed, like a herd of antelope before they break to run. She realized they were staring at her nakedness, for in white culture you weren't supposed to show your body. And yet, they were staring, fascinated. Well, if they needed to look, let them. Náudah walked in beauty again. She took Toh-Tsee-Ah by the hand and they waded into the water.

"It looks delightful!" cried Elizabeth. "I'm going in, too!" She jumped out of the hack, slipped off her jumper and opened her blouse.

"Elizabeth!" shouted Amelia. "Stop that! There are men around."

"Men? There's just Silas. He's my—brother."

"Brother-in-*law*!" said Amelia.

"Oh, he's seen me plenty of times," said Elizabeth.

"That was when you were young," said Amelia. "Before you grew—before you developed—"

"You mean before I grew breasts?" said Elizabeth, opening her blouse to show a firm young breast. Its nipple stuck up like a puppy's nose. She could feel, without touching, that it was moist. She could feel Silas and Elijah staring at her, and she was not ashamed. She was no more ashamed than Preloch had been. She pulled the other side of her blouse from under her skirt band and let the blouse fall to the ground. Without turning away from Silas' and Elijah's eyes, she popped open her skirt band and the long, dark skirt fell to her ankles, leaving her in her bright pantaloons. "I'm going to swim with Preloch," she announced.

"That's it!" cried Amelia, jumping out of the hack with a lurch. "Silas, you and the children drive on around that bend and wait for us. This is it! That woman has got to go! I do everything I can to civilize her, and what do I get? She's corrupting everyone around her. I won't have it, you hear? I won't have her coming in here and ruining everything decency stands for. Go on, now. And quit staring. Elizabeth, put your clothes back on. This is the thanks I get for taking you both in. I knew it would never work. That savage! I knew it would never work."

"But Amelia," said Silas. "There's no place to send her."

"Yes, there is. Let Billy and Serena take care of her for a while. Even if he is wounded, they can damned well do their part."

She swung her gloves at the horses' rumps, as if to shoo them away. "That woman has got to go, do you hear, Silas? I don't care if she is your sister. She's not really your sister. She's too much of a savage. You find another place for her to live. I won't have her in my house another single day, do you hear? I won't harbor that savage any longer. She's hopeless. I try and try, but she just won't learn. She . . . is . . . hopeless. A hopeless savage."

Amelia turned, and there stood Elizabeth, as naked and shameless as any savage.

12

With Serena and Billy Parker,
Fall 1862

Smiling Billy Parker was a Unionist, but he had been con-
scripted into the Confederate Army and forced to fight for a
cause he abhorred. An exploding bombshell had torn chunks
of flesh from both of his legs, so he was sent to a hospital, then
home on furlough. Later, he was discharged because he could not
walk without crutches. Yet he lived in almost daily fear that the
Confederacy would draft him again as soon as his wounds had
healed.

His wife, Serena, was a cheerful young woman who always
looked for the good in others—and usually found it. Discovering
something in others to approve of had made her tolerant of and
even interested in their point of view. She was not driven by an irri-
table urge to reach out and remake those around her.

This young couple lived on an eighty-acre farm two miles south
of Birdville, not many miles from Isaac and Bess Parker. They
attended the same church as the elder Parkers, but the Baptist con-
servatism had not robbed Billy of his smile nor Serena of her good
temperament. Late in the summer of 1862, Cynthia Ann was sent
to stay with them until some other arrangement could be worked
out.

Náudah, Toh-Tsee-Ah, and their little suitcase were turned over to Billy and Serena one Sunday at church. Billy helped Cynthia Ann into the front seat of his hack; Serena and Toh-Tsee-Ah sat in the back.

One of the first things Billy said to her on the way home was, "I know your Uncle Ike kind of went back on his word to help you visit your family on the high plains, Cynthia Ann. I don't know how I'll do it, me being on crutches, but I'll try to help you go out there."

Náudah hardly knew what to say. Was this just another of their false promises? She was reluctant to let her hopes rise, because the disappointment that followed was so painful. To protect herself, she had become suspicious, distrustful. Yet Billy's smile was infectious. She smiled back at him. "Thank . . . you, Billy," she said somewhat hesitantly. "I try. Be a good girl." She had heard the Parker women say that phrase to Toh-Tsee-Ah. She glanced back. Toh-Tsee-Ah was holding up a black patent-leather shoe and talking to Serena. They were obviously enjoying each other's company.

It was a hot day—and going to be hotter. Náudah was glad to get the breeze from the speed of their travel. They had wrapped her in too many, too-tight clothes, as usual. Billy pulled off his church coat and laid it across his knee. Náudah unfastened her collar, feeling a little guilty. She glanced at Serena and noticed that she had already done the same.

They soon got to Billy's farm. The yellow cracker-box house was small, but there were several good sized trees around it. Benches and chairs under the trees told Náudah that Billy and Serena did some of their work outside in the shade.

Billy let the women out at the front door, then drove on to the barn to put away the horses and the hack. Serena immediately helped Toh-Tsee-Ah take off her shoes and stockings. "You can run barefoot around here, dear. It'll be a lot cooler."

Serena turned to Cynthia Ann. "Toatsy-Ann and I had such a good visit on the way home," she said. "Did I get her name right? It was so hard to understand what she was saying, because I'm not

used to children's voices. She's such a sweet little girl. I'm just
going to love having a little one around the house."

Náudah only smiled.

"Oh, me," said Serena. "Here I am talking a blue streak, and I'll
bet you don't understand half of what I'm saying. I'll try to slow
down."

Náudah did not understand all of the words, but she understood
the intent. She liked this woman already.

"Too hot, mucho caliente," said Serena, fanning herself with
exaggeration. "Come on. We'll find some cooler clothes." She led
Cynthia Ann into the bedroom.

"I always wear one of Billy's old short-sleeved shirts around the
house," Serena went on. "It's one thing to dress up for other people to see you at church; it's another thing to continue the torture
at home." She handed Cynthia Ann a shirt. "They're nice and
loose, so the breeze can get in. And I don't wear a chemise or a
bunch of petticoats, either."

Serena took off her blouse and chemise, put on the loose shirt,
and held out her arms. "See?"

Náudah smiled at her. "Toquet."

"Toquet? Toquet? What does that mean, Toatsy-Ann?"

"It's okay.' Mama likes it."

"'It's okay'? Good! I can see right now, we're going to get along."
She motioned Cynthia Ann to change, while she slipped off her
church skirt and her petticoats, then pulled on a light cotton skirt
over her pantaloons.

"And let's go outside, where we can catch the breeze—if there is
any."

She took a bowl of green peas outside with her, put them on the
table under a tree, and started shelling them. "There's always work
to do around here. Since Billy's so crippled up, I have to do a lot of
it. But that keeps me out of meanness. 'Idle hands are the Devil's
playground,' says Uncle James. Have you met Uncle James, yet?
Now, there is one mean preacher. He can preach hellfire and brim-
stone that gets you so worked up, you want to go right out and

commit suicide, but then he tells you that suicide is a terrible sin. So there you are. . . . But he's saved a lot of souls."

"I help?" said Náudah, indicating the peas.

"Yes, of course, dear. Here, you take this bowl, and I'll get another. We have so many of them to do. Your Uncle Isaac came over and helped me with the planting, but then I've had to do the hoeing and the praying for rain all by myself." She laughed lightly at her own little joke. Náudah smiled with her.

"The peas have made a good crop. I'm going to put up a bunch in jars. It's work, but that means we'll have something to eat this winter. And we've got a lot of corn. We're going to have so many pinto beans and black-eyed peas, we'll be able to sell some and still have plenty for ourselves. That means we can buy some of the things we'll need, like flour and sugar. With Billy limping around the way he is, it's sure good that we have such a big garden. But, crippled or not, I'm just so glad to have him home. At least, that limp brought him back to me."

Billy came up from the barn, each step a lurch on his crutch. He noticed Serena and Cynthia Ann shelling peas. "You got enough firewood?" he asked.

"No," said Serena. "I'd appreciate it if you could cut some more. But first sit down and rest a bit in the shade. You deserve a little pause, the same as the rest of us."

"I'll rest when we're safe from the Rebels," he said and continued hobbling toward the house.

"Billy . . . chop wood." Serena made chopping motions.

Náudah smiled, but wondered why, when it was so hot.

"He does what he can. Which is things that can be done standing still. I have to do the rest, like carry water. But he's so good. He works all the time at something."

"I carry water?" said Náudah. "I carry, toquet?"

"Oh, that would be a big help. Come on, I'll show you where the buckets are and the pump. We're going to need a lot, if we're going to get all the peas put up today."

At the pump, Serena leaned close to Cynthia Ann and whispered, even though there was no one within a half mile, "Billy uses a lot of water down there at his still." She motioned toward a clump of trees near the middle of their farm. A cow trail wound through the pasture toward the trees.

"No compren—No understand," said Náudah.

"Billy . . . make whiskey," said Serena. "He's turning a lot of our extra corn into liquor so he can sell it."

"Wis-key?" asked Náudah. "Agua tonto?" *Fool water?*

"You've got that right," said Serena. "Turns men into fools quick enough. But Billy, thank goodness, doesn't use the stuff. He just makes it and sells it to a trader that comes through once in a while. It's a way to turn corn into a cash crop, and Lord knows we need the cash right now. If your Uncle Isaac or Uncle James knew, they'd just about have a fit. That's why we keep it such a secret. You won't tell anyone, will you?"

Náudah shook her head. She didn't understand completely what she was supposed to keep secret, but she understood that a secret existed. The thock-thock of Billy's axe started at the woodpile. Náudah liked these people; they weren't a bit lazy. They were real people.

Serena and Cynthia each carried a bucket of water to the kitchen. Billy had started a fire in the stove.

"Lord knows, this is no day to have a fire going," said Serena, "but we have to process these peas."

"Hakai?" asked Náudah. Then she remembered to try English: "What?"

"Oh, forgive me. I just thought you knew already. See," she said, taking a jar and making signs of filling it. "Summer. We fill with peas." Then she put the jar on a shelf. "Winter . . . you understand winter?" Serena shivered and huddled to keep warm. "Snow, ice, cold. Mucho frío."

Náudah nodded.

Serena took the jar from the shelf again, opened it, and made signs of eating.

"Ah," said Náudah, understanding. They were conserving food for the winter, just as Our People did. She felt a surge of warmth for Billy and Serena. "I help," she said. "Okay? I carry water, help chop wood."

"Good," said Serena, "and then you can help me stuff the jars and cook them off."

Together Serena and Cynthia Ann shelled and cooked the peas, packed them in jars, processed the jars in a boiling water bath, then sealed the jars and set them aside to cool. They hardly noticed that they had sweated through their loose shirts.

13

Peta Nocona at Fort Cobb

At the beginning of the Civil War, Camp Cooper on the Clear Fork of the Brazos River was abandoned and the Union troops sent to various military posts. Those who were Union sympathizers went north with their units. Like many Texans, interpreter Horace Jones joined the southern cause. He was assigned to Fort Cobb, Indian Territory, where the Confederacy attempted to implement its Indian policy. When Peta Nocona heard in the summer of 1862 that Horace Jones was at Fort Cobb, he arranged a meeting.

Peta Nocona set up his buffalo-skin tipi west of the post and waited for Jones. When he came, they exchanged the formal greeting in Comanche, then talked of ponies and weather, the hunt and trade with the Mexicans. Nocona invited Jones into his lodge to smoke. They sat cross-legged on buffalo robes around a small fire. Nocona brought out grass cakes and pemmican on a straw tray.

"Meeku takwu Ta-ahpu makaaruu," said Nocona; *let us feed the Great Spirit.*

Jones politely took a bit of the pemmican and a grass cake and nibbled on them.

Carefully, Nocona prepared a pipe, stuffing it with his best mixture of tobacco, willow, and cedar. He lit the pipe, puffed on it,
offering a brief prayer in each of the four cardinal directions, plus
up to the heavens and down to this world, then handed it to Jones
in silence, who also puffed on it. When the pipe was finished, they
could finally talk about what Peta Nocona wanted to know.

"Many deaths Sul Ross make on Pease River," said Nocona. He
rested his hands on his knees, waiting for a response.

"Yes," said Jones. "Though I was not there, I heard it was a pretty
horrible massacre. And then a blizzard hit within hours."

"We knew nothing of the fight, until I returned from the hunt.
The bodies were stacked up like logs waiting for the fireplace." He
gestured toward a stack of firewood near the door of the tipi. "The
bodies were frozen and stuck together. Most of them, their clothes
had been taken, but they were already dead, so they did not die in
the blizzard."

"I'm sorry," said Jones, studying the fire in the center of the
lodge.

"We pulled at their feet to separate them, so we could look at their
faces and tell the relatives of those we buried." He paused, emptied
the pipe, refilled it, and lit it again with an ember from the fire.

"My wife, Náudah, was not among the dead."

"No," said Jones, looking up to make eye contact with the chief.
"She and Toh-Tsee-Ah-ne were taken to Camp Cooper."

"I heard," said Nocona. "I also heard that you talked with her."

"Yes," said Jones. "That was my duty."

"I only want to hear the truth about my wife, brother." Nocona
held out his hands, palms up, waiting. "Spare none of the details.
Was she tortured? or killed?"

Jones recounted the story of her capture, interrogation and
identification by Isaac Parker. He told Nocona that her white family had taken Náudah to East Texas and that he had not heard of
her since. "She was very much concerned about her sons," Jones
added. "She wept and asked us repeatedly about them. Tell me
about their welfare, brother," said Jones, "and if I see her again, I
can relay the message."

Nocona was hesitant. White men were not to be trusted with information, but Jones had been a friend of the Comanches. As far as Nocona could tell, Jones was an honest man. "My sons are safe," he said reluctantly. "They were out hunting rabbits when the attack came. They are now far away from here, on the high prairie, where the soldiers cannot see them. You cannot see them, now, but someday you may."

"I would be honored," said Jones, laying his hand on his heart.

"I am an old man," said Nocona. "My sorrow has made me old and weak. I have given up leadership of the Noconis, and a younger man named Horseback sits in my place and rides his horse at the head of the column. He is brave and steadfast, while I am doddering. I have not many more years to live. I want my wife. You, you who speak the white man's tongue and the language of Our People, will you lead me to her?"

Now, it was Jones' turn to use the pipe as a delaying ploy. How could he answer this old, desperate, and honest man.

"I would like to, old brother," said Jones, at last. "But I cannot. You, my friend, are wanted by the Texas Rangers; they would kill you at first sight, and I could do nothing about it. You know that, don't you?"

Nocona nodded.

"They even kill white men who have been friendly to the Comanche. They shot our friend, Robert Neighbors, in the street of Weatherford just because he had protected Ketumsee and his band until they were safe at the reservation on Cache Creek."

"I did not know he was dead," said Nocona. "He was an honest man. There are not many such men among the whites; we can't afford to lose them. We will suffer from the loss of him."

"And," Horace went on, "I cannot guide you to your wife, because I don't know where she is. It could take years to track her down, if she is still alive.

"You know as well as I, that the commander of the fort will not give me time to go on such a mission. If it were known in Texas that I was looking for an Indian woman, my own life would be in danger. They might shoot me on the street, too."

Nocona silently studied the fire, then shut his eyes. "You are right, friend," he said at last. "It makes my heart heavy, but you are right. Still, I want my wife."

14

Run Away With Billy

"Por fávor, Billy. Vamanos a la Comanchería. *We go to Comanchería, no?* My heart so crying por mis hijos y mi esposo."

"I know, Cynthia Ann. And I know I said I'd help as best I can; and I will, too. It's just that I need to get around a little better, and we need a plan."

"He's walking better every week," said Serena. "Don't you think so, Cynthia Ann? I'll bet he'll be able to walk without crutches in another couple of months."

"We go—" Náudah began, but language failed her. She made motions to indicate wheels and pantomimed riding in a wagon.

"Now, that's an idea," said Billy. "We could go in the hack."

"Sí, Sí," said Náudah. "Cuando la luna es brillante."

"When the moon is full," repeated Serena. "Yes, it might work."

"I stand—" said Náudah, and she got up in a chair, cupped her hands to her mouth, and yelled: "Nuh-nuhrmuhr kiamah! Nuh-nuhrmuhr-ne kiamah! *And they come. Comanche hear*"—she cupped a hand to an ear—"*and they come.*"

"Sounds pretty crazy to me," said Billy. "But I just gotta get out of here, before they draft me again."

They decided that Billy, Cynthia Ann and Toh-Tsee-Ah would pose as settlers and drive out beyond Jacksboro as if looking for a homestead. When they encountered a Comanche encampment or raiding party, Náudah would take over and find Billy a guide to the North.

Billy and Serena put the roof on the hack and fastened the wagon sheet to it, to make an enclosure around the back. Cynthia Ann and Toh-Tsee-Ah would sleep under the wagon sheet in the hack, while Billy would roll up in a blanket on the ground under the hack. They would take food enough for a week. That way, they could get out far enough on the frontier to meet some Indians and manage to do it with very little money.

They left three days before the full moon and traveled in the daytime. They met several families in wagons or on a variety of mounts, some of them even walking. They were on their way to Fort Worth. "Looks to me like you're headin' the wrong way, mister," said some of them. "Ye c'n lose your hair out there. Whole family c'n lose their hair. I'm ready to give the country back to the Injuns. Some hot-head over by Weatherford killed three Injuns, and that brought 'em out on the war-path. The country jist ain't safe no more."

They traveled to Jacksboro to start their search, thinking that was close enough to the cross-timber country to encounter a Comanche party. A man who operated a livery stable in Jacksboro took one look at Billy's crutch and allowed them to camp in his livery yard for the fee to feed the horses.

On the day of the full moon, they left Jacksboro in the early afternoon, hoping to be five or ten miles from the settlements by moonrise. The wagon ruts degenerated to a horse trail and, by nightfall, even that began to disappear. They were forced to stop, for fear they would break a wheel in an unseen gully.

Náudah gathered plenty of firewood, and they built a big campfire, hoping they could be seen. Náudah went out to the edge of the fire light and called repeatedly, "Nuh-nuhrmuhr-ne kiamah! Nuh-nuhrmuhr kiamah!" until she was hoarse. Suddenly, several horsemen appeared in the fire light. They were Texans. Night riders.

"Ye oughta keep yer woman in better tow, mister," said the leader of the group, a man with a very bushy mustache. "Keep the noise down. They's Injuns likely to be out in these parts on a bright night like this."

"Don't see no saddle horse, Jake," said one of the men in the back.

Billy got up on his crutch and explained to Jake, "I don't sit a horse so well any more. Got my legs bunged up at Shiloh, so I just don't have the strength to hold myself on."

Jake waited, his hands crossed loosely over his saddle horn, his reins hanging slack. Several men had ridden up close enough that Billy could see their faces in the fire light. One had a nasty, three-inch scar on his right cheek.

"I'm getting better every week, though," Billy went on. "Why, I can already follow a plow with one crutch, by holding on to the handle."

"Sod's awful hard to bust out here," said a voice in the back, coughing.

"You better get something for that cough, Henry," said the scar-faced man. "You sound like death warmed over."

"I know," said the coughing man. "But I didn't wanta miss any of the fun."

"Don't look like they got anything worth takin," said another voice.

Jake dismounted, the leather in his saddle creaking with the stress. "We ain't goin to take nothin, then," said Jake. "We'll jist visit with these folks fer a minute, then move on."

"I'd offer some coffee," said Billy, sitting down again, "but I don't think there's enough to go around."

"Tha's all right," said Jake. "It'd jist make us stop and piss. Oh, 'scuse me, ma'am." He touched the brim of his hat. He squatted on his haunches and pretended to warm his hands at the fire. "Ye seen any Injuns?"

"'Fraid not," said Billy. "Haven't even seen any buffalo."

"They's further west," said Jake.

"I hate a damned buffalo," said a voice in the crowd. It was the coughing man.

"Me, too," said another voice. "They ain't even worth the pow-der 'n lead to make 'em drop." Some of the men were already rein-ing their horses away, getting ready to continue their ride in the night.

"You folks a fur piece from home?" asked Jake.

"We lived over by Birdville," said Billy, before he thought he should have lied to them.

"I've killed a few buffs, though, in my time," said a voice in the crowd, ignoring the conversation at the campfire. "It's kind of fun to git 'em in a surround. Ye c'n shoot 'n shoot, till yore gun barrel is melted."

"I kind of like something that'll fight back a little," said the scar-faced man.

Jake stood up, getting ready to mount his horse and ride away. "I'd reckymend you folks pack up tomorry 'n go on back to Birdville."

"But, this is a free county, ain't it?" said Billy.

"No. Not quite free," said Jake. "We's still fightin fer it. 'N, ye know, if Injuns come along and kill you and yore family, then we'd all have to ride out on a vengeance raid. 'R, it might happen that some bad men'd come along, kill you, 'n take everthang you got; then lay it on the Injuns. Either way, it's trouble fer us. We'll come back this way tomorry, jist to see that yo're gone." He got on his horse, turned a complete circle and rode off into the night.

"I sure hope we find some Injuns," said a voice in the crowd.

"Me, too," said the scar-faced man. "Ain't nothin quite as good as huntin Injuns. I've fought ba'rs and I've fought paint'ers, boys, 'n I'll tell you, they ain't nothin to make the blood boil quite like fight-in a Injun. Specially, if ye c'n catch one by hand."

15

Courting Coho Smith

Back in Birdville, after the waning moon forced their return, Billy Parker took six gallons of whiskey to Fort Worth to sell to Ed Terrell at the First and Last Chance Saloon and came back with a new piece of news. He had met a Confederate cotton agent named Coho Smith, who had lived among the Comanches and spoke the language.

"Here's my idea," Billy said to Serena, trying it out for the first time. "I think a person could hire this Mr. Smith to guide me and Cynthia Ann to one of the Comanche villages. She can stay there, and I can hire some Comanches to guide me into northern territory, then I can make my way to Illinois and be safe. Once I'm settled and have a place, I can send for you. We'll just move away from the Rebels and their conscription." He flashed her his big, infectious smile.

Serena was glad to see his smile again. It was a desperate and improbable plan, but she agreed enthusiastically. "Oh, Billy. When can you start?"

"Hold on. We'll have to convince Smith to act as guide first."

"Well, go get him. Bring him here, and I'll cook up a big dinner. Then we can try talking him into it."

"That's a good idea. Only trouble is, he was on his way to Laredo and Saltillo to look for cotton markets. But he'll be back in a few weeks. We'll catch him then. In the meantime, do you think we ought to tell Cynthia Ann what we're cooking up?"

"Oh, of course! She'll be so thrilled."

Náudah immediately began preparations. She tanned a couple of calf skins she found thrown over the fence at the barn and made herself and Toh-Tsee-Ah leather sheaths, sewing them with thick cotton thread and a steel needle. She decorated their dresses with knotted thongs, fringes, and natural pigments of earthen red and charcoal black. It would be important to look Comanche for the homecoming.

Her belief soared in spite of her caution against it.

"Don't be too anxious, Cynthia Ann," said Billy. "We haven't yet convinced Smith to lead us out there."

"He might not be willing, at first," added Serena. "But I'm sure we can get him in the right mind. Why, it's the right thing to do. How can he refuse?"

Náudah forced herself to expect the worst. So many false promises had been made that it was not hard to imagine this as just another. Still, her heart beat faster when Smith finally arrived for the planned dinner.

She sat opposite him at the table, waiting and watching, hardly breathing. He would have to make the first move.

Serena sat at the end of the table with Toh-Tsee-Ah in a high chair beside her. She had taught the little girl to eat with a spoon.

"Well, Mr. Smith," said Billy, smiling. "Have a nice slice of this beef."

"And help yourself to the beans and vegetables. We won't stand on any ceremony around here."

Cynthia Ann took food on her plate, but she didn't touch it, even when the others started eating. Her stomach was upset with excitement. She could not remove her eyes from Coho, wondering, waiting.

"Well, Mr. Smith," said Serena, laying down her knife, "I haven't heard you talk to our cousin yet. I hope you're not like numbers of people that have come here professing to speak Comanche or Spanish, and after two or three words, they are done."

Coho had noticed Cynthia Ann watching him and not eating. "I reckon I can talk all you want me to," said Coho, and he said the first thing to Cynthia Ann in Comanche that came to his mind: "ee-wunee keem." *Come here.*

Náudah sprang up with a scream and knocked about half the dishes off the table, startling Billy. She ran around to Coho, fell on the floor, and caught him around both legs, crying in Comanche, "ee-ma, mi mearo, ee-ma mearo." *I am going with you.*

"It's true," she went on in Comanche. "I was so afraid you'd be just another cheat—and not be able to speak. But I can tell, you can talk the language of Our People. I'm so happy to hear something I can understand. You must talk more. Here, I'll sit by you."[1]

Billy got the table and dishes to right, then placed a chair for Cynthia Ann beside Coho. They began to eat again, but Náudah held Coho by one arm and talked persistently to him in a mix of Comanche and Spanish.

"I want to go back to my husband and sons; I'm so lonesome for them. No one can tell me if they are safe. My heart is so empty; it cries all the time por mi esposo y mis hijos. But Billy has told me by signs and words that he wants to go to my people also. He wants to take me to my family."

Coho put down his knife and fork. So this was their plan. They wanted him to do something for this lonesome Comanche woman. He sympathized with her. He'd been lonesome a time or two himself. He asked, "Billy, do you want to go to the Comanches?"

"Yes, I do," said Billy, "and that's why I sent for you. I want you to guide and interpret for us. I'll pay you as best I can, whatever price you set. I've got to get out of here before they force me into the army again. I want you to take me and Cynthia Ann to the Comanches. I can stay with them until this awful war is over."

Coho repeated to Náudah in Comanche what Billy had said.

"Oh, yes," she said, "That's our plan. You will take us, won't you?"

1. Smith later wrote that the woman was so excited, he thought she would go into a fit. See Coho Smith, "Cynthia Ann Parker," in *Cohographs* (Fort Worth: Branch-Smith, 1976), pp. 69-71.

"But, ma'am," Coho protested, "the Texas legislature has granted you a league of land. You can't just walk away from that."

"Oh, that," she said. "It means nothing to me. You can have it. I'll give it to you if you help us."

"Well, that'd make me mighty happy, except you know that if I was to take you and Billy to the Comanches, I would never dare come back to Texas anymore. They wouldn't let me in, and then even a league of land wouldn't do me any good."

Náudah hugged his arm closer. "You could sell it and buy land somewhere else."

"And you ain't got no horses," said Coho. "That pony I got ain't fit to go on a journey to the upper branches of the Arkansas River."

"Horses! That is nothing!" she said. "There are some first-rate horses running here. Every day, they lick salt out there by the gate. Just let me get my hand on their mane and they are mine. Don't hesitate a moment about horses. Oh, I tell you, my heart is crying all the time for my two sons, mi corazón está llorando todo el tiempo por mis dos hijos."

Náudah tightened her grip on his arm again. "Please, please," she begged, "You will take us to the Comanches, won't you? You'll be well paid, and it's not far. You can do it. Tu puedes. Please say you'll do it."

"Well," Coho said, "you know, I just married a nice young woman. What would she say if I left her?"

"That doesn't matter," said Náudah. "Only take me to my people and they will give you as many wives as you want. Our people are not like the white man, they take as many wives as they wish."

"But I like this one."

"You can take her with you. And you can learn to like as many as you wish. She'll like having other wives to help with the work."

Coho looked around. This woman was sure insistent. How in the world was he going to get out of this? He didn't want to hurt her feelings. He liked her, sympathized with her need, but he just couldn't help her. Billy and Serena were waiting, watching, though they could not follow the conversation.

"Why don't just you and your cousin go?" asked Coho.

"Oh, Billy doesn't know anything about Indians. We might start, and, when we got up in the Indian country, we might be staking out a horse or getting wood, and he would be killed by Tonkawa, and I would be made a slave, and I would never get to see my boys or my people, never, never, never."

"Oh, you'd be okay," Coho said. "Ain't nobody out there now but Comanches. All the others have been put on reservations, or they moved on out to New Mexico."

"You don't understand," said Náudah. "I'm not sure I could find my way. They've turned me around so many times, I'm lost before I start."

"Jist get started in the right direction, and you'll find your way."

"Maybe," she said. "We could go first to the Pease River, and from there to Prairie Dog Fork. But I could not go alone," she said. "Billy can't hunt with a crutch, and I couldn't hunt game like a man to support myself and Toh-Tsee-Ah. You must go, don't say no. Say yes, and I'll give you par-lin pe-ah-et, par-lin tehe-yah, par-lin esposas, *ten guns, ten horses, ten wives*. My people will be so glad if you bring me to them, they will give you anything I would ask."

"Well, I'll have to think about it," said Coho.

The next day, Coho Smith helped Billy bottle some whiskey at his still, because they were going to take some to Dallas and sell it. In the afternoon, Náudah, no longer any vestige of Cynthia Ann Parker in her heart, went out to see how the white man made agua tonto. She wore her calfskin sheath and carried Toh-Tsee-Ah on her arm.

Coho proposed they sample the whiskey as they were finishing.

"You're welcome to, sir," said Billy. "But I never touch the stuff. I just make it."

"That is wise," said Náudah, when the comment was translated for her. "Warriors go crazy with fire water. Americanos bring it into the Comanchería to trade, and we get nothing for it but the morning-after sickness. I would never believe anything a warrior said to me while he was drinking fool water."

Coho took a drink and said, "That's good stuff, Parker."

"Is it?" said Billy. "I never know if I'm doing it right or not."

"¿Cuándo vamanos a la Comanchería?" Náudah asked Coho. *When can we start for the high plains?*

Coho Smith took another drink of Billy's whiskey, eyeing her over the rim of the tin cup. "I don't know," he said at last. "I'd have to arrange my other affairs. Make time in my schedule." He took another sip of the whiskey. "I'll have to let you know."

The next day, Billy Parker and Coho Smith left for Dallas. Billy stayed up half the night in their hotel room, trying to convince Coho to guide him and Cynthia Ann to the high plains.

"Don't you see?" said Billy. "They're trying to kill her."

"Who? No one's trying to kill her."

"The family, the neighbors, everyone she meets."

"Nonsense," said Coho. "She's got every thing she needs: clothes on her back, food on the table, a roof over her head. They's nobody trying to hurt her in any way."

"Not that way," said Billy. "There's something underneath that has a mind of its own. Call it a devil or a demon in us. It's different, can be different, from what we think we think. And that demon in us causes things to happen. It's capable of acting, even when we think we hate what it's doing."

"You're not making sense, Parker. You daft or something?"

"Haven't you ever heard of the better angel in us? Well, we've got a worser devil in us, too. And sometimes, in some cases, that devil is the real us. Sometimes, that devil is our real selves. He takes over and becomes us, and we don't even know it. Don't you see? The devil in the Parkers is trying to kill the spirit of Cynthia Ann."

"You drinking your own whiskey? Come on, straighten up!"

"And they're doing it deliberately, just as much as if they knew in their minds just exactly where they were sticking the knife. They're deliberately trying to kill her. They don't know it, but they're doing the meanest thing they can to her. And that's why you've got to help us. We've got to get out of here, her and me both."

But Smith would not relent.[2]

2. "Parker left me," Smith wrote, "with tears in his eyes and said 'they will never get me into the army again, I will suicide first.'" See Smith, *Cohographs.*

Autumn passed, then winter. They cooked the dried pinto beans with pork rind and ate the jars of green peas. Slowly, Billy's legs healed, so that he learned again to walk with only a cane. Náudah had ceased to ask when they could start for the high plains. Winter was no time to be traveling, especially for people as unused to living on the trail as Billy was—as unused to living off the land as she had become.

Then Billy was gone. Serena was quiet and withdrawn; Náudah could see that she was worried. When a man abandoned his wife on the high plains, people treated it almost as a death: you did not ask about the absent one; you did not mention his name to the wife or any of her close relatives; you went on with life, as if the absent one had never existed.

Still, Náudah sympathized with Serena. Náudah had been forcibly ripped from her family, which had the same effect as an abandonment, especially since no one would even allow her to visit the high prairies. She knew how Serena's heart must be crying all the time. Náudah had come to love Serena, more than just as a sister, almost as a part of herself, a part that understood and shared secrets, because Serena had always been so good and loving to her. She could not resist putting her arm around Serena and murmuring, "Lo siento. Lo siento mucho. I so sorry."

Serena could only smile weakly and withdraw to the bed to sob. Náudah took over most of the housework and brought Serena her food, as Serena had once brought food to her.

Even Toh-Tsee-Ah was affected. She lay with Serena and stroked her shoulder, murmuring, "Don't cry. It will be all right."

Then a letter came. It had no return address on it, but Serena recognized the handwriting. "It's Billy's hand style!" she cried, running her finger under the sealing wax to rip the letter open.

She had read no more than a few lines, before she shrieked with happiness. "He made it!" she cried. "He got through. He got past the blockade! Everything is okay."

"No compren— I no understand."

"Oh, Cynthia, Cynthia Ann," she sobbed, hugging Náudah. "He's safe! He got through." She ignored Náudah and read the rest of the letter.

Náudah stood back, hanging on to Toh-Tsee-Ah, until the little girl squirmed out of her arms, saying, "You're squeezing me too tight."

With a sinking, empty feeling, Náudah began to understand. Billy had not abandoned Serena, but her. She was the one who was forsaken, deserted . . . once again without a support or a hope.

"Oh, Cynthia, Cynthia," Serena went on. "We hired a group of men to smuggle Billy out of the South. They do it as a business, sort of like the negroes use the underground railroad. They've taken him to Illinois. He's safe, and he has a place for us to live, and he has work. I'm going to him, as soon as I can get a ticket. I'm so happy, I could scream."

"I happy, too," said Náudah, but she was already feeling the heavy, icy despair in her crying heart. The beast was bigger than ever; it seemed to have grown while her heart was laughing and smiling with the hope of seeing her family again. But now, it sat on her chest, her head, her voice—she felt she could say nothing, nothing at all; she could not even cry.

Coho Smith would not come to guide them.

Billy Parker would not return.

Serena would leave.

Cynthia Ann would be alone again, rejected. To be bundled off to some unfamiliar place, to be handed over to some insensitive new strangers who would say they loved her. None of her white relatives wanted her. Why, why wouldn't they let her and Toh-Tsee-Ah-ne simply go back to the Comanchería?

Instead, they would continue the torture. They would continue to hold her prisoner in this alien world. She would continue to mourn her losses. Dignity was gone; honor and position were gone; only sorrow remained for Still-She-Mourns.

Sunday School,
Spring 1863

"She's got to go to Sunday school," insisted Orlena, lifting Still-She-Mourns' chin to force her to meet Orlena's eyes. "Aren't you concerned for her soul?"

Still-She-Mourns pulled Toh-Tsee-Ah closer to her chest, as if she could hide them both in the wicker chair. "No. No. I—" She wanted to say she would take care of her baby's religious instruction, but she could not find the word for teach, nor for religion.

"We can't let her grow up in perdition and sin," pursued Orlena, standing straight and clasping her hands in front of her church dress.

Still-She-Mourns did not understand the words, but she understood enough to pull away and look down. Orlena had a brown and gray hooked rug on her parlor floor.

Orlena wasn't about to give up. She leaned toward Toh-Tsee-Ah. "Don't you want to go to Sunday school, Topsannah," she asked the child directly. "And look at the pretty picture books? And learn about Jesus?"

Toh-Tsee-Ah nodded and squirmed to get down from her mother's knee. She liked playing with the other children. She liked the special attention the ladies at Sunday school gave her.

"See?" said Orlena. "She's got better sense than you have, Cynthia Ann. Come along, dear," she added, holding out her hand to the child, "I'll help you get dressed."

Orlena felt victorious. Amelia, her sister-in-law, had told her of the fights she had with the "little barbarian" when Cynthia Ann and Topsannah were staying with her and Silas. Amelia had never adjusted to having an Indian child in the house, but now Toh-Tsee-Ah was speaking English as well as any four-year-old, better than some six-year-olds. It was gratifying to see the progress toward saving her.

"You'd better come along, too, Cynthia Ann," Orlena added, over her shoulder. "No sense in staying cooped up here all the time. You need to get to know other people."

Still-She-Mourns nodded. Yes, she would have to go. She had to see what they were doing to Toh-Tsee-Ah. She had to figure out what they were trying to do to her as well.

After Serena Parker left to join Billy in Illinois, Isaac Parker once again took charge of Cynthia Ann, but he was seventy years old and declared that he and Bess were too old to become nursemaids again, so they hitched up a buggy and delivered Cynthia Ann to her youngest sister, Orlena, whose husband, Ruff O'Quinn, had a farm on Slater Creek in Anderson County, a few miles southeast of Palestine, Texas.

Orlena didn't want to take the responsibility. She laced her arms across her chest and pointed out, "Silas is her guardian. Amelia got the Legislature to appoint him. Let him take care of her."

"You know we tried that," said Isaac, running his hand through his thin white hair. "Amelia couldn't seem to get along with her."

"Yeah, I heard from Amelia how it was," she said, looking away. "It's not like we don't ever see each other. Silas and Amelia only live about thirty miles from here. She said that woman is too much trouble."

"She's your sister!" exclaimed Bess Parker, moving forward to touch Orlena's forearm.

"She's been through unthinkable horrors out there among the savages," said Isaac, waving vaguely toward the west. "It's our duty to help her readjust and recover."

Orlena was silent. *I don't care about none of that,* she thought. *She hasn't been a sister to me. I don't even remember when she was taken from us. And now, twenty-five years later, she comes along and wants to be a sister. I don't have any feeling for her. She's no sister of mine.*

"All the rest of the family have taken a turn at trying to make a go of it," said Isaac. He leaned slightly toward her. "Now, we figured, it's your turn."

Orlena drew herself up straight and took a deep breath. "It's good that you have come here to tell me what to do, Uncle Isaac." The sarcasm in her voice was as thick as icicles.

Isaac was stopped momentarily. He hardly knew what to say.

"I mean, it's good of you to remind us of our Christian duty," Orlena went on, retreating. "We have a tendency to forget, or get so wound up in our own affairs, that we need good family leaders like you and Uncle James to remind us of our ethical and moral duties."

He sighed, leaned back, and said nothing.

Later, getting ready for bed, Orlena said to her husband, "We may have to take her and the baby in, but that don't mean I have to have anything to do with her."

"At least, they say she hasn't been trying to run away, lately," said Ruff, through lips that hardly parted. "That ought to make it a little easier."

Ruff O'Quinn, dressed in his church clothes, brought the buggy around to the front porch and drove the family the few miles to the church in the village of Ben Wheeler. Still-She-Mourns sat on the rumble seat and looked at the countryside. Anderson County was another place with too many trees. Pine trees, the size of a man's waist and bigger—much bigger—were everywhere. She understood that, among other things, Ruff O'Quinn had a sawmill to make these trees into lumber to build more houses. The open places where men had fields only made her more lonesome. She still wanted to return to the prairies of the high plains. But no one would guide her to the prairies.

At the church, dozens of people were standing around, just waiting to meet the strangers. Ruff and Orlena introduced Cynthia Ann and Topsannah to them all. Still-She-Mourns always looked down quickly whenever anyone looked her straight in the eye.

Still-She-Mourns remembered only one of the couples, T. J. Cates and his wife, Frances, because the man had insisted on a proper name. "Jist call me T. J.," he said. "Don't call me Tom, and don't call me Jeff; T. J. will do nicely." Still-She-Mourns knew the importance of correct names. This was the only white person she had ever met who seemed to share that knowledge.

"And is this little Topsannah?" asked his wife, Frances, reaching for the child. "How old are you now, dear?"

"Four," said Topsannah. "Wanta see me dance?"

"Why, sure." She put the child on the ground.

Toh-Tsee-Ah began whirling, chanting a little rhyme:

> I'm a little Injun, Whoop, Whoop!
> I can run and dance...

"Oh, my," said Frances with a stop in her throat. She picked Topsannah up again. "Maybe we'd better not do that one now. Maybe later." She was afraid the rhyme would be "pants" and the meaning would be vulgar. "Wherever did she learn such a thing as that?" she asked Orlena.

Orlena pulled herself up straight and took a deep breath. "Don't ask me. I'm not responsible."

"She's certainly a bright little girl," said T. J., reaching out to touch Toh-Tsee-Ah's hand. "You must be very proud of her," he added to Cynthia Ann.

Still-She-Mourns could only smile and look down. She had no words to express her ambiguity: that, yes, she was proud of a daughter that learned rapidly; and, no, she was repulsed by what the child was learning.

Later, Still-She-Mourns walked in the pasture near her sister's house with Toh-Tsee-Ah. They were right, she thought; it was time for the child to learn about important things. The child could talk well and understand much. Still-She-Mourns had been so wrapped up in her own concerns and so dulled by her own depressions that she had neglected the prairie flower's education; she had hardly noticed how rapidly the child was developing. She resumed talking to Toh-Tsee-Ah-ne in Comanche.

"Your father is Peta Nocona. He is leader of a band called the Noconi, the Wanderers. They are part of a group called Quahada, the Antelope. Do you know what an antelope is? He's an animal about this high"—she made a gesture— "and he runs around on the open prairie. He can run very fast, and bounce and jump even more than you can. When you meet one of them, he stops, lifts his head, and looks at you. His horns curl like this:" She curled her forefingers above her head to imitate prong horns.

Toh-Tsee-Ah giggled and put her fingers up to make the sign of an antelope also.

"That's right," said Still-She-Mourns. "When they see a person, they bounce away, like this." She hopped in imitation of an antelope. "But they're so curious. They don't know what's good for them. They have to stop and look at you." She turned, fingers still up as prong horns, imitating an antelope investigating the approaching hunter.

"If the hunter makes a big motion to scare them, they will run, of course. Or if the hunter just stands still, the antelope will get bored and bounce away, showing his big white rump. They've got big patches of white hair on their backsides"—she bent over, rubbing her hands along her buttocks, to draw the white patches of an antelope— "and they bounce away, showing the hunter their white rumps."

Toh-Tsee-Ah bounced away also, in imitation of her mother.

"So the hunter has to do something to make the antelope curious.

Flashing a mirror is good. The antelope sees the flash and says to himself, 'Now, what in the world could that be? I'll just have to get a little closer look.' So he walks slowly, creeps, toward the hunter"—she crept toward Toh-Tsee-Ah-ne— "and, all the time, he's saying to himself, 'I'm about to get into trouble. My curiosity is about to get me in trouble. I'd better run away.' So, he'll run back, just a little way. But his interest won't let him run very far."

Toh-Tsee-Ah giggled as Still-She-Mourns acted out the part of the antelope.

"So he comes right back," said Still-She-Mourns. "He comes right up close, to see what all that activity is. Then the hunter draws his bow"—she straightened up to became the hunter— "and, thunk, the arrow finds it mark, and we all have food to eat tonight."

She folded her arms and dropped the pantomime. She had almost made herself cry. The little game had brought it all back; she could see the prairie in perfect detail as she went through all the acts of an antelope hunt. For a moment, she had been back there on the plains, where she loved and was loved, where she spent her time working, cutting and drying the meat, making buffalo robes, repairing moccasins or leggings, preparing the food for her husband.

"Then what?" asked Toh-Tsee-Ah, jumping up and down.

"Oh, we'll cut some of the meat in strips and dry roast it for later. We'll hang some on sharp sticks before a fire and let them cook. Oh, Toh-Tsee-Ah-ne," she whimpered, suddenly sitting in the grass and drawing her daughter to her, "I want to be there; the need sits in my chest like a big wolf who is eating my heart away. I want to be there on the prairie . . . and hunt the antelope . . . and cook. . . ."

Her voice began trailing off. Her eyes lost their focus.

She lay in the grass, alive but seriously wounded. She had not intended to go with the war party, but something had happened. Her white relatives had insisted she go. Now, she was wounded in the heart. A Tonkawa sliced away part of her ribcage and held it

over a fire. "This is fine meat," he said. "It will make me stubborn
and loyal, like you." Quanah's bones lay a little way off. Someone
had already eaten him to gain his youth and strength.

A melancholy settled on her like a sudden winter storm. Tears rolled down her face.

"Toquet, pia," said Toh-Tsee-Ah, hugging her mother and beginning to cry with her. "Ka Taikay." *Don't cry.*

But her mother did not respond.

That's the trouble, thought Still-She-Mourns. It won't be all right. They will keep us here, in these stupid clothes, and we will go to their church, and they will never let us go back to the Comanches where all is right. "It won't be all right, Toh-Tsee-Ah-ne," Still-She-Mourns moaned. "It won't be all right."

17

Tecks Ann

T. J. and Frances Cates came often after church on Sundays to take Cynthia Ann and Topsannah for autumn drives in the countryside. "That's good," said Orlena, folding her arms under her bosom. "It'll be good for both them and us to look at something besides each other's ugly faces for a while." She reached up and brushed her hair with the palm of her hand, an indication that she didn't consider herself ugly.

The Cates were very interested in Cynthia Ann and, especially, Topsannah, whom they thought a bright and sprightly child. T. J. was friendly and interested in Cynthia Ann also. He often tried to relay any news he thought Cynthia Ann might be interested in. "I hear the Yankees have made a treaty with the Comanches," he reported one Sunday in the fall of 1863 as they drove toward the river for a picnic. "They're supposed to give them $25,000 in presents and some sort of annuity if the Comanches will stop plundering and terrorizing on the Santa Fe Trail."

In the back seat of the hack, Frances and Toh-Tsee-Ah were talking about an old woman who lived in a shoe.

Still-She-Mourns had learned to understand "treaty," but she did not understand the details. Where was the Santa Fe Trail?

T. J. sketched an imaginary map on his knee and drew a line across it with a stubby finger. "Across Kansas and a corner of Colorado; then along the Canadian River and across country to Santa Fe. I don't know what they want it for. With the war on so heavy, there aren't many people wanting to go anywhere."

"Comanches make war?" asked Still-She-Mourns, looking directly at T. J. as if she wanted to see what his eyes said.

"I'll say they do!" said T. J. "Not a moment's slack. Can't say as I blame them. So many white people moving into their territory. . . . If it was me, I might feel like I had to fight, too."

"Quahada fight?" asked Still-She-Mourns, turning in the seat with excitement. "Noconi fight?"

"I don't know any details," said T. J., giving the reins a shake. "All I know is what I read in the papers, and the Yankees don't give us a lot of news about what they're doing." They rode in silence for a moment. "Course, the Rangers are doing what they can."

Rangers! Still-She-Mourns understood that. A panic beat in her chest; she withdrew into silence. Rangers slipped up on you, killed everyone they could in the first rush, then backed off. Then, when you weren't looking, they struck again. They left stacks of naked bodies. They were worse than rattlesnakes. She hated and feared Texas Rangers, and she was glad when she heard they were shorthanded because so many men had been called to the war in the South.

The couple played little children's games with Topsannah, teased her, taught her Mother Goose rhymes. Topsannah, for her part, responded with cute sayings, laughter, and a cuddly affection.

Walking along the riverbank, the adults were calm and serene, but Topsannah ran ahead of them. She plucked a wildflower, a purple daisy, and came running with it back to Frances. "What is this one called?" she asked excitedly.

"Why that one is a daisy, I believe," said Frances. "Can you say 'Daisy'?"

"Daisy, daisy," repeated Topsannah, in sing-song. And she was off again, running. Almost at once, she was back with a crooked stick that had been washed bare by the river.

"That's a piece of driftwood," said T. J. taking it from her and
running his fingers over the smooth surface.

"Save it for me," said Topsannah, and she was off again. Soon she was back with a colored rock for her mother. "See, Pia! It's the color of a buffalo!"

"Yes," said Still-She-Mourns, trying to respond in English. "Color, buffalo, in spring."

The child continued to run ahead of them, discovering the world of her senses, and T. J. and Frances delighted in rediscovering their own world of the feelings through the child's sense of wonder.

Another Sunday, they took Cynthia Ann and Topsannah on a horseback ride, Toh-Tsee-Ah sitting in the saddle in front of T. J., his arms around her loosely. The child loved riding and often cried out, "Go fast! Go fast!"

"Is that okay, Cynthia Ann?" asked T. J. "Shall we gallop some?"

Still-She-Mourns responded by kicking her horse to make him gallop. It was not a very good horse they had brought for her, not one that could run fast, nor for very long, but it was a thrill to be astride again. She could feel the wind against her face and in her hair. The pressure of the horse against her legs was a lovely feeling she had missed for such a very long time. With a little self-deception, she could almost believe they were on the plains again.

When they stopped for their picnic beside the river, Topsannah stood with a piece of chicken in her hand and recited a rhyme that Frances had taught her:

> Jack Spratt could eat no fat;
> His wife could eat no lean.
> So betwixt and between them both,
> They licked the platter clean.

And T. J. punched her round little belly to tickle her and make her giggle.

They taught her to sing "Dixie" and give the rebel yell when attacking the geese in the pasture at home.

Toh-Tsee-Ah was well-coordinated and learned fast, but she tired easily.

"Well, she's only five," Frances said. "Of course, she needs a nap."

"If you ran off half as much energy as she does," added T. J. "you'd need a nap, too."

1. Literally "long ago, it is said." The "I" in Comanche is pronounced like the vowel in "sit." This is the formal opening of most Comanche stories. The formal ending of a story is "subetl," literally "that is all."

"Soobe-sɪkɪtsa rɪa,"[1] Still-She-Mourns told Toh-Tsee-Ah-ne, sitting in the porch swing at the O'Quinn house and braiding a rope as she talked, "long before your grandfather was born on the high prairie, long before even his grandfather was born, Our People lived far to the north with a people called the Shoshoni. They lived there near snow-covered mountains for a long time, and, for a long time, they were happy with the Shoshoni.

"Then one band began to quarrel with the other band. Some say the quarrel was over a piece of meat, but no one among Our People today really knows why the two bands quarreled. There was no settling the fight. So our band took down the tipis and left. We didn't have horses then, only dog travois. The rest, we had to carry on our shoulders.

"We moved south, onto the prairies of Kansas and the Llano Estacado and into the hill country east of Santa Fe. We caught horses and trained them. We learned to hunt the buffalo from horseback. We made strong bows and straight arrows. We became the strongest and most numerous people of the high plains. No other people dared to come near us for our warriors were powerful and successful.

"These are Our People, Toh-Tsee-Ah-ne. We are strong and proud and—"

"How many times do we have to tell you, you may not jabber that barbarous language?" Orlena, interrupted. "Besides, Cynthia

Ann, you've got to pull your own weight around here. You're not a lady of leisure, here. You've got to do some work."

"I work," said Still-She-Mourns, holding up the rope she was braiding. "I teach Toh-Tsee-Ah to work."

Still-She-Mourns could spin and weave as well as anyone. She had learned to sew shirts with a needle and to repair pants. She loved to braid ropes, whether of sisal, hemp, cotton, or leather. Her ropes were smooth, straight, even, and strong. Whenever anyone in the neighborhood needed a new rope, they came to her. "I teach Toh-Tsee-Ah make rope," she added.

And, indeed, Still-She-Mourns almost never sat idle. She always had some work in her hands. She tanned hides with the hair on them. She made harness for the work horses, saddle bags and bridles for the riding horses, purses and parfleches for the people who came to visit on Sundays.

She cut wood for the stove and fireplace, for she could handle an axe as well as a man. Thick and strong, she carried water for the kitchen, two buckets at a time. She knew how to work and liked it; she was impatient with anyone who was not working. She disliked lazy people, among whom she counted her sister.

"You no work," she said. "You teach Toh-Tsee-Ah be lazy."

Orlena drew herself up straight, her eyes flashing anger, and she took a deep breath to still her frustration. "It's good that you have come here to teach *me* how to live, you barbarian!" She pouted, turned, and left.

No one on the high plains would have acted that way. "Among Our People," she continued to Toh-Tsee-Ah, "many important men have two wives, or maybe three or four. Then the first wife has less work to do. The other wives do it. Or sometimes, a wife has a slave—a Mexican or Texian, whom her husband has captured or bought. Then the slave does all the work, and the wife gets to lie on a buffalo robe and lose all her muscles.

"I have become Orlena's slave, and she doesn't even know it. She is becoming like some termite, eating away inside a log and never doing anything that is good. You break open a rotting log and you'll see them: pale little ants, blind in the daylight, staggering because they are weak. The birds don't even like the taste of them.

"I never let Peta Nocona buy me a slave, because I do not want to become like a termite. Or you go to the river and turn a log. There will be soft, fat slugs or worms under it. I will not be a slug on a buffalo robe."

She went back to her rope. The sisal strands became leather strips before her eyes, and

she was braiding a rope for Peta Nocona. It would be a strong rope, one that would hold a half-dozen captives in battle. It would hold a wild horse when he has first been snared. It would drag home a buffalo or an elk. Strand by strand, she would make it the finest rope in the Noconi band because she loved her husband. And she knew he would be proud of her work.

She laid aside her rope and sat crying. So little. It took so little— and, flip, she was back in the depths of her sorrow. Would she ever see Peta Nocona again? Or Quanah or Pecos? They had not dimmed in her mind; she could still see them as clearly as before, but they seemed further away. They almost seemed to have been transported beyond the sunset. Tears ran down her face.

"Don't cry, Momma," said Toh-Tsee-Ah. "It makes me sad to see you cry."

One Sunday, T. J. and Frances brought a pony hardly higher than a man's waist. On it was a child's saddle, with short stirrups. Toh-Tsee-Ah wanted to be put on the horse at once.

T. J. sat her in the saddle and led the pony around the yard. She glowed with delight and shouted to her mother, "Momma! Pia! Look at me, I ride."

Still-She-Mourns watched with mixed feelings. It was the right thing to do, to be learning to ride, for one spent so much of one's life on a horse. But she was not sure that the whites were the right teachers.

The Cates had brought Toh-Tsee-Ah a pair of boots. She kicked the pony with her little boot heels and wanted to go faster. T. J. jogged around and around the house, so the pony would trot. He watched Toh-Tsee-Ah closely, to catch her if she slipped or fell, but she already had a good sense of balance on a horse.

They came back to the porch, T. J. sweating with the effort. "Whoooo," he moaned. "I've got to take a little rest."

"I want to ride," insisted Toh-Tsee-Ah, kicking the pony again. "I want to go."

"She acts like she was born on a horse," commented T. J. "She'll make some chap a real sweetheart."

"Ain't that the truth," commented Ruff O'Quinn. "She's a real Texan."

Frances took the reins, saying "I'll lead him around the house a time or two, but I'm not going to trot. Come on, Tecks Ann, and we'll have a little fun. I'm going to call you Tecks Ann, because you're a little Texan. Won't that be fun?"

Tecks Ann nodded her agreement.

In the weeks that followed, T. J. and Frances let Tecks Ann hold the reins of the pony and ride between them, as they let their horses walk around the pasture. She soon learned to stay on quite well and could even guide the pony a bit. T. J. and Frances were proud, happy, amused and delighted with the child's progress. They taught her a little verse:

> I'm a little Tex-an,
> See me ride and run.
> Come with little Tecks Ann,
> So we'll all have fun.

When they returned from one ride, Tecks Ann announced to her mother, "When I get big, I'm going to be a Texas Ranger."

Still-She-Mourns dropped into the swing on the O'Quinn front porch, deeply unhappy. Was there no way to protect herself and Toh-Tsee-Ah from the corruption of tosi-taivos? Was there no way to resist the Tejano medicine?

18

A Parker Thanksgiving,
November 1863

When the summer grass had wilted in 1863, Toh-Tsee-Ah, Child of the Prairie Flowers, caught a bad cold.

"That's what you get for letting her nap without a sheet," scolded Orlena. "I always say, don't come in hot and sweaty from a hot day—and a lot of play—and lay down in a draft. You'll catch cold ever time."

Still-She-Mourns felt helpless, trying to soothe her child where she lay in a strange bed. On the high plains, she would have known which flower to steep or which root to powder for a remedy, and there would be medicine people around who would help rather than criticize, people who had puha. She laid her hand on Toh-Tsee-Ah's brow and told Orlena, "Hot. Mucho caliente."

After a moment, Orlena came back with a damp cloth, fluffing it in the air to make the evaporation cool it. "Here. Bathe her forehead with this."

Still-She-Mourns felt a surge of compelling warmth and gratitude for her sister. "Thank. I thank," she stammered.

Orlena put her hand across Cynthia Ann's shoulder in a little hug. "I'll fix her a toddy," she said. "That's supposed to drive the fever out."

And it seemed to help. The mucus in Toh-Tsee-Ah's nose loosened, her fever went down and she slept long hours. She was up and playing halfheartedly in a few days. But the cold lingered, and she was still sick at Thanksgiving when Silas Parker brought his family to visit at the O'Quinn farm on Slater's Creek.

Amelia was dressed as beautifully as ever: in a big, wide-brimmed hat with silk flowers and berries on the crown; a white, puff-sleeved blouse and a dark sleeveless jumper that wouldn't button, but curved away gracefully below her rib-cage; and she wore her usual straight, dark skirt.

Amelia's elegance made Orlena feel like a poor, country cousin; so, as soon as she got the turkey cooking, she went to put on her finest dress—one with a lace collar and peekaboo yoke. She worried her hair around a "rat" into a stylish roll.

Still-She-Mourns and Toh-Tsee-Ah wore their simple cotton shirtwaists and combed their hair with grease and water, straight out from the middle and down to their ears.

Amelia took Toh-Tsee-Ah in her arms and asked, "How's my Little Barbarian?"

Toh-Tsee-Ah just looked at her, not responding to the teasing or the pretended affection. She remembered this woman, and she remembered her sister, who was honest. "Where is Liz-buff?" asked Toh-Tsee-Ah.

"That slut? She ran away," said Amelia, handing Toh-Tsee-Ah back to Still-She-Mourns. "I guess she's entertaining men in some cheap bawdy house in Fort Worth. No telling how soon she'll be pregnant. She's not my sister. I'll have nothing to do with her. She's no better than a savage."

When the turkey was ready, all the children were sent out to play; they'd have to wait until the second seating. Toh-Tsee-Ah would not go with them. She clung to her mother's side.

The table was crowded with food. There was wild roast turkey, sweet potato pone and jellies, gravy and potatoes, green beans cooked with pork fat, apples, mince, and pecan pies.

Silas, as the visiting head of family, was asked to say the blessing.

"Lord, Lord, Lord," he said, sounding almost as if he were swear-

ing. "There's so much here, and we notice it so little. Lord, open
our eyes and help us to see thy blessings. And bless each of these
men, women, and children gathered here today. Amen."

"Well, that was mercifully short," said Ruff O'Quinn, through
his straight, hard lips. He picked up the sharp knife and long fork
and began carving the turkey. "Silas," he asked, "I presume you
want breast?"

"Thigh," said Silas. "I like my meat dark. It's always sweeter,
closer to the bone."

Still-She-Mourns was surprised that she had understood as
much of the prayer as she did. At Uncle Isaac's, the elder had
always called special attention to Still-She-Mourns, calling on all
to thank their God that Cynthia Ann Parker had been recovered,
had been delivered from her dark night of unspeakable savagery.

"Cynthia Ann?" asked Ruff. The service had gotten around to
her. She looked down to avoid meeting his eyes and shrugged her
shoulders.

Orlena picked up her plate. "Give her a little of the wing. She
doesn't need much to keep that broad beam of hers working."

"How about the Little Barbarian?" asked Amelia.

Toh-Tsee-Ah squirmed out of her mother's arms and went out
reluctantly to find the other children.

"Well, I wish everything in life were that easy," exclaimed
Orlena.

After dinner, while the children were eating, the men sat on the
front porch in their shirt-sleeves, smoking and chatting. Silas mentioned that several straps in his horse's harness had broken on the
way to the O'Quinn's, and he had simply knotted them back
together. "I need to fix 'em before I go home," he added.

"I help," said Still-She-Mourns. "I make harness."

Still-She-Mourns worked quickly, with awl and strap, with knife
and mallet. She had not known of such harnesses on the high
plains, but she knew horses and she knew work; it was not hard to

figure out what was supposed to be done. She made wider and softer straps, turning the fur-side of the leather inward where there was stress or rubbing. She punched holes and attached everything with leather thongs. This was the way hands were supposed to be used. She caught herself humming a little Comanche work song. She bit her lip to stop it, before she started to cry again.

"By golly," said Silas, interrupting her thoughts. "That looks better than when it was new. You ought to go into the harness-making business, Sister."

Ruff stood by and nodded his agreement. Cynthia Ann looked up furtively, almost meeting her brother's eyes with hers. She smiled. It was a twinkling of camaraderie, of acceptance, of kinship.

"You ought to 've been born a man, Cynthia Ann," said Silas. "You're no good with woman's work, and you are good with man's. The good Lord should have made you to wear pants. You'd make some woman a good husband."

Again, Ruff grunted his agreement.

For a moment, Still-She-Mourns felt like Cynthia Ann Parker.

The children had finished eating and were running about the yards and barns. When a group was running past, Elijah, Silas' boy, now ten, stopped. He had taken off his jacket and was sweating profusely. His face was red, and snot was running out of his nose and almost into his mouth. "Uncle Ruff," he said, "I don't feel good." And he collapsed in a faint.

Still-She-Mourns knelt at once to pick him up. She put her hand on his brow. "Caliente," she said. "Mucho hot."

"You mean he's got a fever?" asked Silas.

"Sí. Infermo," said Still-She-Mourns. "Need medicine."

When they got to the house, the other women agreed the boy was sick and needed treatment.

"What is it?" asked Orlena. "La grippe?"

"Probably," said Amelia. "There were kids with influenza running around at church the other day. He probably picked it up from them."

They made him a hot toddy—boiled lemon drops laced with whiskey—and put him to bed. When Silas and Amelia went home, they left him behind to be tended in a sickbed.

A few days after Silas and Amelia came to get their recovered son, Toh-Tsee-Ah came down with a fever. She lay in bed, her face flushed and puffed. Orlena laid her hand on the child's brow and murmured, "She's hot; too hot. I'd better fix her a hot toddy."

Still-She-Mourns was very grateful, for that was the remedy that had helped before. She wiped Toh-Tsee-Ah's brow with a damp cloth, trying to cool her down. She couldn't keep a tear from coming to her own eye.

"Ka taikay, pia," said Toh-Tsee-Ah; *don't cry*. But she turned her face to the wall and closed her eyes.

"Here you go, Little . . . one," said Orlena, coming back into the room with a steaming glass held in a towel. "Drink this right down, and you'll feel better in no time." She pulled the child upright in the bed and held the glass to her lips.

Toh-Tsee-Ah turned her face away and refused to drink.

"Come on, Little Tecks Ann. Don't you want to get better?"

Still, Toh-Tsee-Ah would not drink.

"Here, Cynthia Ann," said Orlena, giving up after another try. "You'd better take the glass. Maybe she'll take her medicine from you."

Her eyes glistening with tears about to fall, Still-She-Mourns held the hot glass to Toh-Tsee-Ah's lips. The child took a sip, then made a face at the taste and whispered, "Too hot."

"That's what does the good," said Orlena. "Now, drink it all down."

When the glass had cooled a little, Still-She-Mourns held the glass to Toh-Tsee-Ah's lips again, and the child drank.

"That's good," said Orlena. "Now, cover up real good and sweat it out."

Toh-Tsee-Ah sat up straight in the bed, began to murmur something and vomited at once.

"Oh, crap!" cried Orlena. "Now, we'll have to change the bed." She dabbed at the spume with the towel she held. Toh-Tsee-Ah lay back and turned her head away. "Maybe I made it too strong," mused Orlena.

For the next two days, Toh-Tsee-Ah vomited, even when there was nothing in her stomach. And her bowels ran with diarrhea. She could not eat nor drink. She grew weaker and was in danger of dehydrating. Her fever burned on her forehead.

Toh-Tsee-Ah twisted in the bed with her discomfort, strewing the quilts across the floor when she was too hot, then being unable to retrieve them when she got too cold. "She not get better," said Still-She-Mourns, and she wished there were a shaman or a medicine woman to call. If they had been on the high plains, she would have known someone with puha strong enough to help.

T. J. and Frances Cates came to visit. "Come on, Tecks Ann," said T. J., "you gotta get well."

"Need medicine man," said Still-She-Mourns. "You go, get shaman? Get Comanche shaman?"

"Oh, I'm sorry, Cynthia Ann. I'd really like to, but it's too far away, and there are still too many raiders out there. The Comanches are on the warpath again. The agency at Fort Cobb couldn't make good on their promises to the Indians; so the Indians are mad again."

"Come on," said Frances. "How you gonna become a Texas Ranger, if you don't get over this?"

Tecks Ann smiled for them, but it was a short-lived smile. She rolled away and would not please them with any of her cute sayings.

"Give her some quinine," said T. J. "That's supposed to bring the fever down."

"She's such a sweet child," added Frances. "Our neighbors have noticed that she speaks English more than Comanche nowadays."

But the quinine didn't bring her fever down. The influenza developed into pneumonia. Mucus clogged her lungs. She burned more with a higher fever, her breath became short and gurgly.

Still-She-Mourns sat by the bedside day and night, weeping and trying to comfort her daughter.

Toh-Tsee-Ah, seeing her mother's tears, cried "Ka taikay, pia. Toquet."

But it wasn't all right. Toh-Tsee-Ah-ne, Princess of the Prairie Flowers, died on December 15th, 1863, of a fever that would not be cooled.

When Still-She-Mourns awoke, she knew something was wrong. She touched Toh-Tsee-Ah; her arm was limp and cold. "No! No!" Still-She-Mourns screamed in Comanche. "Wake up! Wake up!" She shook the child by the shoulders; they were cold. She pushed the child's cheeks, slapped her face gently, lifted her one eyelid as if she could help the child come back to consciousness. "Toh-Tsee-Ah," she commanded, "wake up! Wake up!"

There was nothing she could do. She held the limp body of her daughter to her breast and wept. "Aaaiiieeeee, don't leave me, Toh-Tsee-Ah. Don't leave me! Wake up, now. Wake up; the game is over. Wake up and we'll laugh." But though she held the little body erect, there was no life in it to hold it straight. "No. No. No. No. No. Am I dreaming? Will I wake up, and it won't be happening. It's a trick my mind plays on me."

Orlena and Ruff came in. "Oh, Cynthia, I'm so sorry," said Orlena sincerely. And she reached to comfort Still-She-Mourns with an arm across the shoulder.

"No," said Still-She-Mourns, shrugging off the comforting gesture. Then she shifted to broken English. "It nothing. She is play game. She not dead."

Ruff reached to take the child's body, but Still-She-Mourns turned her back, refusing to let him touch the child. "She's mine," she went on in Comanche. "You can't have her. She's mine. No es una Tejana."

She ran with the child in her arms through the door into another room and slammed the door. The little body draped across her arms like a pelt newly taken from an animal, still warm and moist, still containing the feelings of being alive. Except this little body was cold.

She went out on the porch and lay Toh-Tsee-Ah's body in the swing, then knelt on the porch, leaning over the child. She listened at the little chest, but heard nothing. She beat on it gently, afraid she would hurt her daughter and make her cry.

Finally, she had to admit: the child was dead. Her last fragment of life on the high plains, the high plains she loved like life itself, had now been taken away from her by another of the white man's tricks. She screamed in Comanche and wept without control. She beat her forehead against the porch swing and made it bleed. The blood dripped on the child's chest and shoulder.

Immediately, Still-She-Mourns rubbed the blood as if she could rub its life back into the child. "You'll be well," she said in Comanche. "This blood will make you warm. I'll give you my blood. I'll give you all of my blood. You'll stand up, and run, and play. You can even be a Texas Ranger if you want to. Don't leave me, Toh-Tsee-Ah-ne. Don't leave me."

Orlena came out. "Look what a mess you've made," she said, then softened at once. "We'll have to clean her up before we can bury her. Let me take her in the house and wash her."

"No," said Still-She-Mourns gruffly. "No take. My baby."

Orlena stood for a while, her hands on her hips, then left.

The little body was getting stiff. Still-She-Mourns molded it into a sitting position in the swing, and, when she released her grip, the body stayed. She looked like a child, waiting to be entertained.

Still-She-Mourns clapped her hands and chanted:

> I'm a little Teck Ann,
> See me run...

But the child would not dance.

Still-She-Mourns laid her head in the child's lap and cried. The tears wet the little girl's legs and nightgown. "What will I do without you?" wailed Still-She-Mourns. "Whatever will become of me now?" She wept until she could cry no more and the sun had moved halfway across the sky.

"Look, Cynthia Ann," said Ruff O'Quinn through tight lips. "T. J. and I made a little casket."

"Won't you let us wash her and lay her out?" asked T. J.

She pulled the body closer and turned away. "No," she said. "No. Not bury." How could she make them understand? As long as her little body was not buried, Toh-Tsee-Ah's soul would be walking around. Still-She-Mourns could at least be with that soul during the long nights. She might not be able to see or talk with Toh-Tsee-Ah's soul, but she would know it was there, there in the dark, looking for her bones and someone to bury them.

"That's not very nice to her," said Ruff. "You've got to lay her to rest."

Still-She-Mourns wailed and released the body. This quiet man with the tight lips was right. It was not love, but greed, to hold the baby's soul in torment. Still-She-Mourns would have nothing, nothing at all, to console herself, but Toh-Tsee-Ah's spirit had to be set free to go on to the afterworld. Still-She-Mourns would have to allow them to wash the body, clothe her in a ruffled party dress and the patent-leather shoes, and arrange her in the coffin, as if she were sleeping.

Heartbroken friends carried the little casket to a buckboard, and several buggies and hacks that had assembled followed it to Asbury graveyard, eight miles to the south.

At the graveside, Still-She-Mourns felt detached from her own body. Her mind stood over there, by a cypress tree, and watched her body. The poor body hurt so much, it was numb, no more than a log. The body made motions, but they were baffling. She saw the men slide straps under the little coffin and lower it into the hole.

She felt herself lurch when the coffin lurched.

The grave was as large as Palo Duro Canyon, its sides straight up, like the cliffs at the Cap Rock. The sky whirled above it, tipping on its edge and flowing down the sides of the grave to form a puddle at the bottom, like a river of tears as big as Prairie Dog Fork. A fever burned in her mind like a hundred campfires. Still-She-Mourns watched as her body collapsed in a faint. Too much. The heart surrenders. Unconsciousness became the only balm.

Her medicine bag had long since disappeared; so Still-She-Mourns assembled what substitutes she could find and went to a sandy place near the creek, alone she thought, but T. J. Cates was watching.

She smoothed off a place in the sand and drew a circle of the universe with a crossroads of the four directions in it.

At the north end, she placed a dull fieldstone to represent the wisdom of the present time. The eye of the Great Spirit had been clouded over, like an aged man's eyes by cataracts. He could no longer see into the world to guide the feet of people.

At the south end, the quadrant of personal nurture, she laid two twigs which she had tied in a cross to represent the Christopher medal Peta Nocona had once brought her from Santa Fe. Its shiny metal had long since been lost. She encrusted the little stick-cross with mud, in recognition of the impermanence of all things.

She stared long at the eastern fork of the diagram on the ground, the quadrant of beginnings, of creativity, of things becoming. She saw nothing in her future but tears and sorrow. Peta Nocona had once filled her life with happy expectation, and Quanah, Pecos and Toh-Tsee-Ah had fulfilled Nocona's promise. Where were they now? Were Quanah and Pecos in a grave as bleak as Toh-Tsee-Ah's? Or had they been slain on the prairie and their bodies left to rot, their souls doomed to wander until their bones were buried? Was Peta Nocona still alive? Or had he pricked his finger with a thorn while gathering wild plums on the Canadian River and died of the blood poisoning? There was nothing on the path ahead and woe on the road behind, where strangers chided her with failures. Still-She-Mourns felt the grief in her grow as large as the thunder of a summer storm, and she cried in great sobs, huge tears the size of gumdrops. She caught the tears in her hands and sprinkled them on the eastern fork of the universe. "Tears are my becoming."

She had less trouble with the western fork, the fork of dark adversities, the gateway to the world hereafter. She took the butcher knife she had brought with her and hacked off her hair, as short as she could cut it, and piled it in the west. Oh, if only her sad, sad life could melt as easily and be poured through that hole into the other world. But she knew there was no illness to take her strong body, and her white relatives would not let her starve.

She looked around for some of the sky people to participate in her ceremony of sorrow. It was mid-December; they had all gone somewhere. Or perhaps they were cozy in their nests and did not want to help Still-She-Mourns take her tears up to the Great Spirit.

Nor did she see any of the surface people. No squirrels to carry messages, no bugs to bungle things, no snakes, no creepers. Nor were there any of the burrowing people out. The universe was deserted. They had given it back to the emptiness from which it was created.

She doubted even the existence of the All Spirit, who was alive before the universe was made and who was to live after its destruction.

Still, she whittled shavings and lit a small fire in the center of the universe. She fed it with little sticks, then bigger ones, until she could feel its warmth.

She opened her dress, took the butcher knife and hacked at her chest. She caught the drops of blood in her hands and sprinkled them on the fire. They sputtered, as blood always does. She hacked diagonal gashes among the scars on her forearms and held them over the fire so the blood would fall into the flames. It turned to smoke and went up, up into the All Spirit.

She took from a pocket a corncob pipe that belonged to Ruff O'Quinn and stuffed it with the tobacco she had saved when the men threw away their cigarette butts. She lit the pipe with a bloody stick and puffed smoke in the six directions, sing-song chanting:

Your universe is dead, Great Spirit.
It shines no more with beauty, dignity, and grace.
The flavor of life has gone from your food;
The promise of tomorrow has wilted like summer grass;
The dark hole of nothingness stares like a wicked snake.
The bone pickers leave bones to rot in the open;
The fires in the lodges are all cold;
The spirit-messengers are silent because there is nothing to say;
Your Sacred Smoke is absent from the Universe:
Still-She-Mourns has become She-Has-No-Name.

Has-No-Name

"You're downright gloomy," said Orlena. "You turn everybody's disposition sour. Ruff has a sawmill out by the county line, and there's a cabin empty out there. So you can just go there and live alone."

What did Has-No-Name care? She had no child, no family, no life, any more than she had a name. This place, that place, what did it matter? Her blank existence was a harsh dream, and she watched herself, without interest, going through it automatically. One foot stepped in front of the other, but there was no place to go.

Though the board and batten cabin was small for a family that might work at the sawmill, it was spacious for one person. It had a pine table with three chairs, an old bed in one corner, an oak chest beside it, small windows in three walls, and a homemade door in the fourth. Orlena showed her the flat-topped cast-iron stove for warmth and cooking, with a bare metal flue going up through the ceiling and roof.

"You do know how to make a fire in a stove, don't you?" asked Orlena.

Has-No-Name nodded absently.

"Well, that's good. We never seem to know what you know and don't know."

The cabinet had a sliding, metal-covered dough-board and a swinging bin for storing flour. Orlena had even hung thin, white chintz curtains on the windows and put a colorful, hooked rug on the floor. "We want you to be comfortable, Cynthia Ann," she said, as she went out to get more things from the hack.

Has-No-Name stood near the little cast-iron stove. Some of the whites who lived with the Mexicans at Santa Fe had stoves like this. And the bluecoats had given Ketumsee and the minor chiefs of his Penatecka band a few of them when they put them in little square houses on the Comanche Reservation on Clear Fork of the Brazos. The stove was another of the white man's things that weighed one down. It was another demon that threatened to devour the Comanche way of life.

The stove seemed to be growing larger, looming up to bend over her, so she put a hand on it to hold it off and protect herself. It burned her hand slightly, taking her breath, smothering her; she began breathing too fast; she couldn't seem to take a deep breath. They—who were they?—were trying to get her, capture her, take her away? She jumped to run.

Pieces of Quanah lay strewn over the plain. As Has-No-Name watched, they dissolved into pieces of Has-No-Name. There was no blood at the cuts. Frantically, Has-No-Name tried to fit an arm to a foot, but they were the wrong foot, wrong arm. She looked at them, quivering with fear, beginning to cry.

Her heart beat too fast. She began to admonish it like a little child: "Pihi-tie," and then she forgot what she was doing. "Soobe-si," *a long time ago. . . .*

Ruff and Orlena came back with coffee, sweets, bacon. "What's wrong, Cynthia Ann?" cried Orlena. "You're white as a ghost. Are you okay?"

Has-No-Name watched her sister emerge from a cloud of nothingness in the middle of the room. She was coming toward Has-No-Name too fast. Has-No-Name jumped back, crying, "No me

"Silly, no one's trying to kill you," said Orlena. "We've just brought you some things to eat."

A man's hand went into a little sack and came out with a sweet. "Here, have a piece of candy." It was the kind man whose lips never moved. Has-No-Name allowed him to come into focus. She tried to smile at him but felt the smile caught in a tic at the edge of her cheek.

"Thank," said Has-No-Name, taking the candy. "I thank."

"Now, that's better," said Orlena. "Here, let's fix you something to eat. Would you like some bacon and eggs?"

Has-No-Name shrugged. She liked bacon and eggs, but they seemed disgusting at the moment. She held the candy in her hand.

Saying "I'll get the other stuff," Orlena went out to the hack again.

"And I'll start some water for coffee," said the tight-lipped one, putting more wood in the little stove. "You'll want some coffee, won't you?"

Has-No-Name nodded and tried to smile, but she wasn't sure the smile got to her lips.

Orlena returned with a middle-aged woman. "This is Wilma Pagitt," she said. "Her husband, Joe, is one of the sawyers. She'll help you when we're not around."

Has-No-Name tried to look at the woman, but the woman's face and arms dissolved in a dark shadow. Has-No-Name felt herself trembling as if she were someone else. Her upper lip and hands began to sweat.

"Hello, dear," said Wilma. "We'll get along just fine. We're going to be the best of friends."

When Wilma had cooked the bacon, eggs, and coffee, Has-No-Name felt separated from herself. She stood by the door and watched as Ruff led the body of Has-No-Name to the table and helped it sit in a pine chair. First Orlena, then the faceless woman, picked up bits of the food on a fork and put them in Has-No-Name's mouth. Without interest, she watched the mouth chew the food.

Orlena turned away and cried. Ruff took her in his arms, trying to comfort her. "My own sister," Orlena sobbed. "My own sister."

"There's nothing we can do," said Ruff. "Except comfort ourselves that we know she's in good hands here at the mill."

"We'll all do the best we can," said Wilma.

Orlena ran out of the cabin and got in the hack. Ruff paused, touched the shoulder of Has-No-Name, but could say nothing; then he, too, went out and got in the hack. Wilma put food in the mouth and said, "Chew, dear. Chew your food."

The mouth chewed and swallowed.

"That's good!" said Wilma. "And look, we've only got three bites to go." Wilma touched the gashes on the body's arms. "We've got to do something about those nasty cuts, too. How in the world did you get them?"

Has-No-Name became aware of her arms and hands. They had once been strong hands, muscular from work, a little gnarled with age and cold. She wondered what they were doing on the ends of her arms. One of the hands was holding a bit of candy. The arms looked like raw bones, with a slick, translucent cloth draped over them. As she watched, they faded and were gone.

> *Trades-It was on the ground, under her horse. Her arm was bent back under her in a way no arm was supposed to bend. She rolled over, trying to escape. The horse trampled the broken arm again, pulverizing the elbow. There was nothing anyone could do. Paha-yuka pulled it out almost straight, molded it like mud, and tied grass around it. The shaman sang, but the arm was still permanently disfigured and stiff.*

The winds blew, storms came, time passed. Has-No-Name noticed sometimes that she was in a different place, a different chair, or in the bed. Sometimes the door was open. What did it matter? She was already dead.

> *Has-No-Name watched them wrap her body with the finest clothing her relatives and close friends could find—soft doeskin*

against the freshly washed corpse, otter fur around the neck, rabbit
skin next to the tender parts. Peta Nocona came in with the medi-
cine man, Bear Growls, who was the most powerful of all
Katsotecka Comanche medicine men. No Penatecka or Yamparika
shaman had so much puha. And his Bear medicine was among the
strongest of medicines.

Bear Growls coated the face of the corpse with vermillion and
closed the eyes with red clay. One of her close relatives, a woman,
was supposed to prepare the body for burial, but Peta Nocona had
changed that; he wanted the best and strongest medicine for the
burial of his wife. He laid his own medicine bag against her chest,
as Bear Growls bent the knees up and the head forward to bind
the body into a ball with soft-braided ropes, ropes that Walks With
Dignity had made in her lifetime.

Bear Growls and Peta Nocona laid the body on a thick, plaited
rug outside the tipi door and waited for her relatives and friends to
come by and look at the body. Each one dropped some little token
on the blanket beside the body—a sprig of sage, a rabbit's foot, a
small unusual stone that had puha—gifts of love and supernatur-
al power for her spirit to take to the Afterworld. Every person in
the village came to see She Mourns for one last time.

Two strong women of her clan lifted the body onto a horse, then
guided their horses close on each side to hold the corpse in place for
the trip to the burial cairn in a cliff in Palo Duro Canyon above
Prairie Dog Fork. Then Peta Nocona, ignoring all taboos, rode up
and took the place of one of the women and called for Bear Growls
to take the other. All the people of all the villages along Prairie Dog
Fork followed, many on foot, some of the old on horseback. The
wailing and weeping awoke the eagles and the wolves and brought
out the snakes, all of whom joined the cortege.

The procession went west from the village to a big cave that
faced the sunrise, high on the cliff of Palo Duro. It was the best
possible place for a burial. The corpse had opened a place in the
burial wrappings and was watching the proceedings with interest.
Peta Nocona and Bear Growls placed the corpse in the cave and
wedged smooth rocks against its back to keep it firmly in a sitting
position, facing the sunrise.

Then Peta Nocona called his servants to bring forth the horses—
twenty-eight horses. He killed each one there at the mouth of the
cave and threw the bridle, saddle, and blanket into the cave for the
use of the corpse. Then he took the knife and gashed his own arms,
four times on each forearm. No one on Prairie Dog Fork had ever
seen such a display of love.

When the last of the horses had been killed and the people of the
tribe had each given Still-She-Mourns their last token of love, they
all placed sticks, mud, and stones in the mouth of the cave, soon
sealing it up. But the people would not go away. The burial rite
was finished, but they would not go away.

The corpse stirred, breaking the burial bindings and wrappings.
She wasn't going to die this way.

Then Náudah, clothed in a brilliant doeskin sheath, ringed with
four yokes of shining cowrie shells, emerged like a baby being born
through the dirt and stones of the cairn and stood in the bright sun
among her friends and family. The spirit of Náudah was not ready
to die. She Walked Again in Dignity among her friends and relatives in Palo Duro Canyon.

"Y' gotta keep up yer strength, Cynthia Ann. A body cain't jist
roll over and die. You've gotta keep your body healthy, so your soul
will have a chance to heal. C'mon now, 'n eat this."

Walks-Again looked at the chicken being forced into her hand.
Some fingers wrapped her fingers around it. It was a drumstick.
What was it doing there? Beneath it was a pine table.

"Go on. Eat," commanded the voice gently. The hand took hold
of Walks-Again's forearm and lifted it toward her mouth.

The woman was nice looking: a little overweight and her hair
was all tangled. Her bosom stretched the cloth at the buttons on
her polka-dot shirtwaist, and her teeth were dirty, but the woman
was looking at Walks-Again with interest. Walks-Again even forgot to look away from her gaze. Wilma's eyes were friendly; they did
not say savage or dirty or infidel.

"Go on. Eat," commanded Wilma again, guiding her forearm
upward.

Walks-Again opened her mouth and took a bite of the chicken. Little spasms of flavor ran across her tongue. What were they doing there? And then she remembered the taste of food and the satisfaction it brings—not just the feeling of a belly well-fed but also the tingle of well-being that could lay across your shoulders, like a warm buffalo robe. She chewed and swallowed, then took another bite. She began to eat with pleasure.

"That's better," said Wilma. "And don't forget to take some of these vegetables. They put spirit in your eyes."

Obediently, Walks-Again took some of the green from the plain white ceramic plate. What was it? Oh, they were beans—green beans someone had put in jars last summer and stored on a shelf, and now she was eating them. Where had she heard of that? The beans had been flavored with pork rind. They tasted good.

She felt the light coming back into her life, as if the sun were rising. She looked around. Her hands took form over the white plate, the pine table under it. The board and batten walls of the cabin materialized with the little windows that knew where the spring sun was. Where had the winter gone?

A woman leaned forward in front of her. Walks-Again almost recognized her, the one with the dirty teeth. The woman was offering her a glass of milk. "Come on, dear, drink this. Maybe it'll help you get some sleep. Lord knows, you need it."

Where had she seen that gesture before? *Elizabeth was handing her a tumbler of water and saying "Agua. Para tomar."*

Walks-Again felt something tugging at her face. Down by her mouth. It was a smile, trying to form itself in spite of the immobile, slack cheek. She gave it permission to emerge. Hesitantly, Walks-Again pointed to Wilma, then to herself. "You. Me," she said. "¿Amigos?"

"That's for sure," said Wilma, grinning widely. "Amigos."

Walks-Again smiled at Wilma and drank the warm milk.

"She's Getting Better"

"She's getting better," Wilma reported to Ruff and Orlena, her hand on the rounded end of the dashboard of their buggy, as if she were holding it in place. Ruff and Orlena sat in the buggy, ready to return to Slater's Creek. "Some days, she almost seems like she's getting well."

"Getting well?" exclaimed Orlena. "Has she been sick?"

"Oh, no. Not sick in any way a doctor could treat with a pill or a potion, anyway."

"Good! You had me startled there."

"But she hasn't been right," Wilma went on. "You know that. There's something that's eating at her, even if it don't show like a sore would."

"But she's getting better, you say?"

"Yes. I do believe she's getting better."

"Well, that's good." Orlena glanced at Ruff, a signal that they could start when he was ready.

"She likes to bring one of her kitchen chairs outside and sit in the sun, like a squirrel, soaking up the sun."

"I never did understand how she could tolerate the sun so much," said Orlena. "And it as hot as it is this summer."

"Sometimes it helps," Wilma went on, "and sometimes it don't. Sometimes, she'll seem as normal as every day and other times, she just don't seem to be there. It's like her mind is off somewheres else."

"You're doing a real fine job, Missus Pagitt," said Ruff. "Keep up the good work. And let us know if anything new develops." He snapped the horse's rump with the reins, and they drove away.

Wilma watched them go, then went to her own cabin to get the chicken and green beans that she was going to take to Cynthia Ann. "How're you today, dear?" she called, as she entered Cynthia Ann's cabin. "I brought you some more of that fried chicken you like so much."

Gets-Better smiled and ate a drumstick. By eating so much, she had gained back some of the weight she had lost. Chicken was almost the only thing she could taste. That and the green from the jars.

But there were setbacks, too. Often, Has-No-Name had to be fed, because she just didn't seem to understand what food was for, or how to use it. Wilma was always cheerful, putting the spoon to Has-No-Name's mouth, then wiping off the drool. "I'll swear," Wilma would say at such moments, "I've told Joe lots of times that I needed a baby to take care of—besides him, that is—but I never thought it would be like this. Open wide."

One day, Wilma came to Gets-Better's cabin with a comb and a pair of scissors. "It's time we tried to even up your hair a little," she said. "Let's go outside, so's we don't have a lot of sweepin' t' do afterwards."

Gets-Better sat in a kitchen chair near the garden plot and let Wilma comb and trim her hair.

Trades-It, with her crooked arm and bent hand, ran the comb through Náudah's hair, applying the dark grease, while Loves-Horses watched.

"I don't think there is bear grease enough in the world to make her hair dark and shiny," said Loves-Horses. "It always looks like a deer's rump."

"But it's pretty that way," said Trades-It. "I like it that way."

"There, now," said Wilma. "It's still short enough to be a man's haircut, almost. Maybe we'll start a new fashion." She held up a mirror for Gets-Better to look into.

"Who?" asked Gets-Better. "¿Quién es?"

"Why, that's Cynthia Ann Parker," said Wilma. "Don't you even know her?"

So that's what Cynthia Ann Parker looked like. Gets-Better had heard a lot of people talking about her. In the mirror, Cynthia Ann looked worried. At another time, Gets-Better might have liked this strange woman with a wild look in her eye, but today, she already disliked her; she had not suffered grief. Even as Gets-Better watched, Cynthia Ann faded into a dark nothingness.

"Oh dear," she heard Wilma saying, "We're going into another one of your spells."

"You've got to come over to our house and have supper," Wilma was saying. It was another day, a summer day, but they were in the same cabin. "The boys insisted I bring you. I've made a good Mulligan." Wilma had begun to fidget with embarrassment. She went on, talking too rapidly for Gets-Better. "Those Irish are sure clever, how they can clean out a whole pantry and make it eatable. Though sometimes, I think the stew tastes a little like the cans, or at least like some of the pasteboard boxes the thangs come in. Anyhow, the boys, especially Bob, they insisted I bring you home with me."

Gets-Better shrugged again and allowed herself to be bathed and dressed and led to the Pagitt's cabin.

The men had shaved, washed their faces, put on clean shirts and water-combed their hair. "Nice y' could come, ma'am," said Bob, looking at his own feet. "We're all hoping I can—we c'n get to know you better. We know ya'll been through an awful lot. But you c'n count on us. Yo're among friends now."

Gets-Better looked away quickly, hardly knowing what to do.

172 She recognized the tones of courtship, which confused her. She dared not meet his gaze. She already had a husband who loved her and whom she loved. This new prelude was unwelcome. She turned away, started for the door.

"Wait, Cynthia Ann," called Wilma. "Is something wrong?"

"No. No. No. No. No," was all she could say. Even if she had been willing to listen to a courtship, there was no Paha-yuka here to guide her or accept the presents. Everything was all wrong. She ran to her own cabin, jumped into the bed, clothes and all, and pulled the quilt over her. But that didn't stop the memory.

Blue-Eyes walked with the other unmarried girls along the path to the water hole. When the other girls giggled and started falling behind, she knew there was someone waiting behind the clump of willows near the creek, someone who would declare himself a suitor by stepping out into her path. The other girls were in on the secret, but she had no idea who it could be.

In one way, she was happy that it was happening. Because she was Paha-yuka's adopted daughter, the young men had not dared to approach her, for she was socially too far above them; so she had grown past the usual marriage age. And because she was a white captive, many of the more prosperous men had avoided even glancing at her, for they feared that a captive would not make a good Comanche wife.

She was extremely surprised to see Peta Nocona step from behind the willows. He was much older than she, though not so old as to be ineligible as a husband. But she had never thought of him that way. This was the man who had given her her first pony, had braided her first bridle; he had acted like a mother's brother.

He said nothing, but simply stood in her path, the question on his face.

Blue-Eyes felt herself blushing, but she forced herself to keep her eyes on his. In one heartbeat, she had gone from a girl with no suitor, to one who was sought by the leader of the Noconi band. She hesitated only a moment in her confusion, then smiled and whispered, "We will talk."

He smiled, nodded, and vanished, as she knew he would. Our People frowned on courting couples talking in public.

At last, the wedding day came. The presents had been delivered. The feasting and dancing done. The vows had been said for all the village to hear. Peta Nocona had brought her meat, a big chunk of fresh buffalo. In a beaded, white doeskin shift, she stood with Paha-yuka and Elk-Mother in front of their lodge.

Peta Nocona said nothing, but extended his hand to her. Paha-yuka put Náudah's hand in his and he led her to the vacant lodge her father kept for visitors. Neither of them said anything; talking would come later. She untied the shoulder straps of her dress and let it slip to the floor. He took her in his arms and touched his mouth to hers.

She-Mourns awoke, crying. Would she ever see her husband again? Did he long for her, the way she ached for him? Would she ever escape and return to his gentle touch? Why did everything remind her of the happiness she had lost?

Now, another man wanted her. If he had been her husband's brother, it would be proper for her to marry him. If a warrior had been killed in battle or if he were only gone a long time on the warpath, it was expected that his brother would take care of his wife. The brother would bring her meat, and she would sleep in his lodge, sharing the duties of the brother's other wives. When the warrior returned, the temporary marriage would be over. She would return to her husband's lodge, and people would comment about how generous the warrior was to give his wife to his brother. If the warrior never returned, the widow became the brother's wife permanently.

Gets-Better did not even know if she was a widow or not. And this new suitor was certainly not her husband's brother. Still, he belonged to the extended clan of her sister's husband. A sister's husband could act like a husband's brother, if the husband had no brother. Maybe the brother, or clansman, of the sister's husband could take responsibility for a lonely woman.

Gets-Better pushed aside the quilt. Her tears had wet a half-moon in its edge. She turned her head to the other end of the bed and opened the window a crack, so she could hear him murmuring outside her wall, if he should come. But, of course, she knew he would not come; she had not given him an encouraging sign. She had not said, "We will talk."

She-Mourns stood at the edge of a clearing and watched Has-No-Name as she stood by a child's grave. It was Pecos' grave. He had died of smallpox, and the band was moving, hoping to avoid an epidemic among the tribe. Someone—a husband—pulled her shoulders to the side and led her away. Only those who had survived the pox were allowed to handle these dead.

Unable to sleep, she got up and sat in the pine chair by the table, waiting, waiting. But she had forgotten what she was waiting for. Even as she waited, the world began to turn dark, like all the campfires of the universe were burning low, then out.

"I'll swear, I thought you were getting better. And now you have to blink out on me again. Open your mouth, dear; you've got to eat."

It was Wilma, putting green beans in Has-No-Name's mouth again.

"Chew and swallow, dear," said Wilma. "Keep your strength up."

Has-No-Name smiled. In a world that was constantly changing, Wilma was the only thing she could count on.

"That's better, Cynthia Ann," said Wilma. "And it's so good to see you've come back. I brought you some of the chicken you like so much."

In a plate on the table were two drumsticks, golden brown and smelling good from the skillet. Gets-Better reached for one.

"Oh, I'm so glad to see you making sense again," said Wilma, and she reached over to hug Cynthia Ann's shoulders.

"You. Me," said Gets-Better, pointing first to Wilma, then to herself, "Sisters?"

"I reckon," said Wilma. "We might as well be."

As soon as Wilma left, Gets-Better popped the cartilage knuck-
le off the two chicken bones, got out a good knife, and started carving on them, the way Elk Mother had taught her.

> First, Parua-pia (Elk-Mother) sharpened her Mexican butcher
> knife and cut the bones at the point where they started enlarging for
> the knuckle. That was the right length. She talked cheerfully the
> whole time. "I remember how hard this was with a flint knife! It
> sure is nice that my husband brought me a knife from Santa Fe. I
> think I'll go to Santa Fe with him next time. I've heard that Mexican
> women comb their hair differently from the way we do." Then she
> cut a groove along the opposite sides of the bone shank, and
> enlarged the groove with the point of the knife, smoothing it as she
> trimmed. "And my husband says they wear little ornamental combs
> in their hair all the time, not to keep it in place the way we use these
> bone hair pins, but just to look pretty up there on top." She worked
> rapidly, skillfully, for she was making two chicken-bone hairpins for
> a clanswoman.

Gets-Better cooked the finished hairpins in water to remove the
last of the grease and the marrow, then lay them aside to dry and
harden. But she forgot to go to bed and slept the night upright in
a pine chair.

When Wilma came the next day, Gets-Better found the hairpins
in the strange hands at the ends of her arms. She remembered to
ask Wilma to sit.

Gets-Better watched the hands at the ends of her arms as they
combed Wilma's hair, rolled it into a ball at the back of her head,
and showed her how to put the pins in so they would hold.

> Both Trades-It and Loves-Horses pulled Náudah's hair back
> and up, combing it until it lay smooth in their hands. They coiled
> her hair on the back of her head and slipped in the pins, lifting up
> a bit of the hair and inserting the pin under it, so that her hair held
> the pin in place. Náudah felt pleased and pretty.

"Why, thank you, Cynthia Ann," said Wilma, her eyes glistening. "That's one of the nicest thangs anybody ever did fer me."

Joe Pagitt was standing at the door, looking in. "Look at these hairpins Cynthia Ann made fer me," said Wilma, twirling like a proud school girl.

Cynthia Ann smiled without effort, almost looking at Joe. "Wilma and Cynthia Ann—sisters."

On a warm, sunny day of false spring, T. J. and Frances Cates arrived in a hack, with an extra horse in lead. It was a fat, gray, sluggish animal. "We thought you might like to ride a little," said T. J. "And we brought a picnic," added Frances.

"Yes," said Náudah, smiling. "I like." She ran her hands over the rump and withers of the horse. It was not a very good horse, but it was better than none at all.

"You're looking good," said Frances, taking one of Cynthia Ann's hands. "Let's saddle up and go for a ride."

The horses from the hack were soon unharnessed and saddles put on all three horses. Frances and Náudah put on riding culottes, which Frances had brought along. They rode out, along a lane, toward the river. The evergreen trees were bright in the sun, and the leaf trees had a ghost-like halo of tender green from their sprouting buds. The mud underfoot was dangerous. The horses slipped often, so that Náudah reined her horse toward as much high and dry ground as she could. The grass was just beginning to send up green shoots.

Though she let the others lead, Náudah felt good to have a horse between her legs once more. Her arms and thighs tingled, not from the spring chill but from the thrill of being on a horse again. She was with people she trusted so that, if it weren't for so many trees that enemies could hide behind, she could almost imagine she was on the high plains again. "Good," she said to Frances. "Good to ride horse."

When they got to the river, T. J. began looking for a place to stop and eat. Much of the ground had been logged and a lot of the debris left to rot. He had difficulty finding a clearing large enough but finally chose one with several flat-topped stumps around it.

The spring-swollen river rumbled in the background, and mocking birds serenaded them as they flitted about building nests.

T. J. tried to build a fire but had difficulty getting it going, because so much of the tinder was damp. Náudah went into a thicket and came back with a wad of dry moss and leaves and soon had the fire going. Frances put the coffee pot on several rocks around the fire. "That ought to boil soon, if we can keep it from smoking us out," she said.

"Smoke—no problem," said Náudah, moving so that it wafted over her. It wasn't cedar, but perhaps it had some cleansing power. The smell of it brought back a familiar feeling from her many years of happiness.

Frances opened the lunch basket. "It's not much," she apologized. "Everything is in such short supply because of the war. But we do what we can." She offered Cynthia Ann a plate with bite-sized pieces of chicken, sliced cold potatoes and a dilled cucumber on it.

"Thank. We make do . . . with what we have." It was a phrase she had heard often in the houses of the whites.

T. J. poured the coffee into three tin cups. "Be careful. It's hot," he warned.

It was good to eat in the fresh air. "Food sure tastes better in the outdoors, doesn't it?" remarked T. J. "Something about the woods and the feeling of freedom gets mixed in with the food and makes it better."

"Hungry, too," said Náudah. "Hungry make food taste better."

"That's for sure," agreed T. J. and Frances, almost in unison.

When they had eaten and the coffee was gone, T. J. had a proposal for Cynthia Ann. "So many men are away at the war," he said, "that there's a shortage of just about everything and in every trade. There are several men in town that need some harnesses mended—and a couple who want a new harness made. Would you be willing to work on their harnesses?"

"Fix harness?" said Cynthia Ann, trying to verify that she understood correctly.

"Yes," T. J. went on. "They'd pay you just like you were a regular tradesman. Standard rates."

"Pay?" asked Cynthia Ann.

"Yeah. They'll give you money for the work. It'll be your very own money, and you can use it for whatever purpose you want. Buy whatever you want, if you can find anything to buy."

"Good," said Cynthia Ann. "Good to work."

When they got back to the sawmill, T. J. did not hitch the fat gray horse to the hack. "We're going to leave this horse for you. You can ride it whenever you feel like it. Getting out in the fresh air a little more will do you good."

Náudah's heart leapt with a possibility. With money she could buy supplies; with a horse, even a bad horse, she could make her way west and find the Comanchería. It would take some time to get ready, but her mind was already working. "Which way—" She was about to ask which way was west but thought better of it. "Which way—north?"

21

Goes-Blank

A t first, Náudah took good care of the horse and rode often. But, though some men came with gear to mend, there was not much business. With the opening of spring buds, the unfurling of leaves everywhere, she fell into melancholy. To see so much of the world coming alive again only makes one aware of progressing age and weakness. She was not gaining in her attempt to collect supplies and the more she looked at the fat gray horse, the more she realized he was not satisfactory for a long trip to the west. A world-weariness as big as a moonless night squatted on She-Mourns and caused her to sit long hours, idle and staring at a pebble at her feet.

"Le's go over 'n plow up a little garden patch fer her," Bob Pagitt suggested.

"Good idea," said Wilma. "They ain't nothin' quite as encouragin' as watching yer own garden putting out. 'Sides, it'll keep her mind occupied; keep it off of her griefs. She's had a big setback lately. Don't know why. She's jist not all there, like she was for a while."

"What you gonna do to keep our minds off of our grief?" ask Joe.

"Pshaw!" scoffed Wilma. "Your griefs are tiny compared to hers."

"You think so? With things getting so bad with the Indins out west and the Yankees back east both? The army may come along and draft all us men. Our griefs could leave you a widow, and then what would you do?"

"I reckon I'd plant a garden, and go on. A body can't stop just because a body loses someone."

Bob harnessed the fat gray horse to a plow and started turning under the thin sod, preparing it for new planting.

She-Mourns set aside the harness she was working on and watched the gardening with interest, especially when the plow turned up a few earthworms.

Elk-Mother, Parua-pia, stuck the flat digging stick into the soft earth and turned up a wad. Fat earthworms wiggled on the bottom side. Little Blue-Eyes wanted to collect them. "No, No," said Parua-pia, "those are our little farmers. We only plant corn and beans and squash where they live, because they keep the ground moist. They have powerful medicine to make the corn grow."

"Why doesn't father come and help?"

"Farming is woman work, not warrior work. Paha-yuka and his warriors are there on the high places, watching for Tonkawa raiding parties or patrols of bluecoats. That is their part in planting the corn."

"When I grow up, I'm going to be a warrior," said Little Blue-Eyes. "They get to do all the exciting things."

"Well, if Paha-yuka keeps making bows and arrows for you and teaching you how to shoot and ride, you may well become a war woman. But you have many years to grow before we have to worry about that."

She-Mourns watched the earth rolling over in clumps, but she was not able to help. How could she tell them that her feet would not stand under her and her heart was on the high plains? She had been dreaming a lot about the plains lately.

"I'll swear, Cynthia Ann," said Wilma. "You act like you've never seen a garden. Haven't you—didn't any of the Parkers have gardens?"

She-Mourns remembered

"Oh, forgive me. I just thought you knew already. See," she said, taking a jar and making signs of filling it. "Summer. We fill with peas." Then she put the jar on a shelf. "Winter . . . you understand winter?" Serena shivered and huddled to keep warm. "Snow, ice, cold. Mucho frío."

Náudah nodded.

Serena took the jar from the shelf again, opened it, and made signs of eating.

"Ah," said Náudah, understanding. They were conserving food for the winter, just as Our People did. She felt a great surge of warmth for Billy and Serena. "I help," she said. "Okay? I chop wood."

"Good," said Serena, "and then you can help me stuff the jars and cook them off."

"Serena," she said.

"Serena?" asked Wilma, baffled.

"Serena . . . Green in jar. . . . Cook hot hot. . . . Save for winter."

"Well, there you go. How do you think she got all those things to grow, without workin' up the land and plantin' seeds?"

She-Mourns shrugged again. It was a way of saying, "I don't know." How did one know where the buffalo came from? Or how the grass came to sprout? Some things were just there.

"Someone had to put them there," said Wilma, as if reading She-Mourns's thoughts. "C'mon now. This'll do your mood good. Planting is good for the soul."

When the seeds in the garden had sprouted, She-Mourns took an interest. She watched the mustard greens and chard grow, watched the beans and peas bloom and set on fruit, watched the squash vines slither away like snakes from the plant's root, watched the corn as it climbed up past her shoulder before it put out tassels. With Wilma's help, she learned to recognize a weed and learned to cut away the unwanted plants with a hoe.

"You're doing real good," said Wilma. "You're goin' to be all right. And your harness-making business is doing real good, too. As I told the boys, it jist takes time."

"She's been keeping herself cleaner lately," observed Joe Pagitt.

"I've noticed that," said Wilma. "She takes a bath on her own sometimes. And she fixes herself a little food, now and then."

In mid-summer, Ruff and Orlena arrived in a hack with two slabs of marble in the back; on one was engraved, "Topsannah, Dec 15, 1863."

"We're going to place a headstone on Topsannah's grave," announced Orlena.

The Pagitt men washed their faces, water combed their hair, and put on their black suits. Soon the hack and a wagon were winding their way toward the little graveyard. Wilma sat on a jump seat in the wagon, a big bouquet of wildflowers in one arm, her other arm linked with that of She-Mourns.

She-Mourns was shocked by the sight of the grave with its field-stones at the head and foot. She knew what it looked like—carried an image of it in her mind—but mostly she had blocked it out. It was a surprise to be there again.

Her body left her mind. She remembered how the little coffin had lurched, sliding down the walls of Palo Duro Canyon. It lurched again as she watched her body standing by the cypress. The world turned up on edge. Trees lost their root hold and tumbled down beside She-Mourns, tumbling, too, over and over, falling, with no place to stop.

Bob and Joe Pagitt were removing the fieldstones. At once, She-Mourns was with them, helping them to dig up the grave. She was convinced that when she found her baby, there would be life in the bones again. She watched as she slung the dirt everywhere, but She Stands Over There was not moving.

The Pagitts set the flat marble slab in the shallow hole they had dug, while Ruff O'Quinn mixed the mortar to set the smaller shaft in its slot. The men set the gravestone in place and stood back to inspect their work. Wilma arranged the flowers around the monument.

Ruff O'Quinn removed his hat, held Orlena's hand and said a little prayer. "The Lord's will be done, on earth, as it is in Heaven."

The earth had tilted again. She-Mourns was tumbling, falling, collapsing as she fainted. There is a degree of pain against which the only defense is unconsciousness.

Has-No-Name awoke in the wagon bed, where the men had carried her.

"Glad you're back with us," said Wilma, stroking her hand and forehead. "You gave us quite a scare."

Has-No-Name shrugged. Why was she having trouble understanding? She knew the words, had no trouble with the voice; why couldn't she make the sentences make sense? And why was the world going blank?

"We thought you'd be happy to see a stone in place," said Orlena.

Goes-Blank lay on the pine wagon bed and watched without interest as the sound and light went out of everything, as if the sun were setting before a moonless night. Then the moonless night enveloped everything.

There were times when Wilma or one of the men would find Forgot-Her-Real-Name standing at the wood pile, staring at an axe in her hand, as if she could not remember what it was and how to use it. Or they would see her walking automatically back and forth from the wood pile to the cabin, with a single piece of firewood in her arm each trip.

"I hate wood gathering!" cried little Blue-Eyes.

"I know," said Parua-pia, Elk Mother. "I always hated it, too. Even after we had Mexican axes, which made it easier. It's no fun when what one really wants to do is be flirting with the boys. But it has to be done. Now, get on out there and chop some wood."

In defense and for spite, Blue-Eyes carried each single piece of wood she cut to the tipi, then went to cut another.

"Have it your way," said Elk-Mother. "Your way only takes you longer to get the job done."

"She's like a dung beetle," said Joe Pagitt. "Don't know where she's going or why. But she's hanging on to her one piece of dung with all her might."

Late in the summer, Bob Pagitt brought Forgot-Her-Real-Name a bull hide. "We all heard yo're real good at tannin' hides," he said. "So's I thought you might be willin' to make me some boot leather, okay? I'll pay you, jist like ever body else."

Forgot-Her-Real-Name smiled at him and nodded, but she could not find any words.

"I'll hep you get started," said Bob. He had soaked the hide to make it flexible again; he pegged it out on the ground and began scraping away the flesh, striffen, and oily parts. "Now, you can finish it up," he said, handing her the scraping knife, "since you know the secret of how to do it."

Bob came by from time to time to see how the work was going. He would sometimes find Forgot-Her-Real-Name with the scraping knife in her hand, sitting immobile.

Trades-It and Loves-Horses were not surprised that Blue-Eyes had wanted to be a man.

"I was going to be a man, until I fell off my horse and broke my arm," said Trades-It.

"I was going to be a man, until I grew hair around my vagina," said Loves Horses. "Then, all I could think of was a lover and making a nest for children."

Bob had to touch her shoulder before he could get her attention. Forgot-Her-Real-Name refused to look at him.

"They's more trouble out west," said Bob, trying to make conversation. "Damned Indins 're killin' more 'n more of our people. The papers say they've stopped traffic on the Santa Fe road and settlers on the frontier have been abandoning their homesteads and pullin' back. We gotta do somethin', don't you think?"

Forgot-Her-Real-Name heard the words; she even recognized them; but she could not tell where they came from. She heard her own voice asking, "Comanche? Quahada?"

"I reckon so," said Pagitt. "They're the worst sort, ain't they? Folks 're calling for more Rangers. I've been thinking I might give up sawyering for a while, join the Texas Rangers, and go out west to help clear out the country."

Goes-Blank shrugged. A string of sounds made themselves into words, and the words into a sentence, and the sentence into a shadowy meaning. *Why, the man is an Indian hater,* registered in her mind. *He would bring us pox-infested blankets.*

Mopechucopa, Old-Owl, principal chief of the Tenawish band, had the white man's red spots. Many of the people had the sickness. It was killing the Tenawish. Red spots grew on the skin, then became yellow puss pockets, then burst. And the person burned with fever the whole time. Very few who got the sickness survived. Everyone was abandoning those who were sick. Paha-yuka and Parua-pia packed their travois and their three daughters—Loves-Horses, Trades-It, and Blue-Eyes—and moved to another campground on a distant creek. All the families were doing that—going off into small family groups by themselves. Old-Owl had to stay in camp to make sure the women and warriors cared for the sick. But that meant he caught the pox, too. After Old-Owl died, the sickness diminished, but a third of the Tenawish Comanches were dead of white man's spots. Some said the white man brought the sickness to the Tenawish in their blankets, just as they had brought it to the Lakota far to the north. Was there no way to escape their evil intentions?[1]

"I mean, it's all well and good to be a Quaker and a kind man, an' all that, but them Quaker agents up in Indian Territory jist ain't keepin' the savages under control. Peace 'n friendship be damned. I say we gotta get tough. Show them savages who's in charge. This here country was meant to be ours. If the damned war wasn't on, we could send some Rangers out there and get rid of 'em all."

Goes-Blank saw soldiers riding in two straight lines, but they had not been in a battle. They were marking the prairie with boundaries, posts with signs on them. White people were waiting

1. This small-pox epidemic occurred in 1849. As a result of it, the Tenawish band of Comanches, who had inhabited the Cross Timbers region that stretches from just west of Fort Worth to just east of Oklahoma City, ceased to be a presence and a power in Comanche politics.

at the horizon in wagons covered with sheets, ready to make fences for their cattle.

Peta Nocona lay dead, curled up and wrapped for burial. They had not taken his scalp, thank goodness. He looked swollen and red, like he had eaten too much and died of a fever.

Pecos lay dead, too. His face and arms were covered with the reddish-yellow puss bubbles.

Where was Quanah? Was he riding a pinto pony on a raid in Mexico or stretched out on some prairie, food for crows and buzzards?

"Miz Parker?" Something was shaking her shoulder. "Miz Parker? 're you all right?"

Goes-Blank looked toward the man. He was somewhat familiar. Where had she seen him? As she watched, his face disappeared. A dark cloud surrounded him, and he faded into the night.

Later, she found a bull hide pegged out near the place were corn grew. It had maggots in it. What was it doing there?

Then she realized she didn't care what it was doing there. It was nothing to her. If it weren't there, it would be some place else. This place, that place, what did it matter?

Looking at Walls,

1867

Winter came and spring. Then another winter and spring. And another. Forgot-Her-Real-Name was not counting. She had no sense of time. She sat in her cabin, where the walls gave her a measure of safety. It was a little island where the storms outside did not reach her. Sometimes she fixed food, sometimes not.

She watched the walls.

The boards and battens stood vertically in the bare walls. Sometimes, they looked like palisades in a fort; sometimes, they looked like the bars of a cage. Sometimes, she imagined they were the lodge-pole pines inside a tipi of buffalo hides. Then, she could stir the fire, boil the stew, slice the pemmican that had cured like a hard sausage.

> "Come and eat now, Nocona. Call your sons, too. It's time for the family to sit and eat the bounty of the universe."
>
> Quanah and Pecos came in with a cottontail they had just killed, holding the rabbit up by his ears. "See what we've brought home for the stew pot!"

"Wonderful!" exclaimed Peta Nocona. "With hunters like you around, we won't have need for an old warrior like me much (longer."

"Don't say that, father," said Quanah. "What would we do, without you to protect us from the Bluecoats and the Tejanos?"

"Oh? Didn't you know?" asked Nocona in mock surprise. "The Bluecoats are here to protect us from the Tejanos and the settlers both. Nu nuhrmuhr-ne should live a thousand years in the soft, warm arms of the Bluecoats."

"I don't believe you," said Pecos. "You're teasing us."

Ruff and Orlena came sometimes. And sometimes, Silas and Amelia. "Doesn't she know us?" asked Orlena.

"Of course, she does," said Wilma. "She's jist a little distracted."

"She hasn't been real right, since before the war was over," added Joe.

"Do you think she even realizes that the war is over?" asked Orlena.

"Not much sign of it," admitted Joe Pagitt.

"Does she eat right?" asked Ruff. "She's nothing but skin and bones."

"I get a little bit down her," said Wilma. "She won't hardly eat by herself."

"She's probably trying to starve herself to death," said Orlena. "There ought to be an institution for people like her."

Looks-at-Walls studied the side of the cabin. The lines in the boards were not straight, but had the curves and knots of natural wood. She let her eyes move along the lines of a board, studying each curve, each grain. When her stare came to the horizontal board that held the others in place, she let her gaze move along it sideways; and when she came to the milled board that was the door facing beside the opening to the sky, she let her eyes go up the edge of that. There must be some sense, some intelligence, in that arrangement, in the memories, something that would make the world look right. If she could only discover it. . . .

Her glance went back to the boards and battens, and she studied anew each curve of grain, each knot. . . . There had to be some
sense in the world, somewhere.

"Cynthia! Cynthia Ann!"

Looks-at-Walls glanced up and saw her sister, Orlena, briefly,
before the dark cloud of the universe surrounded them all and she
could see nothing.

"We just want you to be comfortable," said her sister's voice.
Then the black cloud surrounded that, too.

T. J. and Frances Cates continued to visit occasionally. T. J. still
tried to relay to Cynthia Ann the news he had heard.

Has-No-Name sat at a pine table and listened while he
explained about the Treaty at Medicine Lodge Creek.

Forgot-Her-Real-Name stood by the stove and watched Has-
No-Name turn into Náudah, who sat up straight and formed a
question, "Who? ¿Quién?"

T. J. looked at the newspaper again, to be sure he got it right:
"The Comanche, Kiowa, and Kiowa-Apache all signed on October
21, 1867—all but the Quahadi and Katsoteka bands of the
Comanche. Chief Ten Bears of the Quahadies has taken his people
back to Palo Duro Canyon."

Náudah slumped back in the pine chair, aware that she was once
enthusiastic enough to exclaim "Quahada! Es mi gente! Palo Duro
es mi país!" or "Ten Bears, Paruacoom, is War Chief now?" Forgot-
Her-Real-Name couldn't remember the Spanish words to say
either.

An apparition of She-Mourns stood by the stove, crying silent-
ly, "¿Vamanos a la Comanchería? ¿Vamanos a la Comanchería?"
It turned into a ghost of Blue-Eyes, who was standing by a tipi and
crying, "I want to go home." But, of course, there was no more
reason now than before to think they would let her go.

"The treaty establishes a reservation in southwestern Indian Territory," T. J. went on, reading from the newspaper.

She-Mourns could remember the word reservation. The blue-coats had made a little island on Clear Fork of the Brazos where Ketumsee and his band of Penatecka were made to sit down and try to live in houses. The children even went to school. Robert S. Neighbors, the agent, was one of the few white men a Comanche could trust. He kept showing the Comanche warriors how to plow.

> "We want each man to fence and cultivate 200 acres; learn to live like white men," he told Ketumsee.
>
> Ketumsee had already talked with his council. "We'll wait and watch. We'll watch and see how it's done."
>
> "Treaties are not good for Indians," Ketumsee went on. "We can't be white men and live anywhere we want; Tejanos would shoot us as we stood at our plows. But we can't be Indians and live free on the prairies, hunting the buffalo and antelope; Tejanos come there and shoot us, too."
>
> "But you'll stay here and try to learn, won't you?"
>
> "As long as all our rations come on time, we have no reason to go outside to hunt."
>
> But the Tejanos had not been satisfied with that; they kept saying that Ketumsee's Penateckas left the reservation to steal horses. And when the bluecoats were away, the Texas Rangers or groups of farmers or ruffians came and killed people, until finally Agent Neighbors moved the 1500 Comanches under his care to a reservation in the Cache Valley in Indian Territory.

"Between the Washita and Red Rivers," T. J. went on, "and between the Choctaw-Chickasaw boundary and the North Fork of the Red River."

When T. J. showed her the map, Náudah knew exactly where that was. The bluecoats had made a little island, a part of the prairie around Cache Creek. . . .

> "Your wife has given you a fine young warrior, Peta Nocona," said Loves-Horses, because Elk-Mother could not speak directly to her son-in-law.

"He will bring home many honors," said Peta Nocona, lifting one of the baby's hands on his own thick finger.

Elk-Mother and Loves-Horses had bathed the baby in a tea made of willow and cedar bark, along with several medicine weeds from the prairie along the creek.

"He smells good," said Ten Bears, who was acting as Peta Nocona's brother. "Let us call him 'Quanah.'"

"Quanah," said Peta Nocona.

"Quanah," repeated Náudah.

"Where the Comanche would be safe from the settlers, the cavalry, and the Texas Rangers," T. J. finished. "There's going to be peace, at last."

Looks-at-Walls watched Still-She-Mourns fall forward onto the pine table. She beat her forehead against the boards until she bled. Huge tears streamed from her eyes. She wailed as if at a funeral and beat the table with her forehead. Nor would she quit.

"There, there," said Wilma, trying to comfort her, wadding up her apron and trying to pad Cynthia Ann's forehead. "You jist cry all you want to. Tears are good for the soul. They clean out a person's insides."

"Do you think she understood anything I said?" asked T. J.

"She must have. Otherwise, it wouldn't upset her so much."

"Well, you can't tell, when she won't say anything, or give a sign."

Náudah, She-Mourns, Has-No-Name, all wept together. It was worse than a funeral for a hundred people. Worse than a whole band being killed by an epidemic of cholera or smallpox. Worse than a defeat by Pawnee, Tonkawa, and Apache combined; for there was no honor in this funeral.

Now, all Comanches would sit in houses and stare at walls.

The Death of Cynthia Ann

In 1869, T. J. Cates read Cynthia Ann the news that the U.S. Government had established Fort Sill on Cache Creek, right next to the Comanche-Kiowa-Apache Reservation in Indian Territory and staffed it with cavalry.

Walks-Again frowned at the word.

"Cavalry. Horse soldiers," said T. J. "They're there to protect the Indians from white encroachers and to keep them in line."

Yes, she understood. Their job would be to maraud all over the high plains. Like Texas Rangers, they would kill everyone, including the women and children, when anyone went hunting for buffalo. They would slay the horses and burn the lodges of Our People.

A band of Our People were camped on a branch of the Washita River so the women could plant corn, squash, and beans in the soft moist places along the creek bottom.

More suddenly than a winter storm, a gang of Texas Rangers swooped into the valley, their six-shooters popping. They swirled through, between the lodges, knocking over tipis and shooting the women and children who were left sitting beside their fires like surprised woodchucks.

Then the Tejanos whirled around and came back, with knives, swords, six-shooters, a few buffalo guns. The warriors hardly had time to nock their arrows before they fell in the storm.

When everyone who could escape had hidden in the bushes and ravines, the Tejanos set fire to all the lodges and storage huts.[1]

"It's the beginning of a new era," T. J. said, referring to the newspaper. "One officer is quoted as saying, 'The government has finally decided to get tough with the Indians and exterminate those who refuse to come in and live on the reservation.' ¿Comprende?"

Walks-Again understood. Those Comanches who were content to sit on the little islands would starve slowly; those who held out and fought would be killed in war with the horse soldiers. Her face began to contort in pain, and tears came to her eyes.

Yes, it was the beginning of something; it was also the end of something. Quanah had been born on Elk Creek, a tributary of Cache Creek. Fort Sill was a just a wrapping they were putting around a corpse; it would only be a short time until some white man piled the last stone on the cairn of the Comanche People.

The bluecoat horsesoldiers swooped in like vultures who knew their victims were already dead. The Comanche encampment on Otter Creek at the west end of the Washita Mountains was caught by surprise, even though they had posted guards to watch. The bluecoats had killed their sentinels before they could give the alarm. The bluecoats raced through the village of women and children, like Texas Rangers. Fifty-eight Comanches were killed in less than a minute.[2]

She-Mourns fell to the ground and wept, crying the funeral wail. Her captors had finally won: she no longer wanted to return to the Comanchería, for there was nothing to return to. Her husband was surely dead. Her sons were dead or would soon be killed in the wars. Her baby was dead. Now, all her relatives, the Real People, the nuhrmuhr-ne, would be dead. There was nothing left to live for.

"Don't take it so hard, ma'am," said T. J. Cates. "You've still got lots of good friends and relatives that love you."

1. This massacre on the Washita by Texas Rangers took place on 12 May 1868; seventy-six Comanche men, women, and children were killed in the surprise attack. A few years later, Colonel George Armstrong Custer would lead a similar attack on a Shoshoni village on the Washita. Thomas W. Kavanagh, "Political Power and Political Organization: Comanche Politics, 1786-1875."

2. The Otter Creek Massacre in October 1858 was different from a half-dozen other massacres only in that it killed more Indians. Twenty-five to thirty dead Indians was considered a good raid in Texas and Indian Territory at the time.

Náudah lay on the ground, her body crumpled into a half curl. She was finally dead. She would not get up from this wound. There was no one to lay her body out straight, no one to wash it. No one would come to bind her corpse and bury her, no one would sing the last songs.

T. J. reported Cynthia Ann's condition to Orlena. "It's like she's just gone to pieces."

So Orlena took her sister back to the O'Quinn household on Slater's Creek in Anderson County so she could care for her.[3] But Orlena had several children of her own. "I declare! I just can't take care of *another* baby!" In late summer, they sent her back to the cabin at the sawmill.

Bob, Joe and Wilma Pagitt still took care of Goes-Blank. Wilma bathed her now and dressed her. And fed her at table. "Come on 'n eat, Cynthia Ann," scolded Wilma. "Ya gotta keep up your strength, girl. A body cain't jist roll over and die. Don't let 'em kill your insides. We c'n kinda keep your body up, but you gotta do the rest. You gotta keep your insides living."

But food had lost its flavor to Goes-Blank.

Someone-Else watched Wilma cut the chicken into little pieces and lift it to the mouth of Goes-Blank with a fork. She spat the chicken out.

Or she would let her mouth hang open, slack, so the Mulligan would drool away.

"Don't do this to yourself, Cynthia Ann," cried Wilma, tears forming in her eyes. "Don't let 'em win."

Someone-Else watched the strange woman who was crying. She could not decipher the woman's words.

Wilma washed, trimmed, and combed Cynthia Ann's hair often. It had grown long in the six years she had been at the cabin near the sawmill. "You like it when I comb your hair, don't you? I can tell

3. Cynthia Ann was included in Ruff O'Quinn's household in the Anderson County census in 1870. See *9th U.S. Census:* Cynthia Ann Parker, housekeeper, aged 45, born in Illinois.

you're more—more 'here' while I'm combing your hair."

Trades-It had become the most skillful person in the village at combing and arranging hair. All the girls, especially the unmarried girls, came to her to have their hair washed and combed with fresh bear grease. Her disfigured arm and bent hand were no hindrance at all when she was doing a girl's hair.

But no warrior wanted a wife with a bent arm; so Trades-It had been forced to go into the lodge of Loves-Horses' husband as assistant wife. She had borne no children and had grown thin and bony as the unhappy years passed.

And then they were all killed at Pease River. It would have been so much easier if Has-No-Name had been killed at Pease River.

"You've got to eat more, Cynthia Ann," Wilma said frequently. "You're getting down to jist skin and bones. And, I declare, your hair doesn't look good. It jist ain't healthy. It's missing something."

Goes-Blank had lost the ability to identify objects. Lines ran along, then up beside the sky, but what was that called? And what did it matter? She looked at the gnarled objects at the ends of her arms. What were they? Why were they there?

Someone-Else watched the strange woman put food in Goes-Blank's mouth, a spoonful of green beans.

"Swallow now, dear," said the strange woman.

The Tonkawa woman had cut strips from Goes-Blank's own arms and roasted them before her eyes. Now, she was forcing Goes-Blank to eat her own flesh.

Goes-Blank's stomach muscles contracted, her face turned red, and the food spewed out onto the strange woman's arm and the pine floor.

"Oh, my goodness," said Wilma. "Must've been something in that disagreed with you." She smelled, then tasted a bite of the beans. "They seem okay," she said. "Let's try another bite."

But the green repulsed her, and she vomited.

"Well, we'll try again later," said Wilma. "Your stomach seems to be upset now."

But it was the same with the fried, the boiled, the baked—all swirled in her mouth, because her throat would not let them pass.

"Swallow now, dear," Wilma would say.

But when Has-No-Name tried, her stomach and throat expelled the strange mass. It was as if Someone-Else was vomiting for her. But what did that matter? What did anything matter? The only interesting thing in the universe was a line that ran along the edge of a board, then up the door facing. Even that was no longer interesting. And, besides, it was going blank like everything else.

Wilma rushed into the cabin and closed the flapping door against the wintry blasts of autumn winds. "Goodness, girl!" exclaimed Wilma. "You'll catch your death of cold. Don't you even know enough to shut the door?"

Goes-Blank did not look at her.

"And you've got to keep a fire going or you'll freeze," said Wilma. She put several sticks of wood in the stove, then warmed some coffee.

"Here, dear, try to drink this," said Wilma, holding a cup to Goes-Blank's mouth. "You haven't been able to hold anything down for several days. You've always liked coffee real good and maybe the sugar and milk will give you a little bit of nutrition."

Goes-Blank took a sip, and the taste brought Has-No-Name there. Has-No-Name reached for the cup and took a small swallow.

Paha-yuka loved too-pah. He would pour a cup from their Mexican kettle beside the open fire, stir in two spoons full of sugar, then sit outside the lodge on a short stump to drink it in the early morning sun. You could hear his sighs of pleasure from two lodges away.

"That's good, dear," said Wilma.

But then Someone-Else coughed and spewed the coffee all over the table and floor.

"Try again, Cynthia Ann," said Wilma. "We've got to get some food into you. You're getting weaker and weaker."

Again, Has-No-Name put the cup to her mouth and sipped. This time, it tasted good.

Uncle Isaac had often given her coffee like this. He loved her, she knew, and, in a way, she loved him; it was just that his love was stifling, thicker than smoke in a tipi.

"Here," said Wilma. "I've put some bacon in a biscuit. See if you can eat a few bites of it."

Has-No-Name nibbled at the sandwich. It tasted good and it stayed down. A feeling of Still-She-Mourns began to spread over her shoulders, like a light buffalo robe on a December morning. She smiled at Wilma and said, "Good. Bueno."

Wilma came in with warm bread and peach jam. "Fresh from the oven!" she said. "I thought maybe you'd like some."

But Goes-Blank lay on the bed with a high fever. Her eyes were watering, not from tears, and her nose was runny.

"Looks like you've caught the flu," said Wilma. "Well, see if you can get a few bites of this down. Open wide."

Has-No-Name appeared and ate the bread. It tasted good. She ate the whole slice. Where had she done that before?

"Ah, there you are, Cynthia Ann," said Bess Parker, approaching with a tray in her hands. "Anna and I have brought you some hot bread and jam."

She-Mourns saw what they intended. She smiled weakly. She took the bread, slavered with fruit preserves, and allowed Toh-Tsee-Ah to accept hers.

Bess and Anna meant well. They just didn't realize that everything they did was another wound.

Goes-Blank's bowels and vomit ran yellow and thin. A fever burned her whole body. Wilma bathed her in cold water to try to bring the fever down. "I'll send Joe to the store," she said, "and see if we c'n find some lemon drops. You need a good toddy."

But she vomited that out too. For days, she had been vomiting out everything they gave her, except plain water.

"You think she could keep a quinine tablet down, if we had any?" asked Bob.

"I don't think so," admitted Wilma. "I don't think she wants to live."

Goes-Blank had a paroxysm of coughing and spat up phlegm.

"And now her lungs are beginning to clog up," added Wilma.

"We'd better send word to Mr. and Mrs. O'Quinn," said Bob.

Orlena was in bed with pneumonia, too, and couldn't come. "Do the best you can," was all she could say. "We'll get out there as soon as I get over this—if I get over this."

Wilma stayed in the little cabin with Goes-Blank all the time now, sleeping upright in a pine chair, or resting her head on the table. Bob and Joe brought wood and kept the fire burning. Wilma rubbed Goes-Blank with menthol and put camphor in hot water on the stove to make the air contain some relief. She heated old dish-towels and made hot mustard plasters.

But still, Goes-Blank's chest gurgled and her body glowed with high fever. Sometimes she could eat; sometimes the food came out involuntarily. Wilma alternately bathed her with cold water and plastered her body with hot cloths.

"It don't look like she's gonna make it," said Bob.

"Don't say that," cried Wilma. "She's getting better. You just can't see that."

But one morning, sometime in the fall of 1870, Wilma awoke to find Cynthia Ann Parker dead. She had not thrashed around in her death throes. She simply quit living.

Joe and Bob Pagitt stood silently at the foot of the bed, while Wilma cried and cried. But Wilma was so exhausted from sitting up with the sick for so many nights that she soon cried herself to sleep.

The Pagitts sent word to Orlena that her sister had died of la grippe complicated by pneumonia.

Orlena told the messenger, "Ask the Pagitts bury her. I'm ill. I can't go to any funeral. Ruff and I will buy a stone later."

"I'll come out when the funeral is ready," said Ruff O'Quinn through his tight lips.

"So, the poor thing finally managed to starve herself to death, hunh?" said Orlena weakly.

"Looks that way," admitted Ruff.

Joe and Bob Pagitt built a plain pine coffin and arranged the simple funeral.

Wilma Pagitt prepared the body for burial. She coiled Náudah's hair into a ball and fixed it in place with two chicken-bone hairpins. Her tears fell on Cynthia Ann's breast. "You poor thing," she murmured. "None of them could forgive you for wanting to be with your husband and children—even if they are Indians."

The Cates, the Pagitts, Ruff O'Quinn, and a small party of mourners hauled the coffin to the Foster Cemetery, four miles south of Poynor, Texas, near the Anderson-Henderson County line. The men had shaved and washed their faces and water combed their hair. They wore the dark suits they saved for weddings and funerals. The women had put on clean dresses. The men lowered the coffin into the ground on ordinary farmyard ropes.

"I can't say I take any pleasure in having to do this," said Bob.

"At least, her soul ought to be happy," Joe responded. "Her bones being properly buried 'n all will let her heart go on to the afterworld and rest. Finally rest."

"Oh, I don't think so," said Wilma. "I think her spirit is going to haunt us for generations."

Historical and Bibliographic Notes

Much has been written about Cynthia Ann Parker, for she was a legend in her own time, and much of it is still available in various archives: The Panhandle-Plains Historical Museum, Canyon, Texas, at the head of the Palo Duro Canyon she so loved; the "Quanah Parker" files, Fort Sill Archives, Lawton, Oklahoma, where many of the newspaper articles, personal letters, etc. are preserved; Western History Collection, University of Oklahoma, Norman, amazing for its range and depth of manuscript materials and photos; the Center for American History, University of Texas, Austin, which owns the best copy I've seen of the Corning daguerrotype of Cynthia Ann, taken in January 1861.

There have been many books on Cynthia Ann and Quanah Parker: An early, biased account is James T. DeShields, *Cynthia Ann Parker, the Story of Her Capture* (St. Louis: 1886; reprint, New York: Garland, 1976). A more balanced account, thoroughly researched, is Margaret Schmidt Hacker, *Cynthia Ann Parker: The Life and the Legend* (El Paso: Texas Western Press, 1990). For general background and specific events in Comanche political history, see Thomas W. Kavanagh, "Political Power and Political

Organization: Comanche Politics 1786-1875," his impressive and packed dissertation (University of New Mexico, 1986) or the book made from it, *Comanche Political History*, (Lincoln: University of Nebraska Press, 1996). William T. Hagan, *Quanah Parker, Comanche Chief* (Norman: University of Oklahoma Press, 1993) is probably best on the details of Quanah Parker's life. Bill Neeley, *The Last Comanche Chief: The Life and Times of Quanah Parker* (New York: J. Wiley, 1995), adds details not otherwise widely known or available. One can get a sense of Comanche religion in David E. Jones, *Sanapia, Comanche Medicine Woman* (New York: Holt, Rinehart & Winston, 1972), who was an Eagle Doctor. *Ride the Wind*, by Lucia St. Clair Robson (New York: Ballantine Books, 1982) is a novel about Cynthia Ann's life with the Comanches; it follows Comanche culture and the available documents pretty faithfully.

For specific events:

In the winter of 1834-1835, elder John Parker secured land and built Fort Parker on the headwaters of the Navasota River in east-central Texas, about thirty miles east of present-day Waco. The fort was a formidable structure—walls of vertical logs ten feet high that leaned outward to prohibit scaling, cabins built on the insides of the walls, and a double gate that was regarded as bulletproof. Today, one can visit a reconstruction of the fort near Groesbeck, Texas. In 1835, there were thirty-four persons at the fort.

Silas Parker, Sr., had been appointed captain of a Texas Rangers troop, which he used more or less indiscriminately to kill indigenous Indians, including the peaceful, agricultural Caddos. On 19 May 1836, a band of Indians, primarily Comanches (but augmented by some very angry Caddos) attacked Fort Parker, probably on a revenge and looting raid. After some subterfuge, the Indians got in at the open gate and killed several of the inhabitants, including Cynthia's father, Silas Parker, Sr., and her grandfather, elder John Parker. The Indians took away five prisoners: Elizabeth Kellogg, Cynthia's Grandmother Duty's widowed sister; Cynthia Ann's cousin, Rachel Plummer, daughter of Reverend James Parker, and her toddler son, James Pratt Plummer; Cynthia Ann Parker, age

nine; and her brother, John Parker, age six. At the time, Cynthia
Ann's younger brother, Silas Parker, Jr., was about three and her sister, Orlena, was still a babe in arms. (See "The Fall of Parker's
Fort," in *Border Wars of Texas*, by James T. DeShields; the story was
widely retold, so one can find other sources with little or no trouble.)

The Reverend James W. Parker, son of John, spent almost the
rest of his life trying to recover the captives. Elizabeth Kellogg was
ransomed within a few months, Rachel Plummer some twenty-one
months later, James Pratt Plummer and John Parker after about five
years. But Cynthia Ann Parker chose to remain with the
Comanches. She assimilated quite completely, married a noted war
leader, Peta Nocona, and had three children. Cynthia Ann refused
to return to her white relatives, thus creating the basis for an epidemic of folklore.

Over the years, a legend developed around "sightings" of
Cynthia Ann, whose Comanche name was Náudah (pronounced:
Ná-u-dah). In the Spring of 1840, when Cynthia was about thirteen years old, Colonel Leonard Williams, a trader, and Jack Henry,
an Indian guide, saw Cynthia in an encampment of the Tenawish
Band of Comanches on the Canadian River. Chief Paha-yuka
allowed them to question the girl. She sat under a tree, stared at
the ground, and refused to acknowledge Colonel Williams. He
reported, however, that he saw her lips quiver when he told her
how much her mother loved and missed her. Colonel Williams
offered twelve mules for the girl, but Chief Paha-yuka refused vehe-
mently, saying "We will fight, rather than give her up." (See Earl
Henry Elam, "The Butler and Lewis Mission and Treaty of 1846,"
West Texas Historical Association Yearbook, vol. 46 (1970), p. 90.

In September 1845, agents P. M. Butler and M. G. Lewis, on
orders from William Medill, the Commissioner of Indian Affairs,
went among the Comanches to look for captives. Among the
Yamparika Band, they found three white children. One, a young
boy named Lyons, refused to leave the Comanches, preferring life
with his Indian family to repatriation. The others, a seventeen-
year-old girl and her ten-year-old brother, were referred to as "the

Parker children." The agents reported that a warrior had claimed the girl as his wife and "from the influence of her husband or from her own inclination, she is unwilling to leave the people with whom she associates." When they offered ransom, the girl ran into the bushes and hid. ("Report of Messrs. Butler and Lewis," House of Representatives, War Department, Document No. 76, 29th Congress, 2d sess., 8.)

On 1 June 1846, the *Houston Telegraph and Texas Register* reported: "Miss Parker . . . has married an Indian Chief and is so wedded to the Indian mode of life, that she is unwilling to return to her white kindred." Noting that many unsuccessful attempts had been made to ransom her, the newspaper concluded: "Even if she should be restored to her kindred here, she would probably take advantage of the first opportunity, and flee away to the wilds of northern Texas."

On 18 November 1847, agent Robert S. Neighbors attempted to ransom a white woman, apparently Cynthia Ann, from the Tenawish Band of Comanches. Again, the Comanches said they would fight rather than give her up. (Letter, Neighbors to Medill, 18 November 1847, in Kenneth Franklin Neighbors, *Robert Simpson Neighbors and the Texas Frontier, 1836-1859* [Waco: Texian Press, 1975], p. 41.)

About 1847, Quanah (whose name means Fragrance or Odor), a son, was born to Peta Nocona and Cynthia Ann, on Elk Creek, just below the Wichita Mountains. Much later, Quanah told Charles Goodnight that he thought he was born about 1850, but he was about thirteen when Cynthia Ann was recaptured in 1860, and his tombstone says he was sixty-four when he died, 21 February 1911.

About 1850, Pecos, a son, was born to Peta Nocona and Cynthia Ann. Many sources say his name was Pecos; Quanah told Charlie Goodnight that his brother's name was Peanuts (Charles Goodnight, "Indians of the Panhandle," ms., Charles Goodnight Papers, Research Center, The Panhandle-Plains Historical Museum, Canyon, Texas). Pecos was still alive in the winter of 1862-1863, when Peta Nocona met interpreter Horace Jones near Fort Cobb, Indian Territory, but Quanah said his brother died young, from an illness, quite possibly smallpox or cholera, both of which ravaged the tribe from time to time.

In 1851, Victor Rose allegedly saw Cynthia Ann and asked her to leave with him. She shook her head and pointed to the children at her feet and the "great lazy buck" asleep on the ground. (James T. DeShields, *Cynthia Ann Parker, the Story of Her Capture* [St. Louis: 1886; reprint, New York, Garland, 1976], p. 32.)

By 1852, Cynthia Ann had ". . .adopted all the habits and peculiarities of the Comanches; has an Indian husband and children and cannot be persuaded to leave them. The brother of the woman [John Parker], who had been ransomed by a trader and brought home to his relatives, was sent back by his mother for the purpose of endeavoring to prevail upon his sister to leave the Indians and return to her family; but he stated to me that on his arrival she refused to listen to the proposition, saying that her husband, children, and all that she held most dear, were with the Indians, and there she would remain." (Captain Randolph B. Marcy, *Exploration of the Red River of Louisiana in the Year 1852*, Executive Document of the House of Representatives, 33rd Congress, 1st Sess. ([Washington, D.C.; Nicholson Public Printer, 1854], p.103.)

About 1858-1859, Toh-Tsee-Ah (Prairie Flower), a daughter, was born to Peta Nocona and Cynthia Ann. She was sometimes called Toh-Tsee-Ah-ne, which means "Prairie-flower-person." "Toh-Tsee-Ah-ne" was probably the source of the name the whites called her: Topsannah.

About 15 December 1860, Peta Nocona left a servant in charge of a women's camp and went on a hunting and trading expedition to barter with Mexicans from Santa Fe, usually called Comancheros. About the same time, thirty-five warriors left to hunt buffalo. The women and children stayed in the camp on the Pease River, near present-day Quanah, Texas, making hides and meat for the winter. On 18 December 1860, this little band was massacred by a party of Texas Rangers. Cynthia Ann and her daughter, Toh-Tsee-Ah, were the only captives, though two or three other Comanches escaped to tell the story. Charles Goodnight and one other tracked them to the main Comanche encampment in Palo Duro Canyon.

For the next ten years, Cynthia was held captive by her white relatives, as detailed in this narrative. She died in 1870, after the U.S. Census was taken.

Quanah Searches for His Mother, 1875-1911

About 1868, shortly after the Treaty at Medicine Lodge Creek, which the Quahada Band of Comanches did not sign, Quanah was part of a raid in Jack County, Texas. The retaliating Rangers from Jacksboro caught up with the Comanches near the Red River. In the skirmish that followed, Bear's Ear, leader of the party, was killed. Though not a chief, Quanah took charge of the defense, gave orders to get the horse herd across the river into Indian Territory, where the pursuers did not follow, and saved most of the war party. That night, he was chosen leader to replace Bear's Ear. Quanah was probably twenty-one-years-old. (See Kavanagh, "Political Power and Political Organization.")

In the fall of 1871, Quanah led the attack against Colonel Ranald S. Mackenzie's 4th Cavalry in Cañon Blanco. The Comanches stole some seventy horses and led their pursuers on a twisting route that left Mackenzie and his troops stranded on the high plains with a Texas blizzard coming. The soldiers would have frozen to death if the Comanches had not inadvertently dropped so many buffalo robes in their hasty flight.

On 27 June 1874, Quanah led the attack at Adobe Walls, a trading post on the Canadian River. The Comanches, including Quanah, killed some of the buffalo hunters, but the large-bore, long-range rifles proved too much for the attackers. On the third day, Billy Dixon, who was well known as a marksman, shot at and hit a Comanche warrior at a distance of 1538 yards, almost nine-tenths of a mile. The warrior, Co-hay-yah, was knocked from his horse and stunned but not killed by the ball, but the strength of the white men—and the "power of their medicine"— demoralized the Comanche warriors.

Late in April 1875, Quanah and the other leaders of the Quahada Comanches, the last of the Comanches to live freely on the high plains, agreed to surrender to their old enemy, Colonel Ranald Mackenzie, who had been appointed commandant at Fort Sill. The Comanches recognized that they could no longer hold out and live. (See William T. Hagan, *Quanah Parker, Comanche Chief* ([Norman: Oklahoma University Press, 1993].)

In mid-May, Quanah was among a small, advance group of Comanches who rode into Fort Sill with the agreement to unconditional surrender and the promise that the Quahadas would now try to live as the white men did, to "walk the white man's road." Quanah identified himself to Mackenzie as the son of Cynthia Ann Parker and asked Mackenzie if he would help Quanah locate his mother.

Mackenzie, to his credit, recognized Quanah's leadership abilities and his potential usefulness. Almost at once, he wrote a letter to Colonel E.J. Strange, of Dennison, Texas: "A Qua-ha-de Comanche, who came into this post a few days ago, is the son of . . . Cynthia Ann Parker. . . . He is very desirous of finding out the whereabouts of his mother, if still alive." The letter was widely circulated in several newspapers. On 5 June 1875, Major John Henry Brown replied through a letter to the editor of the *Dallas Weekly Herald*, supplying the names of several Parker kinsmen and relaying the sad news that Cynthia Ann had died almost five years earlier.

By about 1877-1878, Quanah had become one of the most influential of the Comanche leaders on the Reservation. He worked diligently, as he had promised MacKenzie he would and as he did the rest of his life, to fulfill his oath that the Comanches would sincerely try to adapt to the white man's ways of living. Quanah had become a rancher and cattleman and was wealthy enough to afford at least three wives. He later had seven.

On 5 September 1877, at the request of Quanah, now-General MacKenzie wrote Isaac Parker, at Birdville. Through Mackenzie, Quanah said he was planning a trip to East Texas and wanted to know if his white kinsmen would receive him. Mackenzie added that Quanah was "a man whom it is worth trying to do something with" and that he "certainly should not be held responsible for the sins of a former generation of Comanches." Quanah, however, received no answer.

About 1880, Quanah advertised in several newspapers that he would like to obtain a picture of his mother, if any such existed. A.F. Corning responded and sent Quanah a copy of the daguerreotype he had made of Cynthia Ann and Toh-Tsee-Ah in Fort Worth over twenty years before. Quanah had an oil painting made from the picture, and it hung in a place of honor in his bedroom the rest of his life.

About 1880, Quanah learned of the Texas Legislature's grant of land and pension to Cynthia Ann. He began trying, and continued trying the rest of his life, to secure the money and land for himself. His inquiries usually received silence as their only response, though finally someone in Austin replied that, since the land had never been "located" and patented, the grant had expired and that, because of the questionable validity of the acts of the Texas Legislature during the Civil War, the pension was non-existent.

In November 1910, after many years of searching, Aubrey Birdsong, Quanah's son-in-law, located Cynthia Ann Parker's grave, near Poyner, Texas. Quanah applied for permission and support in moving her remains. The U.S. Congress granted Quanah $800 and permission to remove his mother's remains to the cemetery at Post Oak Mission, near Cache, Oklahoma, where Quanah's "Star" house was located. His Parker relatives, now pleased to have "the greatest of Comanche chiefs" as a relative, did not object. One should also note that the older generation who had firsthand knowledge of the raid at Parker's Fort were long since dead. (For notes and pictures, see *Panhandle Pilgrimage*, by Pauline D. Robertson and R.L. Robertson ([Amarillo: Paramount Publishing Co., 1978]).

On 4 December 1910, Cynthia Ann Parker was re-buried at Post Oak Mission Cemetery. Quanah gave a speech in his expressive, if broken, English. He recounted how his mother had been captured by the Indians, how she had come to love her life with the Comanches and had never wanted to return to her white family. In a gesture of conciliation, Quanah added that the white men and red men were now "all same people, anyway."

A little over six weeks later, on 23 February 1911, Quanah Parker died of pneumonia at the age of sixty-four and was buried beside Cynthia Ann Parker at Post Oak Mission Cemetery.

In 1957, the U.S. Government, needing to expand the artillery range at Post Oak, ordered the removal of the graves. So, on 9 August 1957, the remains of Quanah and Cynthia Ann Parker were removed with much ceremony to the Military Cemetery at Fort Sill, Oklahoma, where they remain today, under impressive monuments.

On 3 October 1965, Toh-Tsee-Ah's grave near Ben Wheeler, Texas, was located and her remains moved to the Fort Sill Military Cemetery, to rest beside her mother and brother, with her own little monument. More than fifty years after Quanah's death and nearly a hundred years after Cynthia Ann's, the reunion they had wanted so badly in life was finally accomplished in death.